# Things that *Shine*

Bria Quinlan
&
Heidi Hutchinson

*Things that Shine*
Copyright © Bria Quinlan & Heidi Hutchinson

# ONE

### EMILY

Over the last three hours, it had become disgustingly clear not only why this job was available, but also why it paid so well.

And when I say disgusting, I mean that literally.

There was nothing like being trapped inside a ginormous burrito to make you want to be sick—except being stuck inside a ginormous burrito that smelled like body odor.

Yup. I was living the dream.

As my shift as the Dancing Burrito came to an end, I struggled to reach behind me to get the prison of a suit off. I had exactly twenty minutes to make it across town to the Brew Ha Ha, and I was cutting it pretty darn close.

"Hello?" I called out as I pushed the door to the garage open. "Can someone get me out of this thing?"

The only sound was my muffled voice echoing back at me.

Well, that wasn't good.

I wobbled into the center of the empty warehouse-turned-garage and glanced around.

Every single food truck was gone.

Even Mama's Pork-Fried Bananas, which had seemed oddly specific and gastronomically questionable at best.

"Hello?"

This could not be happening.

My job was to get the people coming down the street to buy early-morning coffee, donuts, and breakfast burritos from the trucks before they could legally be on the street.

Apparently it was no one's job to get me out of the suit before they hit the road.

Which left me with two options.

Option One: Get across town to the Village while dressed as an insane burrito, then live through however long Abby's mocking would be…if she even helped me out of the suit.

Option Two: Lose my place at The Brew.

The sad thing was, I didn't even have the luxury of that really being a decision.

I grabbed my backpack, tried to pull it up my faux-salsa-covered arm, and trudged down the alley to catch the green line. This downtown stop luckily had an escalator, since bending my knees wasn't an option.

I managed to make it across the street without getting hit…which was great, because I could just imagine the headlines. Things were going as smooth as salsa. I was pretty sure everything would right itself in the world fairly soon, when I reached the turnstile.

Luckily I was a pro at this city girl thing, so my T-pass was in the mesh pocket I could just sweep over the scanner…annnnnndddddd.

Yeah. I was dressed as a burrito. A human-size one.

No matter which way I turned, I couldn't get through the turnstile.

I glanced at the clock in the attendant's glass booth and knew something had to change. I went over and pounded on the glass, trying to get the girl's attention.

Now *that* was a job I wish I had: sitting and reading while ignoring people all day. I wondered what it paid.

"Hey!"

She finally glanced up, and I had a deep feeling that if I were dressed as a human and not a high-calorie food product, she would have just glanced away.

"Can you let me through the gate?"

She just kept staring, and I wondered if she could hear me.

I leaned sideways, since I couldn't really bend, to shout through my mesh mouthpiece into the booth mic. "Can *you* let me *in* through the *gate?*"

Hopefully she got the main points, at least.

A static sound buzzed before she said, "The gate is for people in wheelchairs."

"I don't fit through the stile."

"But you're not in a wheelchair."

This was true. I was pretty rule-abiding, but this seemed special-case worthy.

"What if I were just too heavy to fit?" I shouted back.

She looked really confused by this. With the obesity level of today's society, I found it likely there were people who came in who were too large to fit through...but maybe all of them had a disability, so they used a special pass.

"Listen, I already paid." I glanced toward the track as I heard a train coming and saw everyone on my platform start to push forward. "Please? My train is coming."

The girl just kept looking at me.

I get that a walking, talking, oversized burrito is weird, but not so weird that you can't help a girl out.

I did not need Abby harassing me for being dressed like food *and* being late.

The high-pitched screech of metal-on-metal braking sounded and a dim light broke the darkness of the tunnel's mouth.

As the front of the train came into view, I gave the girl one last look before I did the most desperate of deeds: I jumped the stile.

Okay. I totally didn't jump it. I more like ran at it, then flipped over it, head over feet, watching the ground go by, and landed on my—luckily—padded rear end.

"Hey!" the booth girl shouted, throwing the door open. "You can't do that!"

I gave her an *are you kidding me* look, until I remembered she couldn't see it, and sprinted for the train, diving between the doors as they closed.

Yes! Happy dance time.

It took me a couple bars of self-sung music and happy dancing to realize the entire train was looking at me. Darn commuters.

"Do you have coupons?" The voice came from my right, a little old woman clutching a purse that had to be older than me.

"No. I'm sorry. I'm not actually working."

"You just walk around like this?"

Fair question.

"Not by choice."

The woman stared at me as if what I said didn't make sense, before stating, "This generation makes even less sense every time I leave the house."

We rode in silence, the stares as obvious as the guacamole on my head. Once the train was aboveground, I had to ignore everyone sneaking pics for Twitter or Facebook or whatever, until my stop.

Without the indoor platform, I had to hop down the stairs to the street amid applause and laughter. It was nice that this outfit was good for something. Laughter is often in short supply, and I bet even the grumpiest people had a better start to their day after that commute.

I hurried down the sidewalk, ignoring the atypical hoots and hollers, took a deep breath, and pushed through The Brew's front door. The last of the morning crowd was just heading out. All the regulars still in line turned when they noted the glare Abby sent my way.

Most of them were used to her by now, but even the uncaffeinated morning brewer could tell there was something different about the look she was sending over their shoulders.

"I'm sorry, we don't serve burritos here." Abby's voice was as full of snark as usual.

"Abby, it's me." I waved my hand…well, I waved what I could of it since I couldn't bend my elbow. "Emily."

The whole café had turned now to look at me. Oddly, no one was laughing. They were just kind of staring, as if I were a vision of mass hysteria.

I don't know what I anticipated, but I guess I should have expected her to remain her ever pragmatic self.

"You can't work like that." She crossed her arms across her chest, glaring her typical welcoming morning glare. "We don't even serve burritos here."

"I know." Like I was going to argue with her on that point. "I'm stuck."

"You're stuck?"

"Yup."

And then, a miracle happened.

Abby laughed. Just leaned against the counter and laughed until her face turned pink.

"You're stuck," she repeated. "In a burrito."

"Yes." If only she could see that *I* was glaring at *her* this time.

Talk about role reversals.

"There you are. In a burrito."

"We've covered that."

"Stuck."

"Yes."

"In a burrito."

"You're repeating yourself."

"It's worth repeating."

"Or you could get me out."

"Out of the burrito you're in?"

"That was the plan."

"The burrito plan?"

"If that helps you get through the day."

I tapped my foot, but since I was wearing huge, oversized "shoes" over my sneakers, it just made a faint thud instead of the *tap-tap-tap* I'd expected.

The woman at the end of the line started giggling.

I don't know why I thought this would go better. I'd assumed Abby would make some quick, biting remark and then complain the entire time about me causing more work while she liberated me from the felt and wool hell I was in.

Laughter had not really played into the scheme of things.

"Abby." I all but begged with that one word.

"Well, Emily. You see, we have a problem." She pushed away from the counter and wiped her hands on the little apron around her waist. And now we'd get to the mocking. "I have all these customers waiting for their coffee. *Usually* this is when the new girl comes in to help our rush time…but apparently she was eaten by a burrito. I'm kind of disappointed in her…"

I was about to apologize when she finished.

"…because everyone knows you're supposed to eat the burrito—not the other way around."

We had a stare down—or what would have been a stare down, if Abby could've seen my face—before she finally came around the counter and twirled her finger in the universal sign for *turn around*.

I felt a hard tug on the zipper, but no give. After three tries—and ripping a chunk of my hair from the monster of a uniform—Abby finally got me free and pulled the smelly guacamole hat off my head.

"Oh. Wow. This thing is heavy." She sniffed it. "And, seriously, how are you not dead from being trapped inside this smell?"

I was too busy pushing the costume off me to answer, just glad to be free. I felt like raising my arms over my head and shouting "It will never take my FRRRREEEEEEDOOOOMMMM!" but figured I'd caused enough of a scene for one day.

"Please tell me you don't smell like this thing?" Abby put the guacamole head down and stepped back.

I tried to casually sniff myself, but was afraid I'd built up a tolerance to the inside of the suit in a bid to live through the experience.

"Don't worry." I put my hands up to ward off any further snark. "I have a change of clothes. Give me three minutes to get clean, and I'll be right back."

I rushed through getting cleaned up and changed, before stowing the costume at the far end of the kitchen where we had a little table and chairs by the back door, then headed out front to a smattering of applause.

I glanced at the clock as I rounded the counter—only four minutes late. And, to be honest, I think we could blame that on Abby and her Burrito Plan chatter.

"Good morning, Emily." Mr. Watson stood there, his umbrella under his arm just like every morning, no matter the weather.

"Hey there, Mr. Watson. Nice day to be out and about." I gave him my best smile.

Mr. Watson was a retired widower who came in every morning for his coffee and paper, to get out of the house. He didn't stay. It was as if he still needed a routine to start his day.

"Saw you there in that big wrap thing. Got another job, huh?"

"Yup. But, I think this was a one-day gig. I'm not sure they could pay me enough to get back in that thing."

"What's that make it, six?"

"Five. Well, back down to four since I won't be going back to the Dancing Burrito gig."

Nothing could get me to risk my personal sanity in that suit...well, short of a full ride with room and board.

I handed Mr. Watson his regular coffee and waved him out the door.

The morning rush was starting to wear thin, the last of the commuters rushing off late to work. Time to restock, then reassess.

I was just thinking I should go make myself more presentable—maybe bathe in the sink or something—when the door pushed open again. I glanced over my shoulder, halfway up from a crouch where'd I'd gone to reach a bunch of cups to restock, when...

Oh no.

He's here. Mr. Floppy Hair and Gorgeous Hands.

*Gorgeous* hands.

He'd come in a couple times, starting about two weeks ago, and every time I was just...dumb. I mean, a complete idiot.

Which was the last thing I needed. Boys were off the table for now. Honestly, it wasn't even about the fact that I had five—no, *four*—jobs, or that I couldn't pay my rent or that I was saving to take another course this summer at UMass.

It was more that guys had never been a positive in my life.

Understatement.

No. Guys were...not safe. They derailed and controlled and threatened and needed to be avoided until they were all old enough to have molted and grown into men.

Which, at my ripe age of twenty-three, I knew was not right now.

"This one's all yours." Abby the Obvious gave me a smirk. "I'll be in the kitchen doing...stuff."

Mr. Floppy Hair wove through the café to the table he always grabbed in the window, pulled out whatever was in that sketchbook of his, and pocketed his phone.

I took a deep breath. He's just a guy. Just a guy. I had no interest in guys. No matter how scruffily hot they were.

I reached back, grabbing for Abby, hoping we could switch places, when the door opened again and two cops strode right up to the counter, cutting off He of the Gorgeous Hands.

"Hello, Officer. What can I get you?" We had a couple cops come in each day. Mostly with Max—Officer of Cuteness—on their shifts.

"Are you Emily Tavest?"

"Yes, sir."

"Miss, you're going to have to come with us."

"I am?" I wiped my hands on my apron, my stomach turning over with fear.

Cops weren't high on my To Be Trusted list. Poor Max had worked hard to win me over. I'll admit, the viral picture of him rescuing a kitten hadn't hurt.

"We have a report that you stole a two-hundred dollar character costume."

"Stole?" I echoed. "No. *No.*"

Abby stepped up behind me, looked at the two cops, and shook her head.

"I really thought we weren't going to go through any more frivolous arrests with you people. But, I was wrong." She shrugged. "It happens."

And, without a word of help, she wandered off, pulling out her cell phone and turning her back on me.

I tried not to panic, but my history with the police wasn't exactly a panic-free zone.

"I didn't steal anything," I assured them. "I called them. Told them they left me there trapped in the suit and I'd return it tonight when they got back after their dinner shift."

"Miss, he reported you left the premises with it without permission."

"I couldn't get *out* of it. They *left* me there, and..." Wait a second. "How did you know where to find me?"

The cop pulled out his little notebook and flipped through some pages. "A Mr. Burgess gave us this address."

"He only had it because I called him to tell him I had the suit, I was here, and I'd return it after my shift."

The cop looked at me with a *Law & Order* squint that said, "Sure, *that's* what happened."

"I have the suit." I pointed toward the kitchen as if they could see through the wall. "I'll just give it to you now."

They glanced at one another, doing some type of covert communication thing I can only imagine they teach you in Advance Copness Class.

"We'll have to check if that's acceptable with Mr. Burgess."

"Why wouldn't it be?" I couldn't help but wonder what the point of not getting his suit back would be.

The cop cleared his throat and gave me A Look. "Clarification: We'll have to make sure Mr. Burgess doesn't wish to press charges anymore."

*"What?"*

The officer who seemed to be in charge of this train wreck pulled out his little notebook again and dialed a number he had written there.

"Mr. Burgess? This is Officer McIntyre. We have the girl and your suit."

I couldn't make out the words, but I heard them—loud and fast—mumbling out of the receiver of the phone.

Officer McIntyre nodded as he listened. When there was finally a slight pause, he jumped in. "I understand, sir."

Unfortunately for us, that didn't slow Mr. Burgess down. He just kept ranting. I stood there, waiting, while out of the corner of my eye I watched Mr. Floppy Hair and Gorgeous Hands head back to his table and sit, watching the show but not getting in the way to get his coffee.

Great.

"Mr. Burgess," Officer McIntyre finally broke in. "I have some questions for you as well… Yes, sir. I understand you're a busy man… No, sir. The city has absolutely nothing against small business men. That's kind of what we're built on, actually…uh-huh. Yes. I hear you."

I watched Officer McIntyre get more and more annoyed and frustrated with Mr. Burgess and prayed that didn't get transferred to me.

"Mr. Burgess." Officer McIntyre was obviously cutting him off. "We can have a quick discussion over the phone, or you can answer my questions when you come down to the station to pick up the suit… No, I won't be bringing it to you. I'm not a courier."

There was silence on both ends of the phone. A stalemate.

Behind me, the door opened. A wave of outside heat rushed in with the figure who stood there, shadowed by the sun. As the door fell shut, I made out the broad shoulders and little cop hat.

Officer of Cuteness!

"Max!" I rushed over and threw my arms around him. "They want to arrest me for being swallowed by a giant burrito!"

"Emily." He patted me on the back. "You smell horrible. Go sit over there."

Max pointed to the overstuffed couches by the empty fireplace. I dutifully headed there and sat, Abby coming to join me.

"You called Max?" I asked.

"Of course." She looked at me as if not having my back wasn't an option.

"Thanks."

"Whatever."

We watched Max work things out with the other cops, feeling oddly as if we were under the protection of a local lord.

Once everything was sorted—and I'd agreed I'd drop the suit back off that evening—the extra police left and The Brew fell silent.

Max just stood there for a moment, doing his Man of Silence thing before asking, "Are you sure you're not related to Kasey?"

"Fairly, but anything's possible, I guess."

He just snorted and left before I could thank him again.

Just as I was getting my feet back under me, Prince of Gorgeous Hands was in front of me at the counter.

"Wow, that was crazy, huh?" He gave me a little what-can-you-do smile.

"Um, yeah."

He just kept grinning at me until he finally said, "So...coffee?"

Oh. Coffee. Yeah.

"Um…ah…" I really couldn't deal.

I did what any not-quite-sane woman would do after surviving burritos, commuter obstacle courses, the fuzz, and his Royalty of Hotness.

I turned, walked right through the door to the kitchen, and hid in the walk-in.

# Two

## SAGE

Sage sighed as the sliding door to the back closed behind Emily.

Well, a part of him sighed. Sort of a wistful, reluctant, disappointed, and relieved sigh all at once. It was a smorgasbord of a sigh.

It was all he could do not to declare "Foiled again!" Though that would probably draw the kind of attention he didn't want from Emily.

He chewed on the inside of his cheek, wondering if she'd come back or if maybe he should help himself to the coffee.

He braced himself, pressing his hands flat on the counter. He could hop right over; it seemed sturdy enough. He'd have to mind the register; it was a smallish fit. Though, if Abby caught him, he was a dead man.

Maybe not dead, but probably banned. A banned man. Which wouldn't help him at all in finishing Mrs. Callahan's new dining room or in getting to talk to Emily.

Sage wasn't willing to risk it. He'd wait.

As if summoned by his caffeine addiction, Abby came through the doors and glowered. "Were you mean to her?"

Sage gave his best Han Solo *Who, me?* look—lifted eyebrows and undeniable innocence.

Abby narrowed her eyes. "Yes, you. Why else would my happy burrito be hiding in the walk-in?"

Sage's lips twitched, remembering the cop's accusation and Emily's adamant denial. Because, *obviously* Emily was the poster child for food-costume theft.

"What's the flavor today, Abs?" he asked instead of answering her question. Because he really didn't want to know if he was the reason Emily hid in the walk-in.

Abby blinked.

It was her version of pausing before saying something she wasn't supposed to say.

"They're called *roasts*, not flavors," she corrected patiently.

Before he had a chance at a rejoinder, she turned, pointing to the board behind her.

"Just like yesterday, and the day before, the roasts of the day are always listed right here."

"Yeah." Sage nodded, leaning his elbows on the counter. "I know. But what does *Morning Honey* even mean?"

"Oh." Abby straightened her shoulders and a light smile softened her features. "The beans come from Costa Rica, where they are dried in the fruit instead of being stripped first. The roast is light, to preserve the natural flavor of the bean. It gives the coffee a refreshing, smooth texture. Perfect for the morning. It also makes an excellent espresso."

She measured him with her cool gaze. "Do you want to try something new today?" she asked.

"Hit me," Sage said with a nod.

Abby smiled and spun around. She fiddled with the machines and under counter coolers with an ease and efficiency that was admirable. Like Tom Cruise in *Cocktail*, except without the alcohol and neon lights.

She plunked a shot glass down in front of him.

Well, it *looked* like a shot glass. Except it was square and twice as tall. But otherwise, yeah, shot glass.

"This is two shots of the Morning Honey with a pump of peppermint in the bottom, and a pump of white chocolate on top." She held her little milk pitcher over the glass and drizzled cream into the top, making the layers part and swirl.

Sage stared at the prettiest coffee he'd ever seen. No wonder she got irritated with him and his boring black coffee.

"What do I do now?" he asked.

"You shoot it," she deadpanned. "Like a man."

He took a deep breath, grasped the glass, and obeyed the woman.

"Whoo!" he declared, slamming the cup back onto the counter. Heat rushed down his throat and into his body, followed swiftly by the cooling peppermint. "That's potent."

Abby grinned. "Right?"

She filled his standard to-go cup with black coffee and rang him up.

"Is that on the menu board?" he asked, counting out the dollars.

"It's just one of my own experiments."

"You have a gift, Abs." He raised his cup in salute to her just as the back door opened to herald Emily's return.

Sage paused, his eyes briefly connecting with hers.

He tried the cool-guy chin lift.

She broke their connection, smoothing her hands down her apron before busying herself with a stack of cups that didn't look like they needed to be straightened.

Abby muttered something under her breath and Sage glanced back to the best barista in town. He lifted his eyebrows and she rolled her eyes, turning away.

Sage chuckled to himself as he made his way back to his table. He liked Abby. He liked Emily more, but Abby was pretty kickass, too.

Two weeks ago, he hadn't known this place existed. He'd discovered it in a desperate search for caffeine after his first day working for/with Mrs. Callahan.

Emily had been the one to serve him.

She'd made a joke about the particular light roast blend of the day, and he'd been coming back every day since.

She hadn't actually said much of anything to him since. Mostly she blushed (though he suspected she had no idea she was blushing) and stuttered (but only while helping him). She was quite outspoken and friendly to everyone else.

And that's what he craved.

Her brightness.

She was like a burst of sunshine, no matter the weather.

Kind souls were unbelievably attractive to Sage.

It was so normal to be negative these days. It took honest bravery to be sweet.

It wasn't only her kindness.

Not by itself.

Emily had depth; he could see it in her eyes. The blue ones she tried to hide behind dark square glasses and even darker lashes. Just a hint of a song waiting to be sung.

He flipped his sketchbook open to the hutch he'd been working on.

Given the choice, he would rather spend his time off doing what he really loved—building guitars, writing music, and "loafing," as Heather-the-ex had so eloquently put it the last time they had spoken. He liked to think of it as "not bludgeoning his way through life."

Since Double Blind Study was on temporary hiatus (or "I Hate Us," as Mike had explained during a recent radio interview—which just meant the band loved each other, but even *they* were getting sick of how much they'd been in people's faces as of late. Oversaturation for a band was bad. Like, *bad*. Hence the IHateUs.), Sage had gone back to what he knew—working for his dad's custom carpentry business. It was basically second nature to him, and it paid the bills.

He tried to focus on the sketch on the page again, but he lost interest when Emily crossed the café floor to clear a table.

He shook his head, trying to concentrate on his actual *work*. He didn't need to be flirting with the cute coffeehouse girl. It wasn't professional.

Sage lifted just his eyes and they connected with Emily's. Her tidying of The Brew had accidentally brought her right to him.

"Can I ask your opinion on something?" He seized the opportunity of her nearness.

She frowned and glanced back to the counter, as if it were Home Base. "Uh, sure."

"Cool." He flipped the notebook around and held it up. "What does that look like to you?"

Emily flicked her eyes over the page swiftly while simultaneously flinching, as if she had expected something hideous to leap out at her.

"Oh." She took another look and stepped forward. "Well, I'm no expert, but I do believe that's a place to put fancy dishes."

Sage grinned, flopping the book back onto the table. "Well, you're not wrong. I guess I should've been more specific." He circled the irises Mrs. Callahan had asked him to carve into the woodwork and leaned back so she could see better.

Emily came closer and bent over the table. "Hmm...a dying bird of some kind...?"

Sage barked a laugh and ran a hand over his face. "That's what I was afraid of." He began erasing the failed flower.

"Did you draw that?" she asked, shifting the tray of empty mugs to her other hip.

"Yeah." He blew the eraser dust off the page. "Not my best work."

She straightened and her eyes connected with his before she blushed and stepped away again. "So, you, uh, draw furniture?" She was confused but not trying to sound mean about it, as if she were trying to figure out where this new detail fit in her knowledge of the world.

Sage choked on his startled laugh. Her eyes got round and he immediately regretted his reaction. "No, and yes," he spoke quickly, opening the sketchbook to show her the rest of the designs. "I sketch them before I build them. I'm a carpenter."

She tilted her head to the side, her eyes dancing over the sketches. The front door opened and another regular came in. Emily's shoulders drew back and she flashed the newcomer a brilliant smile.

"Hi!" she greeted, placing a hand on Sage's shoulder as if to say good-bye. He wasn't even positive she meant to do it.

He watched her return to her place behind the counter and help the customer with delighted excitement. Every time.

Sage took a deep breath of the sunshine that seemed to radiate from behind the counter and flipped his page back to the hutch.

Hutches were a crapshoot. Too big, too small, too garish, too plain. This was his fourth attempt. Mrs. Callahan wanted more glass involved than he would like. He'd have to build the thing in her house. Moving it from his workshop would be too risky.

He began to hum as he drew soft lines. Heavy here, light there, move this up, curl this in.

"I brought you a refill." Emily set a new cup of coffee on the table. He hadn't even noticed he'd already finished his first one.

"Thank you," he said with genuine appreciation. He handed the notebook over. "What do you think now?"

Her hands took the notebook and she sat down in the chair across from him. She studied it silently, her fingers moving over the lines with featherlight curiosity.

"Oh yes, I see the flower now. You can really make this into life-size furniture?"

His lips twitched. "I can make it any size, but life-size seems to sell better."

She stuffed down a giggle. "How?"

Sage picked up his fresh coffee and shrugged. "A lot of math, good music, the right tools, practice." He swallowed and took a chance. It wasn't something he normally blurted out to people, but he wanted to—if only because he missed his dream job. "If you turn to the back, that's what I work on when I have time."

She hesitated for half a heartbeat before flipping the pages to where he kept his guitar sketches.

"You make guitars, too?"

"It's a little different from making chairs. I have to rely on the feel more than anything."

"Do you sell them?"

"Mmhmm."

"Do you play them?"

"Well, I have to make sure they work."

She smiled at his jest. A beautiful, soft all-Emily smile.

And look at that. They were having a moment. An actual conversation where she wasn't stuttering or blushing or hiding.

Sage kind of hoped she didn't notice. Not yet.

"McNabb!"

Emily stiffened, not having noticed the front door had opened. Sage twisted his head to see who had yelled his last name.

Oh. It was Blake.

Blake Diedrich was one of the guitar players in Double Blind Study. He had his own tech, but he often groused out loud about how Luke had better equipment. Sage would point out that he would gladly make a few guitars for Blake if Blake would promise to stop smashing them on stage. They were at a stalemate.

Sage stood up, grinning at the tattooed rocker dressed in his customary vintage rock tee, beat-up jeans, and motorcycle boots. "Hey, Diedrich." They met in the middle, clasping hands and pounding each other's backs.

"What are you doing here?" Blake asked, sauntering up to the counter where Emily had returned. "Just a large black coffee to go, darlin'." He fished his wallet out of his back pocket and glanced at Sage. "I thought you were on the road with Christian Ridley."

Sage shook his head once. "Nah, I mean, he offered me an obscene amount of money, but it's just not my scene."

Christian Ridley, newish rock star and lead singer of Riddle Me This, had a reputation for being all party all the time. Rumors of drugs and hookers and drinking were enough to make Sage balk. But the interview was enough to make him decline forcefully.

Christian Ridley had been high as a kite and puked in his assistant's purse.

The rock 'n' roll cliché lifestyle wasn't why he loved his job with DBS.

"I can see that," Blake agreed, placing his money on the counter. "Hey, that guitar you made for Lucy is finally seeing some wear. For ages she said it was too pretty to use. Now she's so connected to its sound, I can't get her to put it down half the time." He turned to Emily as she handed him his change. "Thank you. You're a lifesaver."

Sage felt his smile grow. "That's high praise, Blake. Tell her I'm flattered."

"How about you make me one of those fancy guitars everyone keeps raving about?" Blake asked casually...too casually.

"Will you promise to be nice to it? Not bust its guts all over a stage somewhere in the continental US?" Sage crossed his arms over his chest.

Blake ran his tongue over his teeth as he thought about it. "Uhm..."

Sage chuckled. "That's what I thought. What are you doing in town, anyway? I thought you and Lucy had moved down south."

Blake grabbed his coffee and faced Sage more fully. "We're in the studio this week. I was supposed to meet über-publicist Lindy for coffee here, but he canceled. I figured I might as well get some caffeine anyway." He checked his watch. "I should get back." He clapped a hand on Sage's shoulder on his way past him. "You might want to clear your schedule soon. We might be planning something fun." He turned around and walked backward while dropping his sunglasses onto his face that was lit with a cheeky grin. "But don't tell anyone."

Sage saluted with two fingers and watched the rocker leave. Those guys never stopped working. But he'd be lying if he said the thought of going back on the road didn't sound like the greatest idea ever.

He really needed to finish this dining room.

"You hang out with rock stars."

Emily stood beside him, watching Blake leave.

"Nah." He looked down at her with a half-grin. "I work for rock stars. Occasionally." He was about to explain the whole complication of being a luthier-guitar-tech-roadie-sound engineer when his phone began to vibrate in his pocket. "Ah." He pulled it out and saw Mrs. Callahan's number. "I have to go."

Emily was already retreating behind the counter, their moment over but unfinished. Sage emptied the remainder of his coffee and collected his sketchbook from the table. He paused at the counter and tried to meet Emily's distracted gaze.

He spotted Abby peeking at them from the door to the kitchen.

"Thank you for keeping my brain functioning." He drummed his fingers on the counter, as if it were a regular way to end a conversation. It was obviously lame. "Good luck with your burrito troubles."

He thought about winking, but decided that was both cheesy and creepy at the same time. So he stared at her. Because that wasn't creepy *at all*.

"See ya," Abby said flatly, finally coming out from her not-so-subtle hiding place.

"See you later, Abs." He nodded to the barista and moved his gaze back to Emily. "Thanks for the coffee, Emily."

It was the first time he'd used her name. It felt good on his lips and made him smile just a little wider as he gave a low wave.

Emily's fingers did a little wave-wiggle before she shook her head and turned away.

# Three

## EMILY

He hung out with rock stars.

Rock. Stars.

Blake Diedrich had just walked in here, ordered a coffee, all but demanded a custom guitar from him, and left.

And Artist of God Guitars had turned him down. Just said, *Nope.* No guitar for you.

And what? Did his sketches have summoning powers or something?

He'd shown her a couple pictures of his guitars.

And then, POOF! Rock stars.

"I don't know how I feel about this." Abby stood behind me, watching the door fall shut behind Sage of the Gorgeous Hands.

"About what?"

"Rock stars, guys flirting with you when you should be working…the name Sage." Abby started restocking the pastry display with her latest yummies. "That isn't a world you want to be in. I'm going to have to put my foot down."

She gave me a long stare and I was afraid for a second the next words out of her mouth would be something inane like, "And you're grounded, young lady."

"Um. Okay." Because, what else could I really say to that?

After continuing the long stare a moment too long, she nodded before heading through the divider to the kitchen and disappearing.

From the back room, I heard Abby and John having another one of their "discussions." Apparently with me joining the team, John decided Abby could start doing some specialty catering for events. If a plane powered by fancy pastries was falling out of the sky, those two couldn't agree on what made a "specialty dessert."

Between that, the uptick in commuter traffic, and The Brew After Dark acoustic series they were doing monthly…well, I was lucky to be in the right place at the right time to snag the new barista job.

The pay was good, the tips were decent, and the people were nice… Okay, Abby was a little tough sometimes, but nice in her own weird Abby way.

My shift flew by and I was just trying to figure out how to get my Dancing Burrito back across town when Max walked in, all copped out still.

"All right, Burrito Bandit." He grabbed the coffee Abby slid across the counter to him. "Let's get your stolen goods back to their home."

The problem with this place was that everyone thought they were a comedian.

But, I wasn't going to sneeze at a police escort. It would be a lot faster if Max drove me—not to mention having a cop with me would stop the ever easily confused Mr. Burgess from pressing charges.

Max put the costume in the back and then nodded.

"You want me to ride in the back?" I couldn't believe he'd put me back there.

"Procedure." He winked, and I was pretty sure there was nothing procedural about it.

After an incident-free delivery, Max offered to drop me home. Personally, that didn't sound like the best thing for me. My neighborhood wasn't exactly the Village, and getting dropped off by a cop car wouldn't exactly go unnoticed. Instead, I had him drop me back at The Brew and hoofed it home.

Only I was distracted.

It was distracting.

Anyone would be distracted.

But, there he was—*Sage*—loading tools into a truck. I mean, the hands were bad enough. He was wearing a tool belt. I mean. Seriously. A *tool belt*.

And then he did that thing guys do. He reached down for the hem of his T-shirt and lifted it, wiping the sweat off his face.

I dodged down an alley, knowing that staring was bad. Stalking was worse. And the alley came out on the other side of the block.

I tried to push the picture out of my head. But, the cargo shorts-slash-tool belt-slash-six-pack-abs was a killer combo.

Add talented to that—I was going to have to crush this crush immediately.

I was thinking about my need to focus on the important things when I climbed the three-and-a-half flights to the attic apartment I shared with my roommates, Ash and Megan. We were basically the most illegal apartment you could get. Just over the tracks from a better neighborhood...of course. Everywhere was a better neighborhood.

It was an attic that had been renovated into a slightly-illegal apartment, then cut in half to become an incredibly-illegal apartment, thanks to the world's cheapest landlord.

Our half got one bedroom, the claw-footed antique bathroom, the dining room with ornate built-ins...and the pantry.

That's right. No kitchen. So, we were one of those um...*slightly* illegal apartments with a weird combination of two mini-fridges and a hotplate for cooking.

Also, three girls, one bedroom.

Yeah. When Ash and Megan started struggling with the bills, they put an ad on Craigslist for "a female with little expectation of privacy."

Basically, my room was the dining room you had to walk through to get to the bathroom and pantry.

An ancient tallboy dresser blocked off half the room, creating a short wall and the "limited privacy," as advertised.

But, it was cheap and clean and had great girls in it. So, it was a win.

Of course, the limited privacy also meant life updates were pretty much expected. We didn't have Wi-Fi or TV, so Megan had to live on the gossip our lives created.

Which, for me, was low drama.

Ash, on the other hand, was constantly falling in and out of love. Her latest was a bank teller named Liza. Liza seemed way too down-to-earth for Ash, and Megan wanted to start a pool of how long it would last.

"Honey, I'm home!" I pushed the door shut behind me and wandered through to my little alcove of a dining-bedroom. I adjusted the fan to blow more across the room since AC also wasn't in our budget.

"Hey!" Megan came in and dropped down on my bed-couch combo. "How were the jobs?"

"Job'y." I pulled my shirt over my head, getting rid of the smell of food as fast as possible. "How was your day?"

"Oh, you know." Megan shrugged. "Living the dream."

"Excellent." I pulled my favorite over-washed T-shirt on and reveled in the clean softness.

"So, how *was* the new job?"

"Gone."

I gave her the rundown of my day as Ash wandered in and joined the after-work-summit.

Usually, I just ran through my day so I could get to the rest of the apartment's day summary. I loved hearing about the adventures Megan managed to have just by stepping outside the door. And Ash was probably the coolest person I'd ever met. Okay, I'd just met a rock star, but Ash was still right up there.

Megan handed me an iced tea—our version of after-work drinks.

"Not to be all conspiracy theory," Ash said as she stole my tea. "But, I get the you're-not-telling-us-everything vibe pretty clearly."

Ok, I was stalling...and the near arrest was a good story...until I had to share the final bit of the day.

"Oh, and Floppy Hair Gorgeous Hands is named Sage."

They both kind of looked at me as if I were making it up...because, well, *Sage*.

"At least you're not a Rosemary." Ash grinned as if this was super clever.

"Kind of burying the lede there, no?" Megan was always into gossip. Usually it was celebrity related, but roommate related was just as good.

Which reminded me... "Oh, and Blake Diedrich came in today."

"*What?*" Megan was off the bed faster than panties got thrown on the Double Blind stage.

"I guess Sage works for them." Or something. I couldn't really figure it out. It sounded like he did more than design guitars, but I wasn't going to give Megan anything else to flip out about.

"He works for Double Blind."

"Um, yes."

"And he's gorgeous."

"Yes."

"And you're going to avoid him like the plague, aren't you?" Megan's question sounded more like an accusation.

"Megan." Ash shook her head at her. "Not everyone needs to chase the guy."

"Well, she won't even let the guy chase her."

"Yeah," I snorted. "I'm totally sure a girl with four jobs, no family, on the twenty-two year plan at school...not to mention my past is *exactly* what a guy like that is looking for."

"Em—"

Ash slashed her hand between us, cutting Megan off, and crossed to give me a hug.

"You tell yourself whatever you need to, but you're worth more than a collection of struggles."

With that, Ash ushered Megan out of my room.

I stretched out on my bed, thinking that tomorrow I'd find the obvious flaw in Gorgeous Hands to help with Mission Crush the Crush.

I tried to remind myself that Ash was right. That, not only had I overcome a lot, but I was a good person. You didn't need to be born into a great family to be a good person.

If anything, I worked harder to try to be a good person because of that whole *I'm not worthy* fear.

But, knowing my girls had my back, that *they* believed I was worth something, it meant the world. It meant maybe, just maybe, I was finding my place—my home.

# Four

## SAGE

"I still feel like we're losing the melody," Luke said, his arms crossed over his chest, one ankle propped on the opposite knee.

Blake cast him an annoyed glance.

"Look," Luke arched his eyebrows, "you know I like it when you grunge it up. It's just not supposed to dominate the entire song."

"It's this thing," Blake said, ducking his head and lifting the guitar away from him with a vicious shake. "There's something wrong with it."

Harrison stepped forward and took the guitar. "Let me try." He made some adjustments and tried a couple different chords himself. "Yeah. There's something wrong with this one." He inspected the instrument more critically. "Why are you using this cheap POS anyway?"

Blake grinned. "I have a whole box of them."

"This is because you smash them," Harrison reprimanded, pointing his finger for emphasis. "You're the reason we can't have nice things."

Blake shrugged one shoulder, his lips curled in deep, sadistic satisfaction.

Sage watched all of this with a small amount of wonder, exhaustion, and amusement.

As this was his first time being in Luke Casey's garage-converted-to-studio (With no obvious plan for a backup garage. Luke had three cars parked outside.), he was less overwhelmed than he otherwise would be. The exhaustion was definitely to credit for his maximum chill.

Luke had called him right as he was about to go to bed, asking for him to come over.

It didn't matter how tired you were, or how long your workday was, or what time you had to be up in the morning. If Luke Casey, rock star of all rock stars, called you to come over and "run this thing for him," you went.

No questions.

And that meant being asked to run the soundboard on a super secret and important project for Double Blind Study.

What kind of a rock band thought it was a good idea to record an album in a garage when they could just as easily do it at the professional studio they co-owned across town?

The kind of band that took chances with their art, because it was what they *wanted*.

This one. This band did that.

Luke's garage no longer resembled a garage—it was clean, white, and nearly clinical-looking except for large tapestries that had been hung along the walls, breaking up the white space with vibrant splashes of color that functioned into the acoustics.

Sage had always been curious how the Double Blind Study sound came through on their albums so close to what they sounded like live. He no longer wondered. They played the tracks altogether, capturing the energy of their live performances at once. Doing it that way meant they had a more honest interpretation on each album, but it also meant it took more takes to get the song right. More takes meant more time, and more time meant a lot of money.

It was a producing nightmare.

Which Sage had suddenly been thrust into the middle of.

Luke locked eyes with him on the other side of the glass and lifted his chin. "What do you think?"

Flicking the toggle over, Sage leaned into the mic. "It's muddy."

Luke ran a hand through his hair and closed his eyes. "Okay. Let's take a break for a minute." He opened his eyes and pointed at Sage. "Don't leave."

The band unplugged and shut down, one by one filtering into the soundboard room and taking seats on the couches lining the back wall. Sage shut off the things he knew were safe to disengage, and swiveled on his stool to face the band.

Above the long couch hung a huge painting of the band and their women. It was originally a photograph Sage had actually taken the last time they had all been together.

Zelda, Harrison's wife and the band's official photographer, had thrust her camera into Sage's hands and told him to click ten times. He did. The resulting photo had somehow captured the band's dynamic personalities. They were lined up beside one of the buses, side by side, but in total chaos. Laughing, talking, reacting, *living*.

Harrison's sister, Greta, had taken the photo and turned it into a painting filled with bold and bright colors. It was huge—easily six feet long and three feet high. At the bottom, she'd titled it: The Sound of Happiness.

Sage's eyes wandered over the ten people caught in a moment of life that perfectly captured their hearts, and he was intensely thankful for being able to be there. Being able to witness their lives unfold over the past three years was a humbling feeling.

"So." Luke interrupted his daydream, pulling a chair over and sitting on it backward. "How long will it take for you to be comfortable with the board?"

Sage glanced over his shoulder at the console.

Despite its age and little quirks, he was already fairly comfortable with it. It was the mechanical mind he possessed, one of his many hidden talents. He could look at a piece of machinery, even something unfamiliar, and see all the parts and pieces it took to make it work.

It was vastly different from the one they used on tour, but not so much he would have trouble learning it.

Not that he had tons of experience with the tour board, anyway; just what Greg, the sound guy, had taught him.

"A few hours. If I get enough sleep, anyway." His eyes flicked up to the clock on the wall above the board. Midnight. Awesome.

"Why not your regular guy? Out of town, or what?" Sage asked, confused by their interest. It wasn't unusual for him to be called in to assist in the wiring and miking of different projects, but usually there was a professional here to tell him his job.

Wait; was *he* the professional this time?

Luke exchanged looks with the rest of the band.

"When we sat down and talked about how we wanted this album to sound, your name kept coming up. We discussed having you come 'round to do the checks and wiring, but we always ended up discussing how we *sound* different when you wire us. We sound like a kickass garage band who knows what they're doing."

Sage chuckled lightly, uncomfortable with the compliment.

"Add to that this old console, and we have the potential to make an album as authentically DBS as possible. Besides, for the effort we had to go through to get this board, I don't really want anyone else to run it. So...are you available for the next couple of weeks?"

Sage faced the group at Luke's question and cleared his throat. "I have a dining room to build. Other than that, I'm available for whatever you need." And he'd have to stop at the bookstore and get a manual for this ancient thing.

Actually, he was pretty sure he had one at home.

Luke rubbed his chin and exchanged looks with his band. The mixture of shrugs, nods, and meaningful blinks told Sage very little. But it told Luke what he was looking for.

"How does a producing credit and ten percent sound?" Luke asked directly.

Sage frowned. "What now?"

"Producer, Sage," Luke semi repeated. "You want to do this thing with us?"

Sage's heart lodged somewhere in his throat, making both speaking and breathing difficult. It was still beating, which was good, but it was beating so hard his vision was vibrating. He flexed his hands on his jean-clad thighs.

"You want me to co-produce this with you?" he asked for clarification.

"Yeah."

"Okay."

Luke's lips twitched at his reply. Sage was just happy he didn't spontaneously combust into little tiny pieces of Sage confetti. He knew his response sounded like he was cool, but inside his head he was anything *but* cool.

Because, producing?

Producing was the dream.

Moments later, the band went back to their instruments and Sage went back to work. They didn't shut it down for hours.

By the time Sage crawled up the steps to his apartment above his dad's workshop an hour before sunrise, he was beat.

But happy.

\*\*\*

"Coffee. Please. All the coffee that you have." Sage plunked his money on the counter. Great; his vision was blurry. He was officially experiencing the *blind* part of the Double Blind life.

"You look like crap," Abby stated needlessly.

"Is Emily working today?" Sage asked, ignoring the snarky barista and trying to see through the walls into the kitchen area. Which would have been ridiculous anyway, but it was doubly so since he couldn't see much of anything. And there was the *double blind* part of this life.

"My coffee's not good enough?" Abby asked, filling his order while keeping one suspicious eye on him.

"She's nice and happy, and I happen to like her smile, killjoy." Sage took his coffee from Abby and shuffled over to his spot by the window. He tucked his phone into his pocket and flopped his notebook onto the table.

Was he an idiot for agreeing to all of the things?

This dining room was going to kill him. And if it didn't, then the lack of sleep would. But if he somehow survived that, it would be the pile of dirty clothes in his bedroom coming to life and eating him alive.

But he'd be a complete moron to turn down this opportunity to be a producer for DBS. This was the kind of stuff he really wanted to do. He loved to make music, even if he was only flipping the switches and turning the dials that made it possible.

A bright spot in the outside edge of his vision caught his attention and he rotated his head slowly to see Emily back behind the counter. His slumped-over posture straightened immediately, and he tried a smile on for her. She smiled back and Sage called it a win—even if it was small and half directed at the next customer.

Dang, she was pretty.

Okay, focus on the hutch. He rubbed his tired eyes and watched the lines blur on the page in front of him.

Crap. This was bad.

More coffee.

"Sage?"

Sage picked up his coffee and ignored the voice behind him, convinced it was a hallucination.

Because, why was his mom here?

At The Brew.

"Sage, baby?"

He nodded, surrendering to his tired imagination, and turned around. "Hey, Ma."

Beatrix McNabb, his ma and a southern belle transplant dressed in her customary pastel palette, embraced him as he stood. "I tried to catch you before you left this morning, but I wasn't fast enough."

She glanced at his table and then around The Brew. "I went over to Mrs. Callahan's, since that's where your dad said you'd been workin', and she said you'd be down here. I have to admit, I had no idea this was even here. What a darlin' little place. Is the coffee good?"

Sage grinned at her adorable ramble while she was already heading for the counter.

His ma.

Embracing life, one discovery at a time.

Emily stepped up to the front, Sage caught her eye and winked. "Best coffee in town, Ma."

She set her little clutch on the counter and popped it open, directing her attention to Emily. "I'll take a small hazelnut latte to go, if you don't mind."

"You got it," Emily replied brightly before turning to fill the order.

"Listen, baby," Ma said, turning more toward Sage and dropping her voice to just above a whisper. "Your father and I will be gone when you get home tonight. I didn't want you to worry. I made sure the fridge and icebox were all stocked up."

She sighed and tilted her head, giving him the Concerned Mother Face before patting a soft hand on his cheek. "You look so tired, baby. I know how you like to work yourself to death," she admonished sweetly.

That's when she took two hundred-dollar bills out of her purse and handed them to him. Sage snatched at it, hoping Emily didn't see. But she did. She was openly staring at their interaction, the coffee in hand, the lid half pressed down but temporarily forgotten.

"Here's some money for food while we're gone. In case what I left isn't enough," Ma continued, unaware of her son's discomfort or their audience. She took a breath, her eyes scanning his face with more worry than was needed for a man his age. "Call us if you need anything."

Sage swallowed, his heart beating the drums of guilt and shame. Well, so much for impressing Emily ever again.

"I will, Ma. Safe travels." Sage hugged her tightly and she rubbed his shoulder vigorously, an action she used to prevent herself from getting emotional.

It wasn't her fault.

He was her only. And not even by blood.

She loved him and never apologized for how she went about doing it.

Emily cleared her throat as she set the coffee on the counter, drawing Ma's attention.

"I *love* your glasses," Ma said. "Your entire outfit is cute as a button."

Emily said something. Then Ma said something. They were conversing. Sage could no longer hear the words due to the roaring sound of his own ineptitude beating him over the head.

No way was he going to be able to convince Emily he was cool. Not after all those lovely revelations.

Ma left, and it was just him and Emily and Abby. And the two hundreds wadded in his fist. He didn't meet their eyes. He didn't want to know what pitiful disappointment looked like on Emily's face.

Taking the two hundred dollars, he stuffed them into the tip jar, and turned back to his table.

He needed to finish a dining room.

# FIVE

### EMILY

So, Hot Artistic Guy was also Super Rich Guy. Bummer.

If there was one thing I knew, it was that rich guys didn't do anything long-term with girls like me. They saw us as nothing but toys.

Not that it mattered. I was off boys. Maybe forever. And no, that didn't mean I was on to girls. Maybe *off relationships* was a better way to put it.

"Did you see that?" Abby nudged me.

"What?" I pushed the rolling pastry display stand down the counter and scrubbed at the mess under it.

"He stuck two hundred bucks in our tip jar." She stared at the jar as if she thought it was a joke. As if it would be gone—or fake—if one of us reached for it.

I glanced in the jar—from a safe distance because that was a bucket full of money—and then back up at Abby.

"Do you think it's a joke?" I asked.

She shrugged. A wordless Abby. That was…weird.

"Maybe he's just screwing with us." Because *that*, my friend, is what rich guys did. They screwed with you while trying to screw you.

"Maybe," she said, and turned away, apparently done with trying to figure out the money in the jar.

I grabbed it, making sure it was just the two bills, then headed around the counter, Abby watching me with raised eyebrows.

I got to his—*Sage's*—table and put it down there.

"You dropped this." Because, what was I supposed to say?

"No. I didn't. I put it in the tip jar."

"Right. So, we can't take it." I crossed my arms, trying to look as tough as possible.

There was an insanely loud throat clearing from behind me. I ignored it.

That was the thing with being little and blonde and wearing glasses and having freckles…Yeah. No one took me seriously. I was scrappy. Don't mess.

"Why not?" He honestly looked confused.

"Because we're not here to steal rich boys' allowances. However will you live?" I hadn't realized it till I was done, but I'd picked up his mother's Southern lilt.

"I'll live just fine on *both* of my jobs."

Of course he would. He lived at home. Sounded like he didn't have to worry about food or cleaning…or anything else, either.

"Listen." He lowered his voice. "That's not me. I'm not that guy. I pay my way. I'm living at home because I'm not home much. I'm usually on the road. And 'living at home' is an apartment on my family's land." He shrugged, but I could see the color on his cheeks. "And, trust me, I know how to buy groceries and cook for myself. I was actually going to do exactly that last night, but I got called into work."

I stared down at him, wondering what kind of cabinet building emergencies happened at night, and shook my head.

"I don't know why she felt like she needed to hunt me down and give me money, but it's not because I don't have my own—don't *work* for my own. She likes to…check on me." He took a deep breath and leaned forward. "How about we do this: You keep the tip, I keep my dignity, and we both pretend my mother doesn't know how to find me on my break ever again."

I stared at him, honestly believing he was embarrassed by the whole thing, but thinking there wasn't a lot of space to get past the rich guy part.

Not that I was looking to get past it.

That was Megan talking.

Megan talked a lot.

Just not usually so directly in my head.

"Okay," I said, only because of the dignity remark. Not that Abby and I couldn't each use the extra hundred.

I headed back to the land behind the counter, slipping one hundred in my back pocket and handing the other to Abby.

"Abs," I started, and smiled at her smirk. "He says he needs us to keep this to attempt to buy back his dignity."

She pocketed the money. "I didn't know dignity had a going rate."

I thought about my rent and wondered if I could market dignity on Craigslist.

# Six

## SAGE

"Oh, Sage, darling, you look absolutely exhausted." Mrs. Callahan patted his cheek the way a concerned grandmother would, her head tilting to the side.

It was the same look his mom had given him just the day before.

Apparently mothers everywhere were united in pointing out his obvious fatigue.

"Haven't been to bed yet," Sage answered, setting down his toolbox. Nope; instead, he'd been with rock stars. It had taken all night and he wasn't even a little bit sorry.

Mrs. Callahan tsked. "To have the energy of your youth again," she said wistfully. Sage didn't inform her that she often had *way* more energy than he did most days and she really had nothing to worry about.

He knelt down and undid the latch on his toolbox.

"Don't bother getting set up, sweetie," Mrs. Callahan instructed as she bustled to the closet by the entrance. "I'm heading out. I tried to call you this morning, but you didn't answer."

Sage frowned and checked his phone. He had missed a call at five o'clock. "I must have been in the shower."

"My daughter has run into a bit of trouble and I need to go to Chicago for a few days." She handed her coat to Sage, who automatically helped her into it while she talked. "I'll keep you updated on how long I'll be gone. There's no reason for you to be here if I'm not. Besides, after yesterday, you're way ahead of schedule. I think you've earned a bit of a break."

Sage nodded, glancing around the dining room he'd left in disarray the day before. She wasn't wrong. After yesterday's lovely humiliation, he'd managed to put together three chairs and a table before calling it a day.

Frustration was an interesting motivator.

"Would you be a dear and help me downstairs?" she asked, gesturing to the suitcase next to the door.

"Of course." Sage hefted the case in one hand and the toolbox in the other. He had not been expecting a sudden day off. This would work out perfectly. He had time to have his coffee and study the book he'd found and brought with him before he had to be back at Luke's tonight.

And maybe he'd have a nap.

If he had time.

\*\*\*

You know that hazy fog you develop with lack of sleep and familiarity? The kind where you suddenly feel at home in a department store or gas station simply because you were too tired to activate your "public location" sensors?

Sage was there with The Brew. He'd been frequenting it long enough, and he had passed healthy levels of exhaustion about four hours ago. The Brew may as well have been his living room.

"Again, with the looking like an exhausted sailor."

Sage sighed at Abby's delightful greeting.

"Also, you're early," she tacked on for good measure. You know, in case he didn't feel overwhelmed by her love already.

His eyes flicked to the kitchen doors, waiting for that ray of sunshine to show herself, but they didn't open.

"She's not here," Abby supplied, plunking one of her tall shot glasses of caffeine goodness on the counter. "And I have a new one for you, if you're feeling brave."

"Oh," Sage said with a frown. "Is she okay?" It was too big of a question. He knew it the moment it passed his lips, but by then it was too late.

Abby arched one eyebrow and crossed her arms over her chest. "Yep."

"Cool," he muttered, dropping his gaze to the shot glass. It was pink on the bottom. He took hold of it, held Abby's gaze, and shot it back.

Almond, espresso, finished with...

"Is that raspberry?" he asked, smacking his lips together.

She nodded, a pleased light hitting her face.

"That's good stuff, Abs." He paid for his coffee and the shot and moved away from the counter toward his table when Abby spoke again.

"She'll be here later."

Sage glanced over his shoulder, but Abby was already busying herself and avoiding eye contact. He set his coffee down and then himself, his body feeling like it had aged ten years in the last two days.

Mrs. Callahan's unexpected trip out of town had come at the perfect time for him. He was nearly finished with the dining room. All that was left was the hutch and two more chairs. Easily a week's worth of work. But with the added obligation of recording for DBS at night, he really would have had to push himself.

Now he wouldn't have to.

He drained his coffee and tried to focus on the enormous book in front of him. Most of this stuff he already knew from helping Greg set up the board on tour occasionally. The specific console Luke had in his garage was just slightly different. They were recording on analog—which was flipping sweet; Sage had long dreamed of being able to record on tape. But whoever had owned it last had made special modifications.

He was halfway to the restroom when he wondered if maybe he should take his book with him. He doubted very much Abby would prevent anyone from stealing it. Then again, who would want to steal a used book about recording and audio technique?

You know, besides someone like him.

When he exited the bathroom, his steps faltered. Emily was sitting at his table, paging through his book. He licked his lips, feeling a fresh flush of shame heat his cheeks as he remembered yesterday again.

Yeah, his dignity was completely intact; nothing to worry about there.

She looked up at him as he pulled out his chair.

"I saw your coffee was almost empty, so I refilled it," she said, standing up in haste. "No sketches today?" she asked brightly, nodding to his monster of a book.

He tried to catch a glimpse of those baby blues, but she was looking at the book on the table. He'd considered avoiding The Brew the day after winning his lifetime achievement award for Failure To Adult, as presented by his mother. But the need for caffeine and the hope for forgiveness was too strong.

Considering Emily hadn't completely snubbed him, he felt a hundred times better.

"Nope. Today I need to study for my *other* job," he said. A yawn caught him off guard, and he covered his mouth with the back of one hand while reaching for his fresh refill. "Thank you for this." He saluted with the cup before taking a scalding yet welcome swallow.

"*Audio Cyclopedia,*" she read the cover, tapping the thick book with her finger. "That's some heavy reading."

Sage shrugged with one shoulder. "I read it once already. In college. Mostly, this is a refresher."

"For your second job. Does this have something to do with the rock stars?"

Sage cracked a smile and scratched the side of his neck. "Yeah," he muttered, looking down at the book. "I'm just glad I found it. It wasn't easy to find the first time. I'm guessing it would be harder now."

Emily pressed her lips together and her eyebrows twitched with a thought she didn't share. Which was a shame, because he had a feeling she had a lot to say. Every once in a while he'd be rewarded with little flashes of the inner Emily, but they weren't enough. He wanted more.

Sage sucked in a breath and went for it. "Do you ever have an evening off?"

Emily's head jerked and her smile faded. She recovered and took a deep breath. "I work pretty much all of the time."

Sage nodded. "I gathered that. But I was hoping you might have one night free for, say, food and conversation...?"

Her frown deepened, and she took another step backward. Usually, in his experience, this would be the moment someone would walk in, intruding on his very limited moment with Emily. He braced for the front door to open.

But it didn't.

"I really need to get back to work..." Emily pointed a thumb over her shoulder and attempted an apologetic look that didn't look sorry at all.

Sage didn't realize he was following her until he came to the edge of the counter and wasn't allowed to go any further. Emily whirled around, her sassy edge from yesterday making a comeback.

"Look, it's nothing personal. I don't even know you. But I'm not dating anyone right now. Or for the foreseeable future."

The slight color in her cheeks only made her more adorable and Sage had to fight off a smile.

"Good. Great," he agreed quickly. "I'm so glad you said that, because I don't want to date you, either." He held his hands up, palms outward when her eyes widened. "Nothing against you. I'm sure you're excellent girlfriend material. I just don't see you in that way."

Her eyes narrowed and her mouth got small as her hands landed on her hips. "What's that supposed to mean?"

Sage tucked his hands in his pockets and shrugged, walking down the counter. She followed on the other side. "All I asked was if you might want to eat food with me and talk. It wasn't a date."

She let out a stunted laugh. "That sounds *exactly* like a date."

He shook his head once as he made a small show of thinking it over. "No, I'm pretty sure if I were asking you out on a date, you would know."

She scoffed, her cheeks turning a lovely hot pink. "Oh, really?"

"Yeah," he answered matter-of-factly. "Without a doubt."

She stared at him, suspicion, distrust, and curiosity shining out of her gorgeous blue eyes.

He waited.

"Can I think about it?" she asked in such a way Sage knew there was a very definitive reason for her anti-dating policy. And he suddenly wanted to punch that jerk of a reason right in the nuts.

"Absolutely," he said softly, a thought happening in the back of his mind. He turned it over a couple of times and then brought it to the forefront. "I mean, if you really need to think about just hanging out..."

He shrugged, as if it were no big deal, keeping a close eye on her reaction.

"Sure. Yeah. That's what I need." Emily gave him a look like she was on to his crap.

"All right. Well, in the meantime," he leaned back, trying to act all casual with his quasi-recovered dignity, "I'll just drink the world's most delicious coffee and study like a regular nerd."

Emily rolled her eyes, but she was smiling, so he would take it.

"I will think about it," she reiterated.

"Cool."

It was cool. It was so darn cool, Sage wanted to fist pump in victory, but that would *not* be cool. So he withheld.

He was so tired.

# Seven

### EMILY

"Stop giving him free coffee. This isn't a diner." Abby swept crumbs off the counter and glared at me. "This perkiness has to stop. People are coming in here and wanting to hang out. No more of that."

"Abby, we're a *café*." I shook my head at her. "That's pretty much the definition of what happens at a café."

"Whatever."

I glanced at the door Sage had escaped out after I'd turned him down, and wondered what he was up to.

I wasn't stupid. It had taken me a moment to realize he was lying about it not being a date. I wasn't into guys doing the stealth-dating thing, but since he'd asked straight-out first, that could be forgiven.

It was the "We're not dating—oh, oops! We're in a relationship!" games I hated.

Ash's girlfriends always seemed to pull that crap. Or maybe Ash just managed to always pick out girlfriends who pulled crap.

Abby hovered over me while I restocked everything from the mid-morning shift.

"Go away." I didn't even look at her.

There was something amazingly freeing about not having to be super nice to someone. Abby didn't speak super-nice, so I was learning her native tongue.

I glanced over at her.

"Seriously," I said. "You're off. Go away. Don't you have to study? Or try going outside. There's an entire world out there."

Abby gave me one of her flat muppet-glares before pivoting and banging into the kitchen. I heard her stomping up the stairs at the back of the building to her apartment. Then stomping around upstairs. I wondered if she was hurting her feet walking that heavily to make her point, and went back to my restocking.

It was mindless work that let me focus on other things, like how I was going to finish paying for a class or two next semester.

No matter how you looked at it, I was going to need a fifth job. The Brew was basically paying my living expenses. Let's face it. Living in a dining room had its perks cost-wise. John paid me well on the barista scale, and the tips were good.

But, I put last semester's class on a credit card and still had to pay that off before I could even think about the next one. The interest rate wasn't exactly my friend after missing two months before I found Ash and Megan to live with. If I could get another job and pay off the credit card, I could think about upping my class schedule to two a semester.

Except…when would I work?

I laid my head on the counter with a heavy thud, thinking about how nothing ever seemed to come even. Getting a job was hard enough. I thanked God every day my record was sealed.

I'll never forget the gutting I felt as the pit of my stomach dropped out when Max came in, decked out in all his copness, and shook John's hand before the two sat down to chat.

I was sure—*dead* sure—this was one of those deals where John had run my record and a buddy at the station found something he shouldn't have been able to.

Not being one to torture myself, I strode across the room in a determination I'd honed and sat in Max's seat before John had a chance to call me over.

"So?" I'd asked.

John looked at me as if I were nuts.

And no wonder. Apparently Max was one of his friends and no one had run anything, and John hadn't even thought to.

I came clean about my record—told John the whole twisted story—and thought I'd be out the door for good.

All he said was "Don't be stupid" and headed off to do whatever John did all day.

Now I was just another one of John's adopted baristas…living the life. When Abby came back at the end of the day, I packed up to head out.

"Off to job four hundred?"

"Nope. Three hundred and seventy-two." I tossed the register keys to her and grabbed my bag.

And with that I was off, because a job waits for no woman.

\*\*\*

The next morning, I hit The Brew mid-shift, glancing toward the seat in the window without meaning to.

I was *not* going to be derailed by some mama's boy who was used to having everything handed to him.

"He was already here," Abby said from behind the counter.

"Who?" I asked, barely glancing her way.

"Don't be an idiot." Abby shook her head and wandered off to bake something.

"I'll have a frosty goodness something." I glanced up to find Megan standing across the counter, her gaze flitting around the café. "Goodness that costs less than two eighty-three, please."

Because I could make anything Megan thought of as a treat for less than seven hundred dollars, with how many scoops of chocolate and pumps of syrup she'd want.

I started mixing up something I knew was coming out of my tip jar while I watched her attempt to act casual.

"Megan?"

"Emily?"

"What are you doing here?"

"Oh, you know. Just dropping in to say hi." She gave me a very suspicious smile that was basically an attempt to look innocent.

Whenever Megan looked innocent, games were afoot.

I gave her the look Abby gave me on a regular basis—I'd been practicing in the mirror—and she took a step back.

"Wow, what was that?" She looked over her shoulder as if someone behind her was trying to pull shenanigans too.

I gave her the look again.

"Fine!" Megan dropped her two eight-three on the counter and leaned over it. "Is he here?"

"Who?"

"Don't play games with me, missy." She was practically crawling over the counter, whisper-shouting at this point. "The guitar designer to his godliness Blake Diedrich?"

I should have known this day would come. But no. I was naïve in the ways of Megan. I'd only lived with her three months, and it hadn't dawned on me she'd go all casual stalker on me.

"He's not here." Which, thankfully, was true.

"Fine." She took her fancy practically-free drink and headed over to the corner, where she pulled out a book and settled in.

"What are you doing?"

"I'm a paying customer."

*"Barely."* I looked at my tip jar, annoyed at myself for having enabled her ridiculousness.

Megan sat at her table, reading away. Every time the door opened, she'd check to see if it was a young, hot guy. If it even *might* be a young hot guy, she'd look at me for a reaction.

I considered running to the ladies' room to practice my straight face, but then decided that was too boring. When it came to Megan, a girl had to play sneaky.

The next young guy who came in, I made sure I did everything I could to look interested.

It didn't hurt that it was Brent.

Brent was so full of himself that it was amazing he even bothered to speak out loud to tell me his order. He also thought he was hot stuff.

As soon as he walked in the door, I straightened up, running my hands over my hair and giving him my brightest smile.

Any other guy would have paused, wondering what was going on. But, not him. Nope. He was probably thinking, *It's about time.*

"Hi! How are you!" I smiled, giving him all my perky-cheer in one dose.

"Um, good. You?" Even Brent was realizing he was getting a little more attention than normal.

"Great!" I ran my hands down my side, smoothing out my apron. "The regular!"

It was getting hard to make all these questions into excited statements.

"Um, sure. Sounds good."

Well, crud. Who knew Brent had a regular? He was the person I typically paid the least attention to, so I had no idea what I was supposed to be making now.

As I turned my back on him and reached for the French press behind me—because I could only imagine Brent was the kind of guy to order a French press in the middle of a rush—I caught Abby leaning against the kitchen doorway looking at me like I'd lost my mind.

Since it wasn't out of the realm of possibilities, I just kept staring at the press, trying to remember what I'd made him yesterday.

"Hi." Megan's voice slipped over my shoulder from where she'd moved in on Brent.

I tried to suppress the grin, but since my back was to them, why bother?

"I'm Megan," she said, as if it might mean something to him. Of course, it wouldn't mean anything to Sage either. I didn't know what she thought I did here all day.

"Hi, Megan." Brent didn't sound anywhere near as surprised as he should. But, again. Ego.

"So, I'd ask if you come here often, but I already know the answer to that."

"You...do?" His blurred reflection in the menu board over my head looked surprised for the first time...and maybe a little worried.

"Yup. I'm here just to meet you." She gave a little giggle.

Out of context, I'm sure it sounded like the insane laughter of an obsessed stalker.

"You...are?" Another step back.

Abby sidled up next to me, her back to them as well. "What are you doing?"

"Making a something-something French press something with extra milk?" Because I still wasn't sure what Brent's regular drink was.

"That's not what I mean."

I glanced over my shoulder at where he waited for his drink, Megan all but bouncing on her toes while she grinned up at him.

"Um...she's stalking Sage because I made the mistake of mentioning the rock star guy, and now she wants to get all in on that."

"She's using The Brew to hit on rock stars?"

"Married ones."

Abby's gasp was pure outrage. Although, I'm not sure which part of this equation ticked her off more.

"Plus," I continued, "Brent's a high-maintenance low tipper. It wouldn't be such a big loss, would it?"

Abby glanced over at them, amused, but not admitting it.

"Anyway," Megan continued, totally not catching that anything was wrong yet. "I was wondering...what is it you do?"

"Do?" Brent sounded nervous *and* suspicious now.

Of course, I was kind of curious what he did, too.

"Yes. For work?"

"I'm a fiscal government law advisor."

"Wait. No, you aren't." Megan laughed, and I saw her fuzzy outline reach out and give him a light slap on the arm.

Abby shifted to lean on the counter next to me, watching them.

"Yes. I am. And, did you just hit me?" He sounded outraged, as if she'd hauled off and decked him in the face while wearing brass knuckles.

"That wasn't a hit. It was a...love tap."

Oh, man. I really should put a stop to this.

I started to turn around, my mouth already open to get Megan's attention, when Abby grabbed my arm and shook her head.

Well, at least I could blame this wreck on my boss from here on in.

"No. That was a hit."

Abby snorted. I couldn't blame her, but this seemed pretty much in line with the Brent we've seen here.

"Um, no." Megan didn't sound so sure of herself now. "But, I was just... Anyway, I thought you were a designer."

"Of clothes?" he asks.

I gave up and turned around. The look he gave her outfit was one of such disdain I was afraid her clothes might start crying from having their feelings hurt.

At this, the door opened and in walked Sage.

"Oh." Abby was smiling now. It scared me. "This is going to be good."

"No." Megan crossed her arms and straightened up, all playfulness completely gone. Now he'd done it. He'd judged her clothes. "Of guitars, *Sage*. I'm not sure how you'd pick clothes designer by mistake."

"Right. Do I look like I'd sit around designing toys all day?"

Sage jerked as if someone had smacked him, but kept his mouth shut—and his distance.

"And, anyway, what the hell kind of guy would be named Sage?" Brent sounded so offended I started to feel bad. I mean, not for him, but still.

"I would be." Behind him, Sage stepped forward, glancing between the two idiot strangers arguing over his name, and then up at me. Clearly he suspected I was somehow the silent instigator.

I glanced from Brent—all suited up, tall, and clean-cut—to Sage, who definitely looked like he worked for a rock band—and I knew that no matter how stupid it was, I was getting pitter-pattery over the wrong guy.

Of course, *neither* of them was the right guy since I was a guy-free zone, but still.

Knowing things were just going to get even more ugly, I handed Brent his drink—which may or may have not been relatively close to his regular—and told him no charge.

He didn't bother to stick the five in his hand in the tip jar. No real shocker there. There's got to be some fancy-dancy place over by his financial law advisory whatever office building, so hopefully that was the last time he would skip tipping me, if the coffee gods were kind.

"*You're* Sage?" Megan gave him an incredibly suspicious look, as if this were all his fault.

"Yes." He sounded pretty sure of the fact that he was the Sage she was referring to. Of course, I had to wonder how many Sages were running around town.

"What kind of name is Sage?" Megan asked.

"Actually," Abby leaned over the counter, "I've been wondering that, too."

"Well, if it's a strong enough name for Sylvester Stallone to name his son, then I don't think any of you should be questioning it."

With that, Sage did the closest thing to a manly version of a flounce and swaggered his way over to his chair.

And now, Brent was gone.

Sage was sitting at his table, sans coffee.

Megan was glaring at me.

"So, Megan," I stopped, not sure what I was going to say.

"So, Emily." Megan stopped…probably a little more sure what she wanted to say, but she was using her company manners.

"So, girls." Abby tossed down the towel she'd been holding. "This has been interesting and all, but Emily has to do some work." She raised her hand, interrupting Megan before she could even get going. "She bought you a coffee that's going to cost her thirty minutes of tips, and you deserved the prank for trying to use her friendship. Go back to your corner and think about what you've done."

Megan looked at Abby like she wanted to argue…but even Megan was more socially aware than that.

"And, you." Abby turned back to me. "You make me proud. But don't mess with the good tippers."

She disappeared back into the kitchen.

This job was—in some ways—the weirdest job I had. I mean, especially since the Dancing Burrito thing overflowed into The Brew—I was totally counting that.

"So." I looked up to find Designer of the Gods standing on the other side of the counter, hands in his pockets. "What was that?"

He jerked his head toward Megan without glancing her way.

"That was Hurricane Megan. Otherwise known as my roommate."

"Oh." He nodded, but after a second asked, "Why did she think that guy was me?"

"I may have let her jump to a conclusion." I said it as if I hadn't pushed her over the Cliffs of Conclusions into the Bay of Bad Assumptions.

Sage's mouth kicked up on the right side into a cocky grin I hadn't expected to see from him. "So, you're talking about me, huh?"

Oh. Crud.

"Nope." I shook my head. "But, Abby. That girl can't shut up about you."

"Uh-huh."

Yeah. I wouldn't have believed me, either.

"I may have mentioned you because of the whole Rock Star Buying Coffee and Asking For Handmade Guitars thing." I gave him a *sorry* smile, figuring he was sick of people talking about his connection to Double Blind.

"Oh."

The word was so flat I wasn't sure what to say. But he nodded and walked back to his table, pulling his phone out and probably Googling other coffee shops in the area.

After a few, he came back, and leaned against the counter.

"So, do you want your regular?" I'm trying this again since I actually *knew* what his regular was.

"Sure. Also," he raised his voice, and half turned toward the table Megan was still sitting at, looking like a puppy who'd gotten her nose smacked with a newspaper, "I was thinking, since you don't want to date me—"

There's an annoyed gasp from the vicinity I was calling The Megan Bubble on the other side of the room.

"And, since I figured anything we do just the two of us would be too close to a date for you, maybe you and your friend Megan—"

"YES! Whatever it is, yes!" Megan jumped out of her seat, then sat back down, glancing toward the kitchen door.

Sage turned her way. "Really?"

"Absolutely." She nodded, her curls bouncing around her shoulders.

"Great." He grinned at her. "I hate going to the dump myself, but you find some great stuff to refinish there."

"The dump?"

Poor Megan.

All of us messing with her today.

Me. Abby. Brent—accidentally, of course. Now Sage.

"Yup."

"Oh. Um. Sure." Megan looked at me, her lips pursed and her brows drawn down like there was something important she was missing. "Emily, what does someone wear to the dump?"

I burst out laughing.

"You're not really inviting us to the dump, are you?" I asked, because even Megan didn't deserve this much torture.

"No." Sage shook his head and gave me the best smile I'd seen all day. "I thought you might want to come to work with me tonight."

Megan literally bounced in her chair. But, I could see she wasn't going to make the same mistake twice. She was definitely burning off that extra pump of chocolate I'd given her.

"To make cabinets?" she clarified.

"Well, you could come do that someday too, but tonight I actually have to record some fresh tracks for a new DBS album."

"Oh." I glanced toward Megan, who was nodding like a bobblehead on the dashboard of a car in a high-speed chase. "Tonight?"

"It's your night off!" Megan all but shouted.

Sage turned her way and gave her the super-best smile. "Thanks, Megan."

"No problem." She actually gave him the thumbs up.

I didn't even know what this farce was anymore.

"Where is it?" I asked, knowing logistics weren't going to stop Megan.

When Sage named a town too far outside our area to hit on the train, I had the excuse I needed.

"Sorry. I don't have a car."

And, we already covered the stranger-danger thing yesterday.

"I'll get a Zipcar!" Megan was still bouncing.

"What?" Because, that was not the plan as I saw it.

"A Zipcar!" Megan repeated, still with the exclamation point clearly planted at the end.

"You drive?"

"Yup." She looked proud of this fact, as if ninety percent of people didn't drive.

"But, a Zipcar costs money." Winning point, Emily.

"I have a gift card."

"For Zipcar?" Seriously, were there gift cards for everything?

"It's more of a refund thingy I need to use, but yes."

There was an excellent chance she'd lost her mind. But that probably happened before I met her. The sanity issue was just becoming more obvious now that her favorite band was all but within reach of her code orange level stalker actions.

I knew there'd be no living with her if I said no, so I did the only thing I could.

"Okay. Give us an address and we'll see you tonight."

And, on the way home, I'd have a Zipcar I could use to hide Megan's body.

# EIGHT

## SAGE

"SO, THE COFFEE GIRL, HUH?"

Sage dragged his eyes to the right, keeping his hands steady on the wiring under the console. Blake Diedrich was in a squat, butt to heels, his fingers laced, elbows to knees. As if he hung out like that on the regular.

"Yep," Sage confirmed, focusing again on the connection switch he'd been trying to tighten. "If she shows up."

"Why wouldn't she show up? Doesn't she know about..." Blake waved his hands around the area. "All of this?"

Sage pinched the skin in between his thumb and forefinger in the jagged wood panel as he removed his hand. "Ow, shit, yeah."

Blake backed out of the way as Sage rolled out from under the console. He stood up and flipped the switch that he'd been trying to reconnect. The light blinked on and he grunted in satisfaction. At least he was good at some things.

"When does your date get here?" Sway asked, flopping onto the long couch behind them.

This may have been a bad idea. "It's not a date. We're just hanging out."

Blake, his arms crossed over his Black Sabbath T-shirt, and threw an eye roll to Sway. "You're abusing your friendship with us to hit on chicks, dude."

Sage cracked a smile. It never got old hearing a rock star refer to you as a friend. "Abusing? No. Definitely taking advantage of."

"I love being taken advantage of," Sway declared wistfully.

Sage shook his head. He was surprised it had taken them this long to say something, truthfully. He'd half expected a full inquisition when he'd arrived two hours ago after leaving Emily to finish up her job. But not even Lenny asked him anything about it when she'd let him in earlier. Sage had begun to believe maybe Luke hadn't told anyone else. It was better this way; get the questions and teasing out now instead of later—when (if) Emily showed and caused her to run even faster away from him then she already was.

Part of him felt bad he was basically playing his biggest card just to get a conversation with her. That's all he wanted.

He wasn't stupid; she was not that into him. If anything, she was downright annoyed with him.

But every once in a while... she would smile at him.

That sounded ridiculous, she smiled all the time. She had one of the best smiles around and used it on everyone.

But there was a particular way she smiled at him when she thought he wasn't paying attention.

It was two parts hesitant and one part hopeful, and Sage couldn't get it out of his head. Like she wanted him to ask, but she needed to be able to say no.

She needed to be able to know she could reject him and he wasn't going to turn into a dick.

And she could. She could reject him a hundred times and he would still feel stolen by her smile and thankful for her kindness. He didn't mind being rejected. Not even a little.

He sighed and sat down in front of the console. "The only reason I was able to talk her into coming tonight was because her roommate is very obviously a fan— of you, not me—so it was a little like an unplanned ambush."

He checked the note he'd made earlier and adjusted the appropriate knobs.

"Does she know what a big nerd you are?" Blake asked, fiddling with knobs on his side of the console. Sage smacked his hand away.

"I don't know. I've been leaving my I'm a Giant Nerd sandwich board at home lately." He shrugged one shoulder. "But she's seen my sketches, and this monster." He lifted up his copy of *Audio Cyclopedia*. "My personal favorite was when my mom came in and announced I was still living at home."

Blake whistled under his breath. "And you haven't given up yet?"

Sage snorted a laugh. "What can I say? I have a thing for girls who are too good for me."

"They're the best kind," Sway spoke up seriously.

Blake patted him on the shoulder with the back of his hand. "Don't worry; we've got your back."

"That's exactly what I'm afraid of," Sage said around a chuckle.

"What? Why?" Blake actually looked confused.

Sage shook his head, remembering the last time he had a girl visit him while he worked.

"Oh, yeahhh," Sway said before letting out a deep laugh. "Remember when his ex—what was her name? Heely? Bethel?—"

"Heather," Sage supplied.

"Right! Heather the Clever," Blake jumped in. "We saved you, dude. That girl had issues."

Heather had come out to see him, upon his invite, of course, when the band had played a festival. It had really been the nail in the coffin of their relationship. He had been hoping that if she saw what it was he did, and how good he was at it, and how happy it made him, she'd be happy for him. That was all he wanted.

But she hadn't been impressed.

"I'm still pissed at her on your behalf," Blake rumbled. "You're really friggin' talented and she treated your job like a monkey could do it."

"To be fair," Sage spoke up, "she said *orangutan*. Orangutans are among the most intelligent primates. They use tools, construct elaborate nests...they even develop distinct cultural ideals, and have incredible learning capabilities."

When he was met with silence, he turned to see Blake shaking his head at him.

"Nerd."

Sage grinned.

Losing Heather only sucked because she had been awesome— smart, driven, great sense of humor, wasn't afraid to try new things. But ultimately they had just wanted different lives.

She wanted a steady future, all mapped out from beginning to end. And Sage wanted to travel and create. He enjoyed using his hands in conjunction with his brain to make brand-new things, and Heather thought manual labor was a step below successful.

It wasn't her fault, really; it was just the family she had been raised in and the expectations put on her by her parents.

Finding out they didn't have the same idea for the future had hurt. It had probably hurt him more than her.

Still, he wasn't going to be bitter about it. He was thankful for the lesson he'd learned and even more thankful she'd given him a chance at all.

The indicator light directly beside the one he'd just fixed blinked out.

Sage sighed and crawled back under the console.

He wondered what Emily would think of his job. If she would be impressed, or underwhelmed.

He knew one thing. She was absolutely worth the chance he was taking to find out.

# NINE

## EMILY

MEGAN STEPPED OUT OF HER room wearing a Double Blind Study T-shirt.

"No." I finally found the line and drew it. "Nope. Not gonna happen."

"But I want to show them my love! I mean, this T-shirt dates back to pre-the mess." She smoothed her hands down her side, pulling the fitted tee even tighter. "I've been with them through it all."

I wasn't sure what the band's "the mess" was—and to be honest, I didn't care—but Megan was already going to go mega-fan on them and my job was to mitigate as much embarrassment as possible right up front.

Megan narrowed her eyes, and I knew she would not go softly into this great night.

"What if—"

"No."

"I could—"

"No."

"Fine, but—"

"Still no."

Megan gave me what she thought of as her Death Glare Laser Eyes and swung back into her room to change.

"Don't put a jacket on," I called after her. "I'll just check."

Behind me, Ash laughed. Why couldn't Ash be the fan?

"She's just going to stuff the shirt in her bag," she whispered the words, a fair heads up.

"Thanks. I'll do a bag check, too."

She came back out wearing a little denim skirt, a snap-button cowgirl shirt, and cowboy boots.

I wasn't sure if we were going to a music studio or a rodeo.

"Ummm…" How to say, too much?

"Too much." Ash shook her head. "Way too much."

Okay. Just straight-out, I guess.

"Lose the boots?" Megan asked.

"At least." Ash gave me a look as Megan headed back into their room.

"Do they play country?" I asked Ash, because I'd really thought they were more rock. Maybe they had something out I didn't know about.

"No. Not even a little."

Megan came out wearing a pair of beat-up Converse sneakers and looking a little less like she needed a lasso.

"Let's hit the road!"

I could only hope she meant that less literally than I feared. Megan had gotten up at a ridiculous hour. It was basically her birthday, Christmas, and the last day of school all rolled into one.

She may still have had the cowgirl-snap-shirt on, but her bag was a full tote.

Mental Note to Self: Get Ash a thank you gift.

"Open the bag, Megan."

She completely deflated.

"We're going to be late."

"No. We're not." I raised a hand before she could rush on. "And, your Zipcar is sitting there waiting for us. No one can take it. So, it's not like we'll miss the bus."

Ash had told me this morning while Megan was in the shower that she'd kept her up all night trying to pick out the coolest Zipcar she could find within walking distance.

The fact that it would say *Zipcar* in giant green letters across it didn't seem to kill the cool factor for Megan.

After I'd cleared her of all fan paraphernalia, we headed down the street to grab the car she rented for the day.

Inside the parking garage, she headed straight for the Zipcar station by the stairs. It wasn't until she was unlocking a Mini Cooper that I started to worry.

"That's what you rented?"

"*Right?* It's adorable!"

It was super cute. I was just hoping we'd survive the ride. It was a little…small.

"They have a high safety rating for a car this size." She stowed her bag in the tiny backseat and climbed in.

I was more worried about their Megan Rating. I'd heard stories. Stories that kept me from getting in cars with her.

Of course, living in town meant we could take the T, but if a car was needed, there were a bazillion people who were not Megan you could pay to drive you.

"Well, come on." She was all but bouncing in her seat.

I got in, sliding my seat belt home immediately, and was glad I didn't have anything I needed to leave to anyone since I hadn't done a will.

"Ready?" Megan didn't give me a chance to answer as she backed out of the parking space.

So far, so good. We hadn't hit anything yet—or died in a horrible, fiery crash.

Megan stopped at the entrance to the parking garage, slid her sunglasses over her eyes, and gave me a grin that had chills running down my spine.

"Here we go!"

We zoomed out of the darkness and into the bright morning sun, barely missing a fire hydrant that was "too close to the corner," and cut off an SUV that could have rolled over us without blinking.

Megan reached over, leaving only one of her semi-competent hands on the wheel, and turned on the radio. She then started rifling through her bag until she found a CD, which she popped in.

I would have offered to help, but that would have meant letting go of my death grip on the door's handle.

I thought we might live through this until she got on the Mass Pike. Then, all bets were off.

Megan was having a grand old time, speeding and weaving while singing along to her favorite DBS song at the top of her lungs, completely ignoring that I was about to pass out or pee myself from fear.

Once we got off the Pike, our little car wove through the tree-filled neighborhoods. We passed fewer cars, and the houses got farther and farther apart until my phone told us we were there.

"Holy crap." Megan sat, eyes staring up at the large house at the top of a small incline. "Although, I'm a little disappointed. I expected a big gate. I wanted to have to prove my identity and maybe get frisked by a hot security guy."

Me? I just wanted to make it through the day. Between Megan being Megan and Sage and our non-date-hangout-covert thing, I was hoping I could keep my even-flow flowing.

"This isn't Hollywood." Because, no matter how crazy their life might be, it couldn't be Hollywood if I was involved.

"Yeah, but they're *rock stars*."

True, but there was something about Boston celebrities. Or maybe it was the non-celebrities. There was a cool factor that meant you had to play off that you just didn't care how rich or famous they were. Maybe it was because the list of famous people from the Boston area was out of control.

I worked at a nail salon for three months where Mindy Kaling's mom went. Celebrities and their people were everywhere. And no one was dressed like idiots—most of the time. East Coast Famous seemed to be a thing.

So, yeah. The whole region just played it cool.

"This is the most freaking awesome thing that has ever happened to me in my whole life and I hope I don't pee my pants!"

Ooookay. Everyone in the region *except* Megan just played it cool.

Also, this was the worst idea I'd ever had. Not that it had been my idea or I'd really had a choice.

Sage lost any points he might have gained by using Megan to force me to hang out.

Not that he'd had points or I was keeping score. What I was keeping was far away.

The car lurched forward. I was wondering how fast Megan could get it up the slight incline. We got to the top of the small hill and I pointed to the right where the drive cut around the house.

"He said come around to the garage out back."

We pulled around a large, classic New England house only to find a carriage house with a bunch of cars lined up next to us.

"That's a carriage house." I was a little confused about if this was the garage or not. I glanced at the house to see if there was an actual garage attached to it.

"Yup."

"He said *garage*."

"Of course he did. That's more rock and roll. " Megan was thrilled. "A carriage house! Do you think they have a carriage?"

"I think they have a studio." Which would make sense. Horses would be really distracting while recording.

We found a space left for us under a tree on the far side of the drive and several cars way nicer than what had to be Sage's pickup lined up along the side.

"Aren't you glad we have the Mini now?" Megan smiled, all smug as if the Mini were a match for the brand new Mercedes-AMG GT.

"Yup," I said, not wanting to crush her joy…just keep it from killing anyone. "The Mini is a lifesaver."

I got out of the car as soon as she put it in park, glad to have the ground under my feet, but a little nervous where that ground led.

I headed toward the door at the side of the building, Megan bouncing along next to me.

"Do *not* embarrass me." I felt the need to say this even as I realized it was probably a hopeless cause.

"Would I do that?" Megan looked genuinely insulted.

I guess she'd probably be on her best behavior in front of her favorite band. The hero worship would—with any luck—keep her in check.

I knocked on the door, but when no one answered, I pulled it open enough to peek in. Sage sat at a big panel of button and slide thingys, his head bopping to the music coming in over some speakers.

The room was filled with couches and a gorgeous painting decorated the back wall.

Beyond the glass wall, five guys rocked out until the gorgeous one—the *most* gorgeous one—waved a hand in the air, bringing them all to a halt.

"That sounded soupy." He turned to look more fully at his guys. "We need to back off somewhere."

Next to him, a puppy-eyed hottie nodded and played back something pretty and simple and clean while the rest of the guys watched.

"Sage," Gorgeousness called. "Cleaner?"

Sage sat forward and hit a button. "Yeah, that's crisp in here. Let's hear it with everything else."

The guys nodded and started playing again.

"Wow," Megan whispered. "Sage has the power."

I'd been a little surprised by that as well. The fact that this super famous group of guys trusted him to make their music better seemed insane.

Megan pushed the door farther open and the sunlight fell across Sage, drawing his attention.

He waved us in, and Megan rushed past me so fast I almost landed on my rear. She was over his shoulder, all but pasted to the window, staring in joy and admiration.

Basically, this was a Rock and Roll Revival, and Megan was worshiping at the altar.

Sage grinned at me, a look so comfortable with his surroundings that it was…strong.

Stupid word. I don't know. He obviously belonged there at the soundboard making music happen. There was something incredibly attractive about a guy in his element.

What could he possibly have seen when he looked at me at The Brew? Was that my element? Was that where I'd be living for the next sixty years until I couldn't lift a coffee cup again?

"Hey," he said, turning away from the window. "You made it."

"Yup!" Megan shouted from right next to him. "Here we are! Right here! Watching Double Blind Study do awesome stuff!"

"Okay." It was time to slow the roll. "Megan, why don't you step away from the super-expensive-looking stuff? We'll just watch from a safe distance."

I hadn't finished talking when the music had faded out…each piece ending slowly until the drums just stopped.

I glanced over and saw an entire room of hot rock stars watching us through the glass.

"Hey! It's the caffeine chick." Blake Diedrich looked at me as if I were just in time for something important. "Tell my man Sage here to build me a guitar."

"Omigosh," Megan whispered from beside me.

Sage flipped a switch and spoke into a mic. "What are the chances you won't crash it into a hard object after playing the guitar solo of your life?"

Blake shrugged like this were a regular occurrence. "Slim to none."

"Exactly."

Blake glanced my way. "Come on, darlin'. Be my influencer."

"Oh. My. Gosh." Megan was staring at me now as if I were something new.

"Um…what if he made you a really cheap one to break?"

Sage laid his head down on the counter.

"Sage is an *artiste*. He doesn't do cheap." Blake gave me a killer grin and shrugged again. "Plus, I'd just forget to switch them out and break the good one anyway."

Well, at least he was honest.

"Why don't we take a break?" His Hotness of Lead Singers pulled the guitar strap over his shoulder and set it in a stand. I glanced around at all the equipment, surprised at how complicated everything looked. Who knew there were all these technical thingies at a studio?

Um, probably everyone ever who wasn't me.

The band all came through a door to the right, looking hot, exhausted, and pumped up at the same time.

"You work at a café?" Puppy Dog Eyes asked.

"Um, yes." This did not seem like the lead-in you get with most rock stars. Not that I'd know, but still.

He glanced around, scowling.

"Did you bring any snacks?"

"Harrison." The Emperor of Sex Appeal gave Puppy Dog Eyes—Harrison—a look. "Not every person on this planet was put here to feed you."

Harrison looked like he was going to argue this statement, when Sex Appeal went on, "And, I heard your wife was making sandwiches."

"Still. A pastry of some kind is a polite way to introduce yourself." He shrugged as if it were all the same, when clearly it was *not*. He held eye contact with me, letting me know that next time I *would* be expected to produce some sort of snack cake in order to earn his trust.

"Sandwiches any minute, bro," Sex Appeal semi-repeated with an exasperated eye roll.

Harrison nodded earnestly. "I know. Which is the only reason it's okay."

He *said* it was okay, but I think we all knew I'd accidentally betrayed a sacred oath I didn't remember taking.

Beside me, Megan bounced on her toes and before I knew what she was doing, she breathed out one word: "*Sway.*"

I thought this was a command to dance, until Sex Appeal gave her a saucy grin and said, "And what's your name, honey."

"Megan! I'm Megan!" She started laughing hysterically, and I began to wonder if I should have brought a paper bag. "Hi! *Sway.*"

And then she started giggling like an insane woman. Which I was beginning to wonder if she was.

Behind me, someone covered a laugh with a cough. I glanced over my shoulder at the rest of the band watching Megan corner Sway of the Sexy Aura.

"I was wondering if you could sign something."

"Sure, hun."

Before I knew what was happening, Megan had ripped her shirt open, taking full advantage of those snap buttons, to reveal a teeny-tiny tank top that said Double Blind Study Buddy on it. Her boobs were basically falling out of it.

She held out a Sharpie—which, why hadn't Ash warned me to do a Sharpie check?—and giggled again.

"Well, Megan, hun. I have to say, my boob signing days are a bit behind me." Sway gave her an apologetic look.

"Oh." Megan looked like this was the end of the world. "But, I mean, what's one more boob, right? I mean…how many have you signed?"

"You mean, like a number?" Sway looked intrigued by the question.

"Like, a lot?" Megan seemed to think this was going to change the no to yes.

"Well, *a lot* isn't really a big enough number." Sway seemed oddly proud and disgusted at this at the same time.

I leaned toward Sage, who was making notes in his notebook while all this was going on. "Why doesn't he sign boobs anymore?"

Not that I understood the appeal of having a part of my body I kept covered marked up by a stranger.

Sage didn't look up as he finished noting whatever he was noting in his little book. "Married."

"Megan!" It was time to put my foot down.

"What?" She spun around, her open shirt flitting in the Megan-made breeze.

"He's *married*."

She gave a deep sigh. "I know. I was just…" She glanced around, then smiled up at Sway. "It was a test. You pass."

I couldn't even say anything because he just looked more amused than anything else.

"I'll let my wife know." The door behind him opened. "Speaking of...the girls are here for lunch."

I turned around...and almost fainted.

"Oh. Oh my." I sucked in a deep breath, my gaze focusing in on one thing and one thing only.

My life had just become complete. My idol stood before me in all her wonky awesomeness.

"I...I...Ummm..."

Sage put a hand on my back, warm and actually comforting. "Breathe, Em."

"You're Zelda Fitzpatrick."

# TEN

## SAGE

EMILY'S BODY VIBRATED BENEATH SAGE'S hand and he pressed his lips together to keep from laughing. She wasn't impressed by the rock stars, but show her a wild-haired woman with a plate full of sandwiches and she lost all of her chill.

Zelda stopped short and turned her face a little to the side, her eyes on Emily. "I am," she confirmed hesitantly.

"I love you," Emily gushed, her hands clasped in front of her as if she was trying to keep them from hugging Harrison's wife. "I mean, I love your work." Color crept up the side of her neck and stained her cheeks and ears.

"My work?" Zelda asked, her eyes darting around the room and then settling on Sage, looking for an explanation that she wouldn't find.

How was he supposed to know Emily had a girl crush on Zelda?

"Your spread in *Vanity Fair* two months ago changed my life. I bought an extra copy just to be sure I had a backup in case I wore out the first one. And I don't have, like, any money, so that tells you how important that is to me." Emily was babbling. Full-on fangirl vibrato in her words.

Zelda's eyebrows arched. "My Vonnie Rae pictures?" She slowly shook her head, eyes wide.

"The way you capture the people in the moment. The movement you harness and the light—there's no moon! In any of the photos! I've studied them so many times, and there is no moon!"

Sage had no idea what she was talking about. Zelda had been the band's photographer for a while now. She had documented their tours and single-handedly displayed the DBS life to the public. He knew she did freelance work occasionally, and even more occasionally she would be requested to provide photos for famous whatevers and things.

For example, Vonnie Rae was rock and roll's latest darling. A rock balladeer from the middle of nowhere. Too young to be taken seriously by the industry, but her soulful and almost bluesy representation of life and love in lyrics made her a star to watch. Sage had never met her, but he'd heard Luke and Mike discussing bringing her on as an opener.

"Would you like her to sign your boobs?" Megan held her Sharpie out in offering and Sage nearly lost hold on his laughter.

Emily glanced at the marker and he saw something pass through her eyes as she thought about the offer. She must've remembered where she was and who she was with, because she sucked in a breath as her eyes darted around the people in the room.

Zelda flashed her lopsided and wonky grin. "You're a fan. Of me?"

Emily swallowed and nodded. "The biggest."

Zelda did a little hop. "I've never been fangirled before. This is very exciting."

"I fangirl over you all the time," Harrison said around a mouthful of sandwich.

Zelda waved a hand at him and took a step toward Emily. "I'm so happy to finally meet you."

"Finally meet me?" Emily breathed.

"Oh' yes," Zelda confirmed. "I have had many a daydream about meeting my biggest fan. I'm so glad it's finally happened."

Emily shook her head, wonder pouring out of her every pore. "Can I ask how you did that? I mean, I've promised myself repeatedly that if I ever got the chance to meet you, I would ask you how you took those pictures."

"It was all practical lighting. I didn't have to add to it; I just had to be in the right place at the right time. There may have been some contortion involved.

"Vonnie has a life she's built and I wanted very much to capture her in it. Not orchestrate a false scenario in order to get pretty pictures. I spent several days with her, following her around, watching her routine at home. The night writing sessions in her barn happened to be my favorite part of the day. The old lanterns and the muted surroundings are really reflected in her song styling. I needed to be sure I documented that." Zelda ended with a shrug.

Emily nodded silently, soaking up Zelda's presence and words. Sage couldn't hide his grin even if he'd wanted to. This was a side of her he was really liking.

"Now if I could just get Peter Jackson to return my calls. I'd really love to take Where Are They Now pictures of the original Fellowship," Zelda added with a smirk that said how likely she thought that would be.

"I love *Lord of the Rings*," Emily said.

A stillness entered the room. Hopefully Sage was the only one who noticed. He swallowed and lifted his gaze off of Emily's adoring profile to connect with Luke. Luke half-grinned but took the hint.

"I want to focus on the drum track if we can. Mike, as soon as you're finished eating, get back in there," Luke bossed.

"Of course you do." Mike rolled his eyes, but didn't argue.

Mike had a process. It was a process Sage had heard about but hadn't witnessed until this week. The guy was incredibly hard on himself.

"I'm the worst drummer in the world," Mike lamented as he dusted his hands off on his jeans and stood up. "Let me warm up a minute first." He jerked his head toward the stairs and everyone moved that direction.

Upstairs was the control room. It contained all the analog equipment and was the place where they monitored everything they created. It also doubled as a place to relax—big couches, chairs, tables, and a fridge with refreshments.

"I thought downstairs was where you recorded," Megan asked as she surveyed the equipment with curious but untrained interest.

"It is," Sage explained. "But the console downstairs really just records and sends it up here. This is where we put it together to make the tapes. We can even mix up here, if we want." He waved his hands over the equipment. "This board is actually my favorite thing here. It has a warm but aggressive sound. It's a really fun combination. Very Double Blind Study."

"Sometimes I forget how smart you are," Zelda remarked, handing him a sandwich. "I'm so glad they picked you. When Harrison told me you guys were recording to tape, I got pretty nervous."

"Wait." Megan closed her eyes like she were trying to focus really hard. "Tape? Why not digital? I thought digital was required now."

"Recording to tape is actually really easy," Sage said, leaning against the doorjamb and taking a deep breath as he searched for the right words to describe his thoughts on the matter. "I think there's a huge emphasis on perfection these days. A lot of artists record using a computer because then they can fix the things they don't like. But real life, which I feel like rock and roll is supposed to reflect, isn't perfect. I like tape. It keeps the personality."

"Exactly." Zelda nodded. "It's like how I see things through the viewfinder. I like seeing the rough edges of things. It has an honesty to it. Like that picture of us downstairs. No way would that be considered "perfect," but it is to me, because it's real. That's what we look like, that's how we live. That's our family."

"Pro Tools is great," Harrison interjected. "It really is. But when it comes to making a raw rock and roll record, you really can't beat tape."

"And you have all the power?" Megan asked, her eyes wide with wonder.

Sage chuckled and licked his lips. "Not even remotely. They play their music, and I do my best to keep up." His lips twitched as he remembered how Heather had described it. "An orangutan could do it."

Harrison snorted and covered his mouth to keep from spraying soda everywhere.

"When they take it someplace to be mixed, that's when the professional will make it sound like what you love."

Sway cleared his throat in an obvious way, getting pretty much everyone's attention. Except for Luke, who was talking to Lenny. Okay, they weren't talking, they were canoodling. Sway cleared his throat again. Luke looked at his bassist.

"What?"

Sway jerked his head toward Sage. "You wanna tell the kid who's mixing for us?"

Luke sucked in a breath. "Oh, yeah. Sage, you are."

"What now?" Sage asked, feeling the room tilt.

For a second, he thought he may have misheard Luke. He waited, breathing slowly, trying to keep the chill, his chill, the chill he was known for always having. There had to be some kind of misunderstanding or punch line or prank or something.

The conversations continued around him at a normal rate and volume. No one jumped out to point and laugh at his shock and confusion.

Maybe he should sit down.

Mike's drums pounded through the floor and into the soles of his feet, mimicking his heart rate.

"These guys have a way of not telling you the entire plan," Zelda said, understanding in her voice.

Sage didn't have a response. He wandered over to where the big board resided and sat in the chair in front of it. He would need to do more homework. Because this...this was everything. And if he screwed it up, he would never be able to forgive himself.

If he had to make a list of his biggest dreams that he never thought would ever happen, producing and mixing a Double Blind Study album would be at the very top.

"That board looks more complicated than my cappuccino machine."

Sage looked up into Emily's sweet face, a shy smile flirting with her lips as if it weren't entirely committed to the movement.

"Ah, they're basically the same thing," he said, feeling better the instant she'd come closer to him.

"Megan is in her element," she said, glancing at her friend, who was gabbering at Blake and Lucy. "Thank you for inviting us," she said softly.

"Thank you for accepting the invite," he returned playfully.

She looked away and rolled her eyes, probably because she still wanted to be a little bit mad he had coerced her into hanging out with him. But she had fangirled over Zelda, which meant he was obviously forgiven for a little bit of coercion. Right?

His gaze drifted to the console in front of him and reality sunk in a fraction more. It probably wouldn't hit him full force until later tonight when he was about to fall asleep.

What were the chances a guy like him—with all the weird and impossible requirements he had in his head—would end up not only working for the band of his dreams, but actually work *with* the band to make the kind of music he loved to make?

Creating was his passion. It was the only time he felt like he was doing what he was meant to do. Add rock and roll into the mix and...

Well, *perfect* wasn't a big enough word.

Sage glanced over his shoulder at the white board outlining the tracks and the dailies. Everything looked very official all of a sudden.

He shoved to his feet and gave Emily a grin and a chin lift. "You wanna hear the greatest drummer in the world tear himself apart?"

"Really?" she asked with a soft frown.

He motioned for her to follow him back downstairs and then he sat her in a chair at the board.

"How does it feel, Mike?" he asked into the speaker.

"Like I hate myself, Sage," Mike came back.

Sage grabbed another headset from the cabinet and then sat down beside Emily. He checked the volume on one before handing it her. Then he put his own on. Mike's beats came through clear and Sage flicked the switches over, getting ready to record.

"Tell me when," he said to the drummer.

"Crap, already?" Mike came back. "Okay, go ahead, but I make no promises."

Sage flipped the switch.

Mike played strong for about thirty seconds before a flurry of expletives came through.

"Sorry," Mike apologized. "Broke a drumstick. I'll start again."

He made it to the chorus and then stopped again.

"Wait. Am I supposed to go double on the snare? Or was that something we voted out?"

Sage snickered. "You said you didn't like that. But we can try it if you want."

"Argh!" Mike growled. "I am the worst drummer in the world!"

Emily giggled and Sage felt that hit deep in his chest.

"Stop the tape," Mike said, standing up. "I need to take a walk."

"You got it," Sage said, turning everything down and/or off. Emily handed her headset back to him.

"We picked you on purpose, you know," Harrison said at his shoulder on the other side of him.

Sage rotated his head the other direction and his eyes connected with the guitarist. Of all the guys in the band, Sage related to Harrison the most.

"It wasn't as unplanned and last minute as it appeared. We wanted to produce this one ourselves because the songs are so personal. You were an obvious choice."

Sage stared at him. "I don't get why. You can have your pick of any of the leading producers out there. I'm a...hack."

Harrison grinned. "Look at Luke's guitar."

Sage did. It was the blue, hollow-body with diamond-sound holes Sage had made for him four years ago. He would never forget that day.

Luke Casey had walked into a local music shop while Sage had been in there trying to talk the owner into selling some of his designs on consignment. It hadn't been going well. Apparently there wasn't a big demand for hollow-body electric guitars. And if someone were looking for one, they'd go with a tried and true brand, like Gibson—not an unknown self-taught luthier.

But Luke Casey had taken the red pearl finish out of Sage's hands and asked for an amp. Thirty minutes later, Sage had his first commission and a job offer. Changing the course of his life forever.

"That guitar is the sound of Double Blind Study," Harrison said. "It just is. And since you made it,"—he stuck a finger in Sage's chest as he spoke—"you're a part of our sound, too. We wanted this album to reflect us, as musicians. You have that ear, you know us, we trust you, you don't blow smoke. It's really that simple."

Sage dipped his chin to his chest, uncomfortable with the praise. "You're a lot nicer when you've eaten," he said, looking to change the subject and get back to work.

Harrison stepped backward and his eyes flicked over to Emily. "Don't forget to show her your Thorin Oakenshield tattoo. Fangirls love to share their fandoms."

And there it was.

Sage closed his eyes and pinched the bridge of his nose. He thought it would be Blake that would out him. Not Harrison.

"You have a Thorin Oakenshield tattoo?" Emily asked. He couldn't tell if she was curious or disgusted. And he wasn't mentally prepared to look at her to figure it out. "Like, a portrait of Richard Armitage?"

"It's so awesome," Harrison went on with a chuckle. "We were in LA and had finally talked him into coming out with us for drinks. But Sage isn't a big drinker, so it didn't take much for him to have too much." Harrison leaned his hip against the console and crossed his arms over his chest.

Sage pulled his hat lower over his eyes.

"He expressed a desire to get a tattoo and Mike and Blake walked him down to a place they had used before." Harrison smacked his bicep with the back of his hand. "Show her," he encouraged with a happy grin. "Show her the quote."

Silently, Sage reached a hand over and pushed the short sleeve of his T-shirt up to his shoulder, revealing the one and only tattoo he had ever gotten. It was a black ink replica of Thorin Oakenshield's family crest from *The Hobbit*. It took up the entire head of his shoulder. The artwork was actually very good; it just didn't belong on Sage. Below the crest, in bold and masculine font it said: Loyalty, Honor, A Willing Heart.

"Isn't that badass?" Harrison asked with genuine awe. Only another nerd would be able to appreciate and admire a tattoo like that.

Emily glanced at Sage's resignation and smiled. "It's something, all right."

Sage felt his lips curling up on the ends. He lowered his shirtsleeve, thankful Zelda seemed to be making an approach. Maybe she could get her husband to stop embarrassing him.

"So, I was thinking," Zelda started, zeroing in on Emily. "I'm taking pictures of this whole process." She waved a hand around the garage. "For the album jacket and promotional materials. Capturing the guys in their element, stuff like that." Her eyes flicked to Harrison and landed briefly on Sage before returning to Emily. "I could use a second camera...if you're interested."

"Huh? What?" Emily asked, her back going ramrod straight.

"You'd be paid, of course," Zelda went on. "Technically, you'd be working for me."

Emily was shaking her head and Sage saw her eyes gloss over. "I can't," she forced out. "I don't have my own camera."

Zelda smiled warmly. "That's okay, because I'd want you to use one of mine anyway."

"But you haven't even seen my work," Emily pointed out. "I could be terrible."

Zelda laughed at that. "You could be. It's a chance I'm willing to take."

"Why?" Emily whispered.

"Because I was given a really big chance once, and it changed my whole life. I always swore to do the same for someone someday." She checked her phone as it chirped. "I have to take this. Think about it. I'd love to at least have you around to tell me how amazing I am."

Sunlight filled the studio as Zelda opened the door and stepped outside, Harrison on her heels. Emily watched them go. Sage tucked a strand of hair behind her ear and she turned toward him. He let go immediately, but his fingers buzzed with the small connection.

"Is she for real?" Emily asked, her voice strained.

"It appears so, sunshine," Sage replied quietly. He watched her closely, trying to gauge where she was on an emotional level, but he didn't know her well enough yet. It was a fact he understood but also hated. He wished he knew her better. So he knew how to talk to her, give her what it was she needed in this moment.

"It's how it happened for me," he said, going with his gut. "I was offered an opportunity, and I would like to say I was smart enough to recognize what it was before I jumped." He shook his head, turning to face her fully. "But I hadn't a clue."

"But you jumped."

He nodded. "I did."

"Do you regret any of it?" she asked, looking away from him.

"Em, I don't know what kind of answer you're looking for." Sage took his hat off and held it in his hands, turning it over. "I'm a dropout. I left college to hang out with rock stars. My girlfriend broke up with me because she didn't see a future in what I was chasing. I live at home with my parents, and I justify it by working as hard as I can doing what I love. It could have all blown up in my face. And I have some regrets mixed into all of the chaos of the good. I don't feel great about dropping out, or how I handled everything with Heather..." He sighed, staring at the floor. When he looked up, she was watching him closely. "I feel bad about the bad things, I feel good about the good. But...no matter what, I'd still jump."

# Eleven

## EMILY

I WANTED TO JUMP. I wanted to take this risk, and I couldn't believe it was even on the table. But I thought of how many of my jobs this would probably conflict with.

I wasn't really in a place to take a week off to take pictures of famous people.

John would just work at The Brew that week and not worry about it. Mrs. Hansen could listen to an audiobook instead of me reading her great-grandfather's journal to her. Glamour Paws would be ticked, but if I could take pictures of rock stars or glamour shots of overdone poodles, it was a no-brainer.

I was a little worried about Michael finding coverage for the overnight babysitting. But maybe Ash would do it. She was actually getting her master's in early childhood ed, so the worst that could happen was she ended up with my job if he liked her better.

"Hey. Where'd you go?" Sage asked.

Glancing up, I realized we were alone in the sound room. It was the first time I'd been solo with him and I felt…well, I didn't feel like at any moment he was going to wreck my life.

Improvement much?

"I was just thinking how I've never really been given an opportunity before." I'd been given jobs—jobs pay bills, but don't really move your life forward. But actual opportunities? Not so much.

"No?" He cocked his head to the side. Not really challenging me, kind of just letting me go where I wanted with this.

"I bet you have." I tried to say it like it was just a passing thing, but Sage narrowed his eyes and leaned forward.

"I have." He turned, shifting his body away from the board and toward me. "You just saw one. Luke buying my guitar was the first step to becoming his guitar tech. I never would have ended up here without that opportunity."

That wasn't really what I'd meant.

I tried not to scowl at him, thinking about all the chances he must have been given just being who he was. Growing up well off, opportunities were handed out like balloons at a fair.

"You don't mean something I worked for, though, do you?" He didn't sound accusatory. He didn't even sound upset.

I pushed back, afraid I'd said too much, wondering what he was seeing now as he looking at me. I felt like ninety percent of my life was just keeping the past from sneaking up on me again.

Not that it mattered.

I was a relationship-free zone.

I was here strictly because he'd blackmailed me into coming with the invite to Megan.

Which...where was Megan?

I stood, glad for the chance to escape a conversation veering too quickly toward something too personal.

"I better find Megan before she kidnaps Sway." I turned away and headed toward the door when I heard Sage get up to follow.

Sage snorted. "Not like that hasn't happened before."

"What?" I spun around, smacking right into him.

Sage's arms came up, catching me in the most cliché awkward moment ever.

I stepped back, trying to get out of his way.

"Sorry."

"No worries." He grinned, a bit like he knew something I didn't. "You wanted to go rescue Sway?"

"Right." I stepped back again. "Sway."

Because rescuing His Sexiness was vital.

I took another step back.

"Whoa, there." Sage reached out, grabbing both my shoulders, and pulled me back. "Watch the chair."

"Right." I started to step back again, then remembered imminent death, disfigurement, and dignity destroyer lay behind me. "Chair. To sit in, not fall over."

He stepped forward, just a bit. "Sway's used to taking care of himself."

"Right," I said. Again.

"And, Megan isn't really that threatening."

"No." Unless obsessive energy was scary.

"We could just hang out up here for a while."

"Ummm..." I glanced over my shoulders at the stairs.

"Unless I make you too...nervous?" He didn't seem to be flirting anymore. It seemed to be a real question.

I was trying to figure out how to answer when Mike's voice came over a speaker. "Okay. I'm back. I worked out why I sucked at this."

Sage closed his eyes and took a step back. I found myself leaning forward, my body wanting to follow him as he moved back into Work Sage mode.

Just as I thought he was shutting me down, he held out his hand, watching me, giving me an out I knew he'd shrug off.

But instead, I took that leap he'd mentioned...and I took his hand.

# Twelve

## SAGE

EMILY TIMIDLY SLID HER HAND into his and Sage held his breath.

He'd held it out on an impulse. His expectations had been realistic and very, very low. Actually, he'd half expected her to bolt and leave an Emily-shaped hole in the door.

Seriously, if he ever got to meet the person or persons who had made this girl so wary, he was going to give them at the very least a stern talking to, and at the most, a punch to the nuts. Assuming they had nuts. Which he was assuming.

But she was currently holding his hand. And watching him. With an obvious question on her face. It said, "What have I just done?"

Sage gave it a gentle squeeze and tugged her back to the soundboard and to their seats. He reluctantly let go of her hand as she sat down. Wordlessly, he handed her the headset as he took his own seat.

"Okay, Osborn, show me what you've got." He flipped the switches over again, his palm still tingling from the touch of her skin.

Mike started his track expertly, showing exactly why he was named in *Rolling Stones'* Top 10 Drummers of All Time. The hesitation and second-guessing was completely missing, and in its place was a solid, steady rhythm that had Sage nodding his head and making the proper adjustments with ease. When these guys were on, they were so on.

They wrapped the track and Sage showed Emily how to pull the tape and cut it with a razor blade and set up the board for the next track. Her visible trepidation when he sliced through the tape and tossed the excess had him feeling just a little tougher than he was. Of course, he knew it was fine to cut through it, but she didn't.

"What are all those?" she asked, pointing to the trash can of used and crumbled tape.

"The first three hours of that track."

Her eyes widened. "Three hours?"

"Yep." Sage blew the air out of his mouth and grabbed a handful of the used tape. "Three hours of cursing and broken drumsticks and off-color jokes." He dropped the tape back into the bin.

"How long does this usually take?" she asked just as Mike joined them, sweat coating his face. Her words drifted off as she assessed his now sweaty apparel. Mike was the only member of the band who wore shirts displaying the name of his own band.

"Normally it takes weeks," Mike answered for Sage. "But Sage has us ahead of schedule. Should only be a few more days."

Sage pursed his lips at the unintentional lie. No. This would not be wrapped up in a few days. And he was beginning to get increasingly frustrated with their verbal praise. Especially since he hadn't earned it yet. Realistically, they could finish this up and hate everything. They'd have to take it somewhere else after that; maybe one of the bigger producers would happen to be available. It's not as if it was unheard of. Luke hated their sophomore album so much, he had scrapped half the songs and rerecorded everything in a weekend in a studio overlooking San Francisco Bay. It had been the right choice; they'd won a Grammy for that album.

Sage's eyes drifted to the side and connected with Emily's as she watched him. Always watching, measuring, listening, observing. What she was looking for, he had no idea. He'd be happy to fill her in if she ever asked.

"How did that turn out?" Mike asked.

"Good." Sage nodded. "It definitely has a more driven feel than the previous ones. I know that's what you had talked about doing."

Mike ran a hand through his sweaty hair, nodding as he headed out the door, leaving Sage and Emily alone again. Sage wondered if he could hold her hand again. Probably not.

"It's starting to get kind of late," she said softly after neither one of them had spoken for a solid minute.

"Right," Sage agreed. "And you have to make caffeine bright and early."

"I should find Megan and detach her from whichever band member she's fused herself to."

Sage couldn't help grinning. He was glad for Emily to have a friend like Megan. She seemed like a handful, to be sure, but everyone needed at least one friend that kept them on their toes.

"Do you need help with that?" He offered his services.

"I don't know," she said dryly. "Do you have any industrial-grade solvents handy?"

Sage barked a laugh, noting the tiny, pleased smile she tried to hide.

They found Megan outside with the rest of the band.

"Hey!" Megan greeted, hurrying over to her friend. "I was just leaving."

"What?" Emily asked, panic outlining her one word.

"Yeah, Marcus lives really close to here. I wanted to drive by his house with my hot new car."

"It's not a new car, Megan. It's not even *your* car," Emily explained patiently. "It's a Zipcar. It says *Zipcar* right on the side in big green letters."

"So? It's like wearing a borrowed shirt you look hot in—it might be borrowed, but you still look hot."

"That's—no, that's not a thing..."

Sage split his attention between watching Emily's face morph slowly from patient exasperation to horrified panic, and Megan skip over to the Zipcar, get in, and leave. It took all of four heartbeats.

"How am I supposed to get home now?" she asked the empty parking space, a touch of venom lacing her words.

"Yeah, McNabb, how's she ever supposed to get home now?"

Sage shot a warning glare to Blake, who cackled gleefully until his wife stuck an elbow in his gut. He had been ready to make that suggestion; he didn't need Blake making it sound like the tawdriest of options.

"I would be more than happy to give you a ride back into town," Sage offered. "Or maybe Megan will be right back...?"

Emily crossed her arms over her chest, her eyes dancing over the empty space of the driveway as if the vehicle would magically reappear any second. She sighed. "I don't want to put you out."

Sage fought to hold the smile in. Put him out? It was exactly what he'd wanted.

But, she still wore that look. That *Someone has screwed with me and I'm afraid you probably will, too* look that frustrated him. Probably because he couldn't do anything about it except show her he wasn't that guy.

Sage tugged his keys out of his pocket and gave a low wave to the onlookers calling out their good nights and "come back again, y'alls." He walked Emily to the passenger side of his Dodge and pulled the door open, examining the seat and inner door. It was clean, objectively speaking, but a thin layer of sawdust coated the seat, dash, and door. It was the curse of the carpenter. He reached behind the bench for his stash of extra towels and rags, selecting an overly bleached bandanna.

Emily stood silently as she watched him run the soft cloth over her seat and door. He returned it to its location and tagged a larger towel, which he used to spread carefully over her seat. Then he held the door open and stood back, offering a hand to help her up.

She paused, staring at his hand on the top of the door and the one reaching toward her. "What's the towel for?"

"My job usually means everything I own is covered in sawdust. I didn't think you'd want to get it all over your nice dress," he explained with a shrug, wondering if maybe he was overthinking it.

Emily took his words and analyzed them internally, like she did with everything he said, before taking his hand and climbing up into the cab. She let go as soon as it was physically possible to do so without falling back out of the truck. He closed the door and took a deep breath.

Pretty girl in his truck. He could totally handle this. It shouldn't matter it had been almost three years since he'd had a girl in his truck. It was just a ride, and she was just the most skittish and confoundingly beautiful, mysterious girl he had ever met. He'd foolishly thought all he would need to do was spend some more time with her and he'd have some answers to his questions. Nope. He only had more questions. And damn if he wasn't even more interested in her than ever before.

He turned the creaky old truck around and carefully maneuvered down the drive.

"Where to?" he asked, his voice sounding louder than it ever had in his truck before.

"Toward The Brew," she answered solidly.

It didn't escape him the way she refused to look his way, keeping herself separate even as they shared the ride.

"I would offer to let you pick the music, but my radio actually died today," he said with a grimace. "I'm sure I can fix it; I just didn't have time."

She nodded silently, her eyes fixed out the window.

"How long have you been friends with Megan?" he asked, trying to fill up the silence with something easy.

"Uh, long enough that I shouldn't be surprised by her ditching me," came the quick reply that wasn't exactly an answer. "We're roommates."

He almost said, *I know*, but was just happy she was willing to share *anything*.

"So, you go on tour with the band and stuff?" she asked.

Yes, something he could talk about. He nodded. "Yep. I really lucked out by getting in when they went dry. Otherwise I probably wouldn't have stuck around." He tugged the bill of his hat a little lower.

"Dry? What do you mean?"

"Well," he started to explain, knowing how it sounded and hoping he told it right. "They did the rock star thing. All the clichés ever. The women, the drugs, the booze, the wild parties—every single rock-and-roll story you have ever heard, they did it. But Mike overdosed somewhere in Europe while they were on tour—Germany, I think. I guess it was really bad; he almost died.

"Luke doesn't have any family; the band was it for him. So it shook him up pretty bad. It tore them all up, to be honest. The media doesn't know half of what they've fought to get back, as a band and as a family. I was brought in on their first tour, where drugs and alcohol were banned on the buses. That's what I mean when I say *dry*. No contraband."

He chuckled as he remembered telling his parents he was taking the semester off to become a roadie. "I was nervous, honestly. I was afraid it was a publicity stunt and I was going to regret it. I was a music major. I had always planned on becoming a music teacher. I wasn't interested in the rock star lifestyle. But Luke had won me over. Not just with taking a chance on my guitar, but he talked to me. About music theory and writing. He didn't make me feel like being such a nerd was the worst thing. If you ever get a chance to talk to Luke Casey, do it. That guy can make every conversation he has feel like it's the most important conversation he's going to have that day. He's the real deal.

"So, I joined the tour and I haven't looked back. I was allowed to have a front-row seat to their rebuilding years. It wasn't at all like what the movies want you to think. I mean, maybe it can be. Maybe that's what it used to be like; I've heard some of the stories. But it's mostly a lot of hard work and a lot of driving." He laughed lightly. "It's just a lot of people working together and hanging out."

He was talking too much; he could feel it. But now that he had started, he couldn't stop. Sweat beaded along his hat band on the side and he felt it trickle down his neck. He used a hand to wipe it away and rub at the tension. Not that it helped.

"It's really unlike anything else. Being surrounded by all the music and getting to travel..." He shook his head. "It's something else."

"Sounds like it," she remarked.

He glanced to his right to see her studying him; he gripped the steering wheel tighter with both hands. "Sorry, I tend to ramble when I'm geekin' out."

His eyes flicked over again in time to see her hide another smile. He took another deep breath and tried to stop acting like a fifteen-year-old on his first date. After all, this wasn't a date. Not even close. If this was a date, he would have bought her dinner and he'd be holding her hand.

"This is your work truck?" she asked, looking around at the interior of the cab.

"Yeah," he said, heat touching the back of his neck. "It's..." He cleared his throat. "It's my everything truck." He loved his truck. He knew it was beat up and old and probably not the best idea for the environment. But he'd bought it with his first dozen or so paychecks. He planned on keeping it until he couldn't. Every time he drove it, it reminded him where exactly he fit in the world.

"You don't have a different one for when you're not working?" She sounded both skeptical and surprised.

"No... Why? Embarrassed to have me drop you off in this beast?" He shot her a grin.

"No, I was...never mind." She sat up a little and gave some more detailed directions as they got further into town.

"You can stop here." She pointed to the side of the road, unhooking her seat belt.

Sage frowned at the lack of parking. "There's nowhere to get out."

"I can just get out here." She waved her hand again. The road was as narrow as any other old Boston street and there really wasn't a better place to stop.

"Emily," he called as she jumped down from the cab. She turned back to face him. "Thanks for hanging out with me."

She nodded at his grin and slammed the door.

Climbing up a little stoop, she fit her key into a typical oak-and-glass door of the old-school walk-up she lived in, putting her shoulder to it to push it open. Before she let it drop shut behind her, she turned and waved, one of her glimmery Emily smiles ticking her lips up on each side.

He grinned to himself, watching the top of her head bob up at each of the stairwell windows as she climbed to the attic floor and disappeared.

Good things tonight. Good things.

He put his truck back in drive, thinking that one of these days he was going to ask her what had happened. When he'd earned the right to ask, and when he'd earned the right to hear her answer.

# Thirteen

### EMILY

"Ash!" I tried not to slam the door as I rushed into the apartment.

"Ashley!"

Her bike was locked up in the hallway, and her bag was at the door.

"Ashton!"

Our apartment just was not this big.

"Ashleyton!"

"Stop calling me that!" she shouted back from the bathroom. "I'm getting out of the shower. Give me a minute."

I went into my dining-bedroom and pulled off my shoes, tucking them in the cubby at the end of my mattress on the floor. With the space I had, I was lucky I only owned a couple pairs of...well, everything.

Ash wandered around the edge of my dresser into the dining-bedroom and bounced down on my mattress.

"What's up, oh, Impatient One?"

"I like him." I threw myself down next to her, tossing my arm over my eyes. If only I could swoon.

I bet Megan could swoon.

"The guitar guy?" She ran the brush through her hair, looking me over like I was nuts.

"Yes. Sage. The guitar-slash-carpenter-slash-sound-guy-slash-Brew patron."

"That's a lot of slashes."

"Right?" I sat up and looked at her like this was an aha moment. "I mean, how do you get around a guy with that many slashes?"

I felt my body clenching up, the weight of worry settling over me like a hair blanket on a July day.

"So, I have a couple questions," Ash began, always the reasonable one. "First, is it time to let go of whatever the past crap is? Next, is this the guy to do it with? And, finally, where the heck is Megan?"

"Megan took the Zipcar to go show it off to her ex." It didn't make any more sense now than it did an hour ago.

"Let me guess. She made this announcement and jumped in the car, zooming off before giving you a chance to join her."

"Pretty much."

Ash shook her head. "I love that girl, but her world view doesn't go past her nose."

"True fact."

"Which means... Everything-slash-everything-else guy drove you home?"

"Yup."

"And you survived!" she all but shouted. I could feel her need to add *Hallelujah!* on the end.

When she didn't, I gave her a second to get it out of her system before going on.

"Okay. I get it." Well, as much as I could.

It wasn't like every guy out there was the kind to completely take advantage of a girl and ruin her life.

"Your life isn't ruined." Ash read my mind. Or maybe she just knew what I was thinking because I'd mentioned the Life Ruining Event Not to be Mentioned before.

"My life isn't what it could have been."

I tried not to dwell on it, not to just let myself settle into how that one betrayal cascaded into even bigger ones. Not to let myself wonder how all those people who had promised me a good life threw me away.

"No one's is." Ash gave me the saddest smile I'd ever seen from her.

I knew she wasn't dismissing anything she knew or assumed had happened to me—she was just saying everyone had their thing.

"Multiple-slash guy sounds like a pretty good deal." She scooted back, setting her back against the wall. "Why don't you try taking a chance on him, see what happens?"

I thought about it, the chance she was telling me to take. It wasn't like I'd climbed so high I had a far way to fall. And, Sage seemed like a decent sort.

Of course, Troy had too, but…

"Okay, I guess I could spend an hour or two with him."

Ash rolled her eyes; apparently my take-a-chance and hers differed a lot.

"Way to go out on that limb, Em." She hopped off the bed, turning back for just a second. "You know, because I want your sanity to return, I'm going to suggest we maybe not tell Megan about this."

Right. Because Megan and Sanity were passing friends, at the most.

\*\*\*

"Would you stop looking at the door?" Abby stood in the kitchen doorway, hands on her hips. "Do you know something I don't? Are we going to get robbed or something?"

"Um…not that I know of." Because wouldn't that just ruin my plan?

"Then, the staring…what's up with that?" Abby had come to join me at the counter.

A couple of her friends were sitting in their usual overstuffed chairs doing whatever they did. On the other side of the room, Mr. Grouchy did whatever it is he did. The mid-morning rush was over and we were restocking for lunchtime.

Abby had started making small gourmet sandwiches on fresh bread, and we were seeing a pickup in the midday time.

"Oh." Abby grinned at me before she turned away, looking pleased with herself.

"Oh, what?" Because that wasn't suspicious.

"Just, oh. I know what you're waiting for…or should I say *who?*" She cocked an eyebrow at me, and before I could come up with some witty comeback, she wandered off and dropped into a chair with her friends.

Fine. I was obvious. Whatever.

But, Sage might not even come in today. Or this week.

He said he wasn't doing the carpentry thing for a few weeks, and now that I knew where his other job was, it made sense he wouldn't be here.

Not that I was worried.

Nope.

The door opened and, for just a moment, the person in the doorway was haloed by the sun—just a tall, lean silhouette. My heart jumped. It wasn't about Sage, per se. It was that I was going to reach out to someone. Nothing to do with him specifically.

Nope.

The door fell shut as he came forward, and the guy came into view.

Not Sage.

Oh.

"Hi! Welcome to The Brew." I smiled at Nick, Connor and Hailey's assistant, as he swaggered on in.

"Hey there, Emily. How's the day treating you?" He smiled his broad, warm smile and I thought, well, he doesn't seem overly threatening, either.

"Better all the time." Because, staying down isn't where I wanted to be.

"Sounds like the right way to go." He leaned against the counter, comfortable wherever he was. "I'm going to need some caffeine to go, and a favor."

Oh. A favor. That sounded...risky. Guys always put things they wanted in soft language. They knew how to make you think something was a little deal, and then next thing you knew—BAM! You're dealing with the cops and explaining your living situation to strangers.

"Wow, no need to panic." He laughed and stuck his hands in his pockets. "Nothing illegal, or anything."

He laughed again, as if this was such an unthinkable thing.

"What are you looking to do?" I asked.

He leaned forward, a conspiratorial look on his face that made my heart rate ratchet up further than it had in a while.

"Connor is surprising Hailey by coming home during his road break." He glanced over his shoulder and dropped his voice again. "He was supposed to stay out for some interviews, but he's coming back a day early and wants to take her to dinner."

He slid a little box you might get chocolates in across the counter.

I glanced down at it as if it were a bomb.

"What's in that?"

The suspicion must have come through in my voice because he looked at me like I'd asked, *How long until it detonates?*

"It's a little embossed invitation to Il Giardino for dinner tonight." He opened the box and the invitation sprung open with it, a cream page with lovely gold print scrolls shaping a formally worded invitation. "Do you think after I leave you could walk this over to her on one of your little trays?"

Ah, my trays. Abby hated those trays.

"Sure!" I glanced down again as he folded the invitation in and closed the lid again. "That's actually really adorable."

"Thanks." Nick looked so proud of himself I must have given him a look. "What? Who do you think arranges all these romantic ideas Connor has?"

With a wink, he grabbed the coffee I'd set in front of him and swaggered out, leaving me to think about the fact that the richest, best-looking, most famous guy I'd ever met was sending his girlfriend embossed invitations to meet him for a surprise dinner.

I thought again about taking that chance with Sage and knew I could do it. Knew I could take this one small chance.

It wasn't as if I were asking him to marry me.

And that's exactly what I was thinking when he finally wandered in.

"Hey!" Geez, Emily. Chill.

Sage gave me a smile that looked like I'd shouted *Duck!* instead.

"How are you? Good? Things good? The music thing? Good?"

"Yup, good. All good." He leaned against the counter and pulled out his wallet. "And you're…good?"

"Yup! I'm good!" Oh my gosh. Even I could hear this was too cheerful.

I glanced across the room and Abby was shaking her head, eyes closed in disgust.

"So, the regular?"

"Um, yeah."

I made him what I was pretty sure he'd had last time and slid it across the counter, trying to figure out how to dive into this.

"So, you know, I thought since we got to go spend a day with you—at your job, not, you know, just randomly—that maybe, if it doesn't sound too boring—you might want to spend a day at work with me." I sucked in a breath, afraid at any second he'd start laughing at me. "Unless you got enough Emily time and never want to see me again and are trying to figure out how to get your coffee when I'm not here so you can live in peace or something."

I could see Sage struggling not to laugh. I glanced at him, and Abby had gone from shaking her head to literally laying it down on the table and hiding from me.

"You want me to come in and make coffee with you?" Because, yeah. That sounded lame to me too, since he was here pretty often already. And Abby would kill me.

"No. I thought you could come to my other job. Well, *one* of my other jobs." I brushed my hands down my apron, hoping they weren't leaving sweat marks behind.

"Oh. What other job?"

Well, that wasn't a *yes!* But, I guess it was the question a sane person would ask.

"I have this job where I take pictures." Because explaining it further than that was just embarrassing.

I knew this was the job I wanted him to see me at because it was the closest to my dream that I had. He'd gotten to show me his dream and how he was living it. I tried to channel Ash and realized that I was worth the same as he was. That working a bunch of jobs and going to school didn't mean I was less worthy than a guy living his dream.

But, the old fears died hard: That he either knew this and was setting me up, or he had no idea how far ahead in life he was.

So, I'd take him to my job and hopefully I'd win him over with the charm of it all.

But, before that, I had to check one thing.

"You don't have any allergies, do you?"

# Fourteen

## SAGE

I HAVE ZERO ALLERGIES. AND, little known fact, I am also hypoallergenic and made from 100% organic materials." He waggled his eyebrows and grinned at her responding tiny eye roll.

"Well, good," Emily replied, her hands smoothing down her apron again. He wanted to tell her that she didn't need to be nervous with him, but somehow knew that would only make it worse. "But I suppose you're already working tonight...?"

Sage shrugged one shoulder. "I'm heading over there right now. I'll tell them I need a hard out by whatever time you need. They won't mind. They're in rewriting mode right now anyway."

"Wait." She eyed him suspiciously. "You're going over there now? Isn't this basically an hour out of your way?"

He lifted his cup. "I take my coffee very seriously." Seeing she was unimpressed, he added, "And I had to pick up a couple of pedals and some other spare parts a block from here." He didn't tell her the part about him volunteering wholeheartedly when Luke had called him that morning to ask about that particular errand. Because he did take his coffee seriously. And also, it was the perfect excuse for him to stop into The Brew to see if Emily had had enough of him already.

Her soft blush and happy smile when she saw him had been pleasantly surprising.

The allergy question was irrelevant. He was so smitten with her at this point he could be deathly allergic to strawberries and he'd allow her to drop him onto a vat of jam.

The pastries nearby caught his eye. "Can I get all of your muffins?"

"What now?" she asked, taken off guard.

Sage grinned. "Harrison will be able to smell the fresh pastries on me when I walk in the door. So can I get all of your muffins? Every single one you have?"

This would guarantee him time off tonight for sure.

Emily's smile was so big and so bright as she packed up the muffins, Sage couldn't wait until later. They made plans for where to meet, and he left.

\*\*\*

For the record, the muffins worked like a charm. Sage was able to get home and shower before going on another non-date with Emily.

He threw his fifth shirt onto the closet floor. Okay, so getting ready for this non-date was beginning to stress him out. He didn't have "date" clothes. Which was fine, because, not a date. But he was hanging out with a girl he liked. A lot. At the very least, he didn't want to dress like a toddler.

He looked to the ceiling letting out a long sigh.

"This is so dumb."

Okay, so jeans. He opened the third drawer down on his dresser and scooped up every pair of Levi's, tossing them onto the bed. Dimly, he realized that this was the exact behavior that left his apartment in shambles more days out of the month than not.

He parceled out the jeans, ranking them from greatest to least by frequency of wear.

Really? He tossed a pair into the corner that both back pockets had ripped out of. Those were just garbage. Before they had even settled into their corner, he was chasing after them. He could use them downstairs for textured rags.

A dark wash denim caught his eye and he snatched them up in suspicion. Where had these come from? They looked brand new. He flipped them over to look at the backside. Oh, nope. Oil stain on the back pocket. He needed to learn how to check where he was sitting before he actually sat. But the stain was small, comparatively. And, hey! No holes!

Okay, those were the jeans.

He jerked the top drawer open to get a pair of boxers.

"Of course, Sage. Why would you have clean underwear? You're a responsible adult who does his own laundry." He cursed at himself as he held the towel around his waist and ran into his living room. The Target bag was way too light to give him hope. He pulled out the empty underwear package and his heart sank.

"I suck at this," he hissed, stomping back into his bedroom. He stared at the jeans. Would going commando on a second non-date be considered slutty? "I just won't tell anyone," he rationalized, dropping the towel.

Buttoning the jeans, he stepped back to look in the mirror. He really wished he would have paid attention before to see if wearing boxers was obvious. Because he couldn't tell the difference.

He spun back to the closet.

Shirt.

Why didn't he own anything marginally nicer than his five-dollar Hanes T-shirts. But the next step up was a plaid button-down. And since he wasn't picking her up in 1994, he should probably leave the plaid at home. Maybe she wouldn't notice it was a Hanes. He yanked a dark green one off a hanger and slipped it over his head. Then he backed up to look in the mirror.

No holes, no stains, no underwear.

He was as ready as he could be.

# Fifteen

## EMILY

THE BUZZER SOUNDED, AND I cursed the fact that I had to wait for Megan to get out of the shower for my turn. I'd thought about skipping, but this was so not a job you could go to smelling like food.

"Did the buzzer just go off?" Megan stuck her head out from the bedroom.

"Yup." I slung my bag over my shoulder and headed toward the door. "Danny probably forgot his key again. I'll check when I get down there."

"Oh." Megan glanced around as if someone were supposed to have brought her some great surprise and it had been canceled. "Sure. Have fun at work."

I gave her a wave and pulled the door shut before she could try to peek down the staircase. Deep breath. In. Out. Okay, Emily. It wasn't a date. You were going to work. You were just bringing a guest. It was a work-guest thing.

I should have made him a guest badge.

But then, not everyone gets my humor, so maybe not.

I ran down the stairs, slowing as I reached the last turn in the bottom flight. I came around the corner and…there he was. On my stoop. The late afternoon sun hitting him in his Ray-Ban sunglasses, those lean arms crossed over an almost-fitted hunter green tee.

He looked good. Too good.

"Hey!" I pushed the door open, and almost took him out.

He hopped back a step, almost missing the edge of the sidewalk, but caught himself.

"Sorry!" Okay, Emily. Seriously. No killing him, and enough with the exclamations.

"No worries." He ran a hand through his hair, probably wondering if I'd wrecked it with the wind of the door I pushed out at Mach-some-number-I-should-know. "So, where are we headed?"

"Can it be a surprise?" Because, I'm not sure there was a sane way to describe this job.

"Sure. Surprises are great." He didn't sound like he was feeling too sure about that. More like he knew that was the right thing to say.

"Anyway, we can walk there from here." Which was the best way to save cash.

I was too embarrassed to ask him to drive. And, what if he wanted to bail early? There probably wasn't a *what if* about it. He'd probably stay as long as he thought he had to and make a run for sanity.

But, if I was going to take a risk on getting to know someone, out here in the open where he had the chance to run was probably the best place.

"So, you sound kind of anti-partying…" Which, let's be honest, with my past always two steps behind me, was probably a good thing. "How in the world did you think you were going to travel with rock stars and be in a drug-free zone?"

Beside me, Sage stutter-stepped as if I'd taken him by surprise. But—seriously—obvious question much?

"You know how you met my mom?"

"The one who brought you your allowance so you wouldn't starve to death?"

"It's not like I live in the house. I have my own apartment." Sage let out a long-suffering sigh…which, really. He had a free apartment, how much suffering could there be? "Yes. Her."

"Okay."

"She's technically my stepmom. My birth mom died shortly after I was born." He sucked in a deep breath, and I held mine. "Of a drug overdose."

"Oh." I stopped. My brain stopped. My feet stopped. I just stopped.

Thanks a freaking lot, Ashleyton. *Get to know him. Go out on a limb. What harm could there be?* Oh yeah. Piece of cake. Dead birth mom.

"Soooo…" I stumbled around, looking for the right words. "You're pretty straight edge about the drugs and booze, then?"

"I'm not much of a drinker…thus the Tolkien tattoo on my arm."

"And so, yeah. Still…rock stars?"

"Well, music. It's music." Sage smiled, and I could see passion for the music was what really drove him.

"And so, if you hadn't found this magically clean—"

"No magic. These guys work their asses off to have the tour go like this. They've been through hell together and I'm lucky they welcomed me in their safe world afterward."

I heard it all in his voice. The respect, the awe that he was where he was, and maybe something more. Maybe something girls would call love and guys would call…*whatever*.

We crossed the street, the big pink awning of Glamour Paws sticking out just after the ironic hipster T-shirt store that sold only T-shirts, and for some unknown reason, key chains.

Wow. Did I know how to kill the vibe on a non-date or what?

I had to get this back on track. I didn't want him to think of death, drugs, a lost mom, and any other weird things that scared him when he thought.

"Sorry. I guess I have a gift for accidentally hitting someone's weak spot." Understatement. "But, you're going to love my job. It's stupid, but it's a lot of fun."

I stopped in front of Glamour Paws and pointed up.

"What? Here?" Sage looked at the pink awning as if it might collapse on us and suffocate us, and then maybe roll him up and hide his body in a basement.

"Everything okay?" I asked.

"Sure. Great." He took a step up the stairs and pushed the door open. "I mean, how weird could it be, right?"

In the doorway, a large white poodle with an oversized pink bow and a tutu sniffed at his feet.

"Right. Weird." I reached down and pet the pup. "It's not weird at all."

Except for the part where I took glamour shots of pets for people with too much money and not enough ways to spend it.

"You're going to have a great time."

# Sixteen

## SAGE

It rapidly became clear to Sage what kind of nightmare he had willingly and willfully walked into.

Of course, this made sense for the way things had been going with Emily. Why wouldn't she be a photographer of dogs? Why wouldn't that come up in regular conversation?

"Are you okay?" she asked, her hand landing on his forearm, concern evident in her tone.

Sage smiled tightly. "Yeah, no problem. Why?"

She eyed him, amusement twitching her lips as if she didn't believe him.

He sighed and slid his hands into his pockets (fingers couldn't be bitten if they were in pockets). "What can I do to help?"

She pointed to a stool nearby, but out of the way. The kind of stool he'd expect to find in any other photography studio. One that people would sit on. Not animals. "You can sit there for now. If I need you to freak out, I'll let you know." Again with the amusement.

"I'm not freaking out," he mumbled more to himself than to her, as he carefully stepped around the tutu'd poodle.

Once he was sufficiently settled on the stool and no other oddly dressed animals had presented themselves, he began to relax. He could do this. Not a big deal.

Emily spoke with her boss and consulted a clipboard, nodding at whatever instructions she received. Sage took the opportunity to look around—without leaving the stool, of course.

It looked like any other photo studio. Except all the pictures on display were large, glowy photos of glamorized dogs. He squinted at a big dog in a frame to his left, its fur long and straight, blowing in artificial wind. Was that dog wearing makeup? Sage shook his head. No, people weren't that weird. Were they?

Instead of offering any kind of explanation on her return to him, Emily just began taking props out of a huge trunk.

"Do you not like dogs?" she asked, arranging a blue satin backdrop that pooled on the floor. She sounded genuinely concerned, like she was second-guessing having him come along. He must have been emoting more than he realized.

"I like dogs." Sage tried to sound nonchalant. Did that sound nonchalant? As long as they were about the size of the poodle, he'd be fine.

Emily lightly laughed. "Sure, you do. You're a picture of composure."

Sage licked his lips and crossed his arms over his chest. He knew his body language wasn't doing him any favors, but he was feeling just a little exposed at the moment. Probably because on the walk there he had shared so much and she had shared so little. He still hadn't processed that fully.

"I like dogs just fine. I'm more inclined to liking bigger dogs than the smaller ones."

She arched an eyebrow.

He took a deep breath, feeling the phantom pain in his inner thighs where he'd had to get eleven stitches—five on the right and six on the left—when he was thirteen. All because he hadn't seen the angry furry attacker in time. "I had a bad experience when I was younger."

"What kind of experience?"

"A bad one," he reiterated flatly, returning her eyebrow arch. He had already told her his biggest heartbreak. He wasn't looking at listing off every one of his insecurities in the immediate follow-up.

She must've sensed his point, because she ducked her head and went back to work—though he didn't miss the smile she thought she was hiding.

The information he'd shared about his birth mom wasn't exactly a secret. People who knew him, knew about it. But he'd thought maybe if he'd showed his soft spot, she might...trust him? Show him hers? He wasn't sure what he'd been expecting. And now that it was out there, it felt different between them somehow. Nothing had changed, not really. He'd made a statement of fact about his life.

And yet, he couldn't help but feel something new had bloomed between them.

A barrier, a normal one that belongs in between strangers, had been removed. With his small revelation, he'd announced his intention to trust her. To hear his information and...stay. In his space. In the place he occupied.

Maybe that was why he was feeling strange. He'd offered an invitation, and he was hoping her smiles and her laughter were an indication of accepting.

That maybe, just maybe, she might eventually trust him.

"Which job do you like more? This one, or The Brew?" Sage asked, trying oh-so-hard to hold onto whatever cool he thought he may have possessed before this non-date.

"That's a tough one," she said, pulling out a pink feather boa from the trunk and tossing it onto the satin. She sat back on her heels and pushed her glasses back into place.

Dang, she was cute.

"I like this one because of the obvious benefits. I get to be around adorable animals and play with cameras the entire time." Her smile changed and her eyes lost focus. "But The Brew...and the people there...I really love being around them."

Sage watched as her thoughts tumbled around in her beautiful head, mesmerized by the purity in her expression. She was completely without guile. Her eyes locked on him and she offered a new Emily smile, one he hadn't been gifted with yet, but was easily in his top five favorite Emily Smiles.

"I actually love all my jobs. It's hard to pick a favorite when I can't stop feeling grateful for them. But if I'm being completely honest and a little bit selfish, I think my favorite is the overnight babysitting." She shrugged. "It's hard not to love getting to sleep in a real bed and have just a little"—she held up her thumb and forefinger while scrunching up her nose—"bit of privacy. Not that I hate living with Ash and Megan." She snorted and rolled her eyes. "But my room is basically a dining room, so...yeah, the little bit of alone time is nice."

Her revelation sparked something and his chest warmed with the unexpected heat of it. He had to take a very slow, deep breath. She went back to what she was doing (he didn't want to know—it involved tiaras and teacups). He didn't want her words to go unappreciated or unacknowledged. He knew it wasn't her whole story, but it was something, and it felt like a gift. One he wasn't going to take for granted.

"I like you," he stated plainly.

When she glanced up at him, she smiled shyly.

And he grinned.

Because that's what you did when the girl you like smiled at you; you smiled back with everything you had.

\*\*\*

Tiny mob of tiny dogs. Tiny mob dogs.

That little gray one with the blue eyes was obviously in charge.

Sage sat as still as he could. He knew his feet had migrated to the top rung of the stool, pushing his knees up to his ears. He probably looked ridiculous. But he was concentrating too hard on deep breathing and staying calm to care. They could sense fear.

The gray one was sensing it right now. They locked eyes and Sage's pulse kicked up.

"This is my nightmare," he said matter-of-factly.

Emily let loose with a riot of giggles, which is what she'd been doing a lot over the past couple of hours. Sage hadn't figured out what was so damn hilarious, but he was fairly certain it had something to do with adorable animals and his aversion to them. Not a strong aversion... he wasn't a monster. But he had a healthy respect for the damage one of those furry creatures could do if you weren't looking.

He was having a hard time being upset about any of it.

Maybe if Emily had been irritated with his lack of manliness, that may have made the evening less enjoyable. But she was perfectly delighted with his hand-wringing and chin rubbing. Not one of the dogs she'd taken pictures of that night had been the size of the poodle. Not even close. It was almost as if she specialized in teacup breeds. It was okay—up until they stopped coming in one at a time and an entire gang of little dogs showed up at once for their "appointment."

Seriously. Ten tiny dogs of varying breeds and colors swarmed around the girl he was currently and quickly growing attached to, demanding her attention. And her allegiance. And her lunch money.

Sage couldn't decide if he should attempt to save her, or flee for his life.

The giggles and gentle admonishments told him she was fine. Still. He was sweating.

"Can you hand me that string of pearls?"

Sage jerked his head up to see Emily staring at him expectantly.

He pointed to his chest.

She laughed and nodded. "Yes. It's in the trunk. I forgot to grab it."

That meant he would have to leave the stool. Sage uncurled his hands from around the lip of the stool where he'd tried hanging on to keep from hand-wringing. His legs made a slow descent to the floor and he straightened his torso, trying to pull his shoulder back to look bigger and discourage a sneak attack.

He made it to the trunk, found the pearls, and was handing them gingerly over to Emily when it happened.

The Blue-Eyed Boss barked, signaling the attack he knew was coming. Sage's eyes darted down to the penned-in area surrounding Emily and the dogs. He lost focus on what he was doing with his hands and his body weight shifted, causing him to lose his footing. He tripped over the eight-inch plastic wall, knocking it down, and fell headlong into the swarm.

Tiny dog bodies pummeled into him and he let a loud (masculine) yell. He tried to cover his face with his hands, but there were dogs everywhere. Ten had multiplied into a thousand and he was doomed. This was it. This is how it would end. He was going to be eaten by novelty dogs dressed as royalty.

It was the laughter that really brought him out of it. The loud, unabashed, delighted, laughter. He opened his eyes to see Emily wiping tears from an eye with one hand while trying to man the camera with the other.

"Are you taking pictures of this?" Sage asked, horrified at her lack of compassion.

"Oh, I have to. Abby is gonna love this."

"You can't show Abby!" He rose up on his elbows and froze. The Boss was standing on his chest. Of course he was. Why wouldn't he take part in his victory? "Heyyy," Sage greeted casually. The Boss attacked. With his tongue. Covering Sage's face in a million tiny kisses.

Well, this was unexpected.

"You're too cute."

Sage's eyes came up to connect with Emily's and he suddenly didn't care if she was talking to the dog or to him (he was going to tell himself later that she was totally talking to him). He grinned, she grinned, and then she took the picture.

Best non-date ever.

# Seventeen

### EMILY

Puppies.

Sage's kryptonite was puppies.

Not rottweiler or pit bulls or ninjas... I mean, I'm *way* more afraid of ninjas than basically any dog out there, so...yeah.

Puppies.

When Mrs. Tennent had brought in her herd of teacup dogs, I thought Sage was going to pass out and fall off that stool he was hiding on.

But, no. It took me asking for props to be his downfall. Literally.

And then he kept calling Rumplefluffkins "Mob Boss"— which made about as much sense as anything else that day.

I pulled the door shut behind me, double-checking the lock while Sage waited at the bottom of the stairs, glancing down the street. Probably waiting for the next influx of tiny dogs.

He scanned the area and all I could picture was him creating an in-depth retreat plan in his head.

"So, you think we can get home safely?" I asked, trying not to laugh out loud.

I'm sure he was aware enough that I was laughing in my head.

But the problem—the *real* problem—wasn't that he had microcynophobia (thank you, Google). It was that I thought his microcynophobia was adorable.

A-freaking-dorable.

It was hard to believe a guy who was afraid of tiny dogs could purposefully set out to use another person. I had to believe this was one more tick in the Safe column.

We walked side by side, him glancing down at me, then away. Rinse, repeat. I thought he was going to take my hand, but instead he shoved his in his pockets.

Which was great. Totally great. It meant I didn't have to dodge the hand-hold.

Yup. Super glad he did that.

I think.

Darn it, I couldn't get Ashleyton out of my head telling me to give him a chance.

"So, the last guy I went out with kind of ruined my life."

His sneaker scraped on the pavement, as he stutter-stepped but didn't otherwise react.

I walked on, trying to figure out if that was enough sharing for one day.

I mean, that was more than I typically told anyone. It was almost the total of what Ash and Megan knew. So, yup. Maybe I was done for the day.

I took a deep breath, congratulating myself on opening up like that.

"So…" Sage spoke up after about half a block. "So, when you say ruined your life, you mean, broke your heart or something, right?"

Did Troy break my heart? Maybe. But his actions weren't the most heartbreaking to me.

"Kind of."

Sage nodded. I could almost hear him thinking, *Well, that's not so bad.*

"Did he…" I watched the run of emotions on his face, looking to ask questions without prying.

His trying to be sensitive instead of nosy made me feel more comfortable. I knew it wasn't going to be like other people. The questions. The pushing. As if being outside the normal expectation they had for me meant they had to know everything about me right away. As if they had the *right*.

Sage cleared his throat before finishing his question. "Cheat?"

"Oh. Probably." I guess I hadn't really thought about it, but my money would be on yes.

Sage looked at me funny and I realized my answer was really dismissive of something that should be a big deal.

"But that wasn't the thing, I take it." It wasn't a question, and he went on, his hands fisting at his side, his gaze staying straight ahead. "He didn't…hit you, right?"

I was really thankful in that moment Troy had never laid a hand on me, because for a moment Sage's rage at the idea rolled off him in a way that screamed Guy Retribution.

"No." I reached out, surprising myself when I felt my hand touch the skin of his arm. "No. He never hit me."

I saw that this opening up thing was way more complicated than I'd expected it to be. I could tell Sage was just going to keep going to horrible places in his head over and over. I could also tell he felt like his questions were limited and he'd reached that limit.

We walked on, Sage quiet at my side, me cursing Ash and her "just open up" advice.

I couldn't leave it like this, but I also didn't want to drag it out. I started spitting out words faster than I knew I'd stored them up.

"He was rich." I guess everything felt rich to me, but money was a thing for his family. "He was dealing on the side. For fun or rep or something. And, when he got caught, he said it was me. That it was all my stuff." I glanced over as Sage stopped walking, knowing there was no turning back now.

He pulled me down a side street to a little park for families.

"And, people believed that?" He sounded so shocked that my heart double-timed its thumping in my chest.

That this guy wouldn't believe that when he just barely knew me compared to—

"Yeah. Everyone did." I sucked in a breath. "Actually, one person didn't believe him."

"Your mom." He nodded like this was obvious.

"No. The prosecutor." I watched as my answer hit him like I'd smacked him upside the head.

"Your parents believed him?" The shock was so clear that he might as well be carrying emotional emojis around with him for clarity.

"Yes…well, no. But, yes."

This part seemed rougher than the rest. It seemed to say something more about me than I wanted it to. This was the part that hurt every time I thought about it. The part where my life switched its course and never changed back.

I'd been trying to catch up with how to make things work since that day, and was still struggling with it. Emotionally, financially...obviously in the trust-bank.

"So, I was in foster care." I took a deep breath and pushed the words out as fast as I could. "I'd been with the family for almost three years. The plan was for me to stay on with them. To be part of the family. To go to college on scholarship. But holidays and such would always be with them. I felt like I had a home. But when Troy accused me, when they believed him and his rich family and his powerful dad over me...they kicked me out."

"They *what?*"

I'd never seen someone so angry before.

Sage got up, pacing across the small children's park before stalking back.

He opened his mouth. Shut it. Turned and stomped across the park and back again.

"Just kicked you out? Boom. Just, see ya, Emily. It was nice having you as part of our family, but we obviously don't know you one bit and we're not freaking human beings?"

Part of me, a small corner of my heart, healed just a little bit at his anger.

"Basically." I cocked my head to watch him where he bounced on his toes, energy tightly contained. "Yes."

"So, what did you do?" He ran his hands down his jeans. I watched as he pushed the energy out of himself and a calm fell over him—centered him. It was like watching someone change their soul for a moment.

People didn't usually want to know that part.

"Well, the Kingstons gave me the money they'd set aside from their monthly foster care payments they didn't spend. They said it was for college, but I was obviously going to need it now."

"Generous of them."

"So, I moved in with some girl I met on Craigslist. It was okay. Except her boyfriend was always there. He was the one who got me my overnight babysitting job. I think it was a way to get me out of the apartment. But, that first job let me figure things out. Then I'd get another job. Then another. I had been accepted to school, so I changed it to two classes so I could work."

"But what about financial aid?"

"Well, when I had to cut my class load to pay for food and shelter stuff, the financial aid changed to almost nothing."

This had become my normal over the last few years, something I just dealt with step-by-step.

I'd been lucky to find Ash and Megan this past spring. And another job at The Brew with good pay and good people. And now, because of Sage, a chance to work a couple days under one of my idols.

Sage spit out a breath that sounded of all things frustrated.

"Don't do that." I all but smacked him as I said it. "Don't do the pity thing."

I stood up, done with this all. Pity was the last thing I wanted. Embarrassment at being betrayed like that was bad enough.

"It's not pity." He shook his head, looking at me with a gaze that I couldn't read. "It's…respect and frustration. For you. Both for you."

I stood there, shocked that he *respected* me. It wasn't something I expected from people. It was a high goal.

"Are you walking me home?" I asked, because I really needed to change the topic since any more of this chatter would have me in a puddle of humiliation on the ground. No matter how accepting he was, it was still embarrassing when your "family" gave you away.

"Of course." We walked back to the sidewalk, the comfortable silence different now. I knew he was thinking about what I'd just told him. I tried to trust that he was being honest about the no-pity thing.

But, trust…yeah. I wasn't exactly great at the trust thing.

This putting yourself out there—sharing stuff you didn't tell people, trusting they wouldn't think you were an escaped criminal thing—was scary.

I hadn't realized how much Sage's reaction mattered to me, what he thought, until the words had started flooding out of my mouth.

And then it didn't just matter. It *mattered*.

Sage was the most easygoing guy on the planet, and it made life around him easy. But, I was still afraid of that good life he'd lead and that laidback style of his wouldn't leave room for the grey area of being wrongly accused.

My heart skipped a beat, and I forced down my fear. I kept trying to put up self-protecting road blocks, but I questioned those now.

Glancing up at him, I hoped. I *hoped*.

And he, calm and sure, stood in the middle of that hope.

And that hope turned to calm, and that calm turned to cheer.

He glanced down at me.

"What?" he asked, giving me a confused smile.

Probably at the stupid grin I was wearing after spilling my guts.

"So, puppies, huh?"

# Eighteen

## SAGE

Sage thought he saw something move out of the corner of his eye and jumped, rolling his chair slightly to the left.

He took a deep breath and tried to calm his heart rate.

No puppies.

Nothing.

Just his imagination.

He chuckled an embarrassed laugh at himself as he flipped the switches on the panel of the old soundboard.

The studio was quiet; everyone had gone home for the night save Sage, who was catching up on the takes he'd missed while he'd been with Emily.

His thought had been in a constant swirl since he'd left her at her door. They were starting to settle and fall into place as he worked the dailies.

Emily's hesitancy, her fear, her walls. It was all making sense.

You know what wasn't making sense? Her smile. Her gentleness, positivity, her kindness.

Sage couldn't imagine...any of it. He couldn't relate. Not even a fraction of a faction of an iota.

It wasn't even the guy—even though he was clearly a dick—that had Sage so upset. It was her family. The people she'd trusted to protect her and love her and believe her.

Her words rang through his head again and his limbs trembled with negative energy. He needed to get rid of it.

Sitting down at the table, he cued up the track they'd been working on earlier. He settled the headphones over his ears and tried to let the sound of loud rock and roll distract him.

The day of the stolen burrito incident replayed. As hilarious as it had been at the time, he remembered her panic and fear. He hadn't even really known her at the time, and he knew what a ridiculous idea it was that she'd steal something, let alone from her employer. But looking back, no wonder she'd been scared. And that wasn't right.

Someone who walked through this world with the kind of integrity that was obvious to a nobody coffee customer (granted, he had only come in for one cup and kept coming back because of the pretty girl behind the counter), shouldn't be accused of and found guilty of dealing drugs.

Drugs!

Sage swallowed, closed his eyes, and leaned back in his chair.

She had had the kind of life where being bitter and cynical would be understood. Even expected. But, no. Not this girl. This girl smiled at every stranger, took delight in the feel of a real bed, was thankful for her job at the coffee shop where she worked with, well, Abby. She worked hard, she was kind, funny, smart.

She was, quite possibly, the most beautiful person Sage had ever met.

***

"Hey."

Emily's head came up and her eyes went round. "Hi."

Sage ran a hand through his still-damp hair and then shoved both hands in his pockets. It had become almost a reflex when he was around Emily now. If his hands were in his pockets, he wouldn't reach for her. Why he would reach for her was beyond his comprehension. Okay, that was a lie. He knew why he would reach for her.

He wanted to know what it felt like to touch the sun.

So, hands in pockets, no one lost their minds. By "no one," he meant him. He was the crazy one here. Totally sack of hammers bananas.

Still, seeing her, even though he'd just seen her last night, it was like finally waking up. Maybe his brain had been trained with the gallons of coffee he'd ingested over the past several weeks and seeing her face at the same time. It responded either way. It was science. Clearly.

He tried his most disarming smile. Relief washed over her face before she schooled her features and returned his smile.

"Surprised to see me so soon?" he asked after he'd made it to the counter.

Color crept up her neck and she glanced away. "A little. I know it was a lot to dump on you—"

"No, Emily," he stopped her. "It's not a lot to dump on anyone. It's a lot to carry alone."

She glanced away as if she wasn't sure she could believe what he was telling her. Sage didn't want to make it about him. He didn't want to use a lot of needless words to explain to her exactly how he felt at the moment. She'd mentioned not wanting to be pitied. And he didn't. Pity wasn't even in the realm of what he was feeling. It was a whole lot of respect with a dash of admiration and a dollop of humility. He pressed on.

"I'm going to need a coffee." He fished his dollars out of his pockets. "And then I'm going to sit over there." He nodded to his usual table. "And if you have a minute at all"—he held her eyes and gave her his best crooked smile—"I would enjoy your company for any seconds you have to spare." He spotted Abby hovering near the kitchen door, so he waved a hand at her. She gave him a look that made it clear if there were sides, she knew which one she was on.

Emily made his coffee, took his money, and he did exactly as he said he was going to do. It didn't take more than ten minutes before she slid into the chair across from him and rested her chin on her fist, elbow to the table, attempting (and failing) to hide her smile.

"I thought maybe you didn't want to deal with…everything," she blurted out.

Sage chuckled. "No. The gang of thugs you choose to do business with aren't enough to scare me off. I'm much braver than you give me credit for."

Her blues eyes danced and her smile grew even as her blush did, too. "You know what I mean."

He nodded; he did know. He glanced over to Abby behind the counter. "You didn't, by chance, happen to show…?"

Emily pursed her lips and avoided eye contact.

"Right." Sage nodded, accepting the inevitable remarks that would be made in the future. "So, I was wondering," he started out, trying to sound as casual as possible. "For our next non-date, would you be interested in letting me surprise you?"

She narrowed her eyes but didn't look as fearful as she would have, say, a week ago.

"Now, before you answer, I want to give you some more details."

"Okaay," she drew out slowly, amusement touching the corners of her mouth.

Sage nodded sternly and pressed his palms to the table. "I would pick you up and feed you and get you back home safe. I will also promise intelligent conversation and an appropriate number of topical jokes." He gave her a flat stare. "I cannot stress enough how much this isn't a date, despite how it sounds. This is me being purely selfish and just wanting to eat food and have conversation with a girl who I think is totally kickass."

She smiled hugely and Sage sighed.

"You know, after I said all of that, I hear it. It does sound like a date."

"You think?" she asked, her eyebrows lifting.

Sage dropped his flat expression and grinned. "Okay. Maybe not, then. Maybe the thing that sounds like a date happens later." He took a deep breath, lost a little in her glow. "Just say when."

# Nineteen

### EMILY

"YOU'RE GOING TO HAVE TO just go out with him." Abby was greasing a pan with what I really hoped wasn't lard, leaning against the kitchen doorway.

"What?" I wasn't actually playing dumb. Abby just confused me that much.

She nodded her head toward the front door Sage had just rambled out of.

"Him. You're going to have to just go out with him. On a date. A date you call a date."

"I—"

"Listen," she interrupted. "I've been through this too many times. You people come in here and have no clue how to run your own lives. You'd think love was this commodity you had to save for. Maybe earn up enough to get some later. Don't worry about this guy. Either you'll save enough for an upgrade or once you do some research on whatever you think the

Consumer Reports of Love is, you'll circle around and he'll just be waiting for you to get your act together."

"That's—"

"And, I'm kind of not going through the whole rigmarole with you." Abby put the pan down. "I get it. I totally get it. *Trust* me. I get it so much you wouldn't even believe me. I'm not sure what your past is. John is way too good a guy to do that—to either of us. But, you can't just swish away from something good."

I stared at her, completely bewildered by this version of Abby.

"I'm not swishing." Because, that was really the only thing I felt qualified to answer right off the bat.

"Uh-huh." Abby gave me the oddest smile and nodded toward my phone. "Just text him and let him off the hook."

With that, she wandered back in the kitchen.

I stood at the counter, rag in hand, staring at the door Sage had walked through moments ago and wondering...

Wondering if Abby was right, and risk was worth it. Wondering if Sage was safe and I could trust him. Wondering if now, with everything going on in my life, was really the time to take that risk.

Wondering if I was worth the risk.

I didn't let myself over think it. I just did it.

I picked up the phone, brought up his number, and texted him.

And, I even hit SEND.

# TWENTY

### SAGE

**Emily:** OK
**Sage:** OK?
**Emily:** Yes. OK.
**Sage:** Did you mean to text me? This is Sage.
**Emily:** I know.

SAGE STARED AT THE SCREEN on his phone. The time stamp said Emily had sent it shortly after he'd left The Brew, but he hadn't checked his phone until he'd parked in Luke Casey's driveway.

That was all it said. Just "OK." No context.

He was still staring at the screen when he came into the garage. He nodded to the greetings of Sway and Mike, but didn't look up. They were supposed to be adding the bass track to the drum track that they'd finally settled on. Sage set the phone down on the console and began turning the switches.

Ok, what?

If she had meant to send it someone else, who was it meant for? And what was Emily agreeing to? "OK" was an agreement of some kind. Right?

"How's it going with the coffee girl?" Mike asked from the couch behind him.

Sage turned around and shook his head. "What does 'OK' mean?"

Mike's eyebrows dipped. Sage snatched the phone off the console and handed it to the drummer.

"Ooh, can I see?" Sway asked, sitting down on the arm of the couch and looking down at the phone in Mike's possession.

"Okay what?" Mike asked, handing the phone back.

Sage shrugged again; it felt more frantic than the last one. "I have no idea. The second non-date went...well." Sage wasn't going to reveal Emily's secrets to these guys or his near-death experience with the Pound Puppies, even though they were basically his closest friends these days. How weird was it that his former idols had turned into his friends? Really freaking weird. Too bad he didn't have time to think over all of that right now. "I saw her this morning before I came out here."

"This morning?" Sway's eyebrows went up. "Did last night go very well?"

Sage glared at the bassist. "You're hilarious." He ran a hand through his hair. "I have no idea what she could be OKing to. I'm trying to remember everything we talked about in the previous twenty-four hours, but I appear to have blocked almost all of it out."

"Almost?"

"I remember her smile," Sage clarified, trying to press his lips together to keep from grinning like an idiot.

"Ask her." Mike crossed his arms over his chest.

**Sage: What are you OKing to?**

"While we wait for Miss Emily to reply and confirm what I already know," Sway said, arching a single eyebrow, "can we try out my track? I'm feeling funky. I want to funk it all up in here."

Sage jerked his head slightly. "What do you already know?"

Sway stood up and headed for the recording room. "You're in dating purgatory. That super-fun middle ground between non-dates and actual dates."

Sage stared at the space Sway vacated, wondering if that were true. Was this just a transitional period? Was this the space where two people decided to invest in a future? Because if they started to real-date instead of non-date, it put a whole lot more on the line.

**Emily: I'm saying OK to you.**
**Emily: And your idea.**

He couldn't stop it that time; he full-on grinned at his phone. Like an idiot. Then he handed the reply to Mike.

"Clearly, you had an idea and she is OK with it," Mike said with a chuckle, handing the phone back.

Sage tossed the phone onto the console and bent in half, the fingers of both hands sliding into his hair. "Why am I so scared I'm going to screw this entire thing up? We're not even a thing." He sat back up and slapped his hands onto his knees. "And yet the idea of us not being a thing feels ludicrous."

Mike's mouth tugged up on one side.

"The more I learn about her, the more time I spend with her, I just..." Sage closed his eyes and shook his head. "She's better than me. And when I'm with her, I feel like the two of us have an honest shot at something amazing. And it's freaking me out."

"You're in it deep." Mike confirmed what Sage already knew.

"I spent years with Heather," Sage said, his stomach twisting. "I wasn't ever worried about losing her. I assumed if we ended, it would be because it was time." He sighed heavily. "And now I'm freaking out about losing a girl I haven't even been able to real-date yet." Something clicked in his memory. "Wait a second." He grabbed his phone again and typed out a quick reply.

**Sage: Are you saying OK to a date?**

Holy crap. If she was saying yes to a real date...

"Hey. Loverboy, let's roll tape," Sway interrupted Sage's thought explosion.

Sage turned around and cued up the drum track, waited for Sway's nod, then hit RECORD and PLAY.

A real date could—no, would, because Sage recognized early on that Emily wasn't the kind of girl you let things fizzle with—a real date would lead to a relationship, which would lead to...everything.

Sage was completely fine with that.

\*\*\*

## EMILY

"For the love of everything with sugar in it, put it away or I'll take it away." Abby glared. She was a pro, but this one seemed a little more glarey than normal.

But, I couldn't help it, I smiled at her because... "You sound like a mom."

Not that I'd really know too much about that firsthand, but she did. She sounded like a mom.

The look she gave me then only reinforced the mom thing...horror, but still mom.

"I mean it." She pointed at the phone.

I giggled. She *meant* it.

"Stop that."

I covered my mouth, trying not to laugh at Mom Abby.

"If I have to—" She cut herself off, obviously knowing where that was going before I could even point it out.

"Are you going to pull this café over?" I asked, trying to keep a straight face.

Without another word, she spun around and stormed into the kitchen.

I glanced down at the text Sage had just sent.

Was I saying okay to a date? That seemed so official.

Maybe a baby-step chance would be a better start.

**EMILY: I'm saying we could hang out.**

**SAGE: So, a date.**

I tried not to roll my eyes at my phone.

**EMILY: Hang out. Gotta go.**

I turned my phone off before this could get ridiculous.

***

## SAGE

"Impossible," Sage muttered at his phone. Emily could ride a unicycle through The Brew, wearing a sombrero and juggling kittens, and he'd still be enamored with her. He bit his lower lip, that now familiar warmth spreading through his chest again.

She was giving him a chance.

She was giving *them* a chance.

All Sage had to do was not screw it up.

"So what did she say?" Mike asked. He'd moved to take the seat next to Sage when Harrison had joined them a minute before. He had also taken it upon himself to update Harrison on Sage's current dating obstacles. It was bizarre how interested they all were. Though, now that they all had their "one," they seemed to be focused on making sure others found their "one."

Sage flipped the toggles that would save the length of tape they had recorded. He slid his phone with one hand along the console in Mike's direction, Emily's reply still lit up on the screen.

"Gentlemen, we have a date in play," Mike announced to the room. He slid the phone back and lifted his chin at Sage. "Where are you gonna take her?"

Sage's mind swirled with possibilities. He didn't want to do anything too flashy since he was aware of her sensitivities toward money and what a distraction it might be for a first date. A first date should be fun and exciting. At the same time, he didn't want to be a total doofus and go too far the other direction.

"I have an idea."

# Twenty-One

### EMILY

I STARED AT MY CLOSET—otherwise known as the bar that ran across one corner of the dining room I hung my clothes on—trying to figure out what to wear.

I didn't want to think *too* hard about it, but at the same time I wanted to put some effort in.

Megan stood near the break in the furniture, holding up one of her club dresses with Ash hovering behind her, shaking her short curls wildly.

Man, I'd kill for those curls. They were all chestnutty and bouncy. She managed to look classic and hip at the same time with the ice-blue tint woven through. A perfect juxtaposition to Megan's adorableness.

"Em, do you like the dress or not?"

"Sorry. I got lost in the splendor of Ash's hair."

Ash tussled the curls on one side, giving me her best Mae West grin. "I can't help it. I distract all the girls."

"Annnnd, no. Today is about Emily." Megan gave her a shove. "Put your ego away."

My roommates were nothing if not girls with big personalities.

Man, I loved those two.

"You really don't know where you're going?" Ash asked as she brushed by Megan, holding out a dress I absolutely was *not* putting on my body.

"Nope. He said casual and comfortable." I pulled my favorite jeans back out of the jean cubby.

"Guy casual is not girl casual." Megan all but stomped her foot.

I really should not have told her I'd kind of agreed to a kind-of date.

"I don't think Sage would take me somewhere not casual." I pulled a brush through my hair, looking at my meager assortment of clothes tossed all over my bed.

"So, he's cheap?" Megan sounded put out by this—as if she were the one going out and had just been told dinner would be at Burger King.

"No. He said 'It's fun and super casual, but I think you'll get a kick out of it.' Not like he made it sound cheap." But what did I know?

I pulled on my favorite jeans and glanced around.

"Fine. Jeans." Megan took all my dresses—the usual Emily Uniforms—and hung them back up. "But you're wearing Ash's emerald-green third-date shirt, then."

"How do you know that's my third-date shirt?" Ash asked, looking more surprised than anything.

"I've been living with you for three years. I know you."

"You know my clothes," Ash mumbled as she went to get the drape'y, green gorgeousness.

I pulled the shirt over my head, rolling my eyes at the up-and-down both girls gave me before nodding to themselves.

"You look great."

"Great in my shirt."

"No. She just looks great."

"Yes. She always does. But right now, she's looking great in my shirt. My third-date shirt." Ash crossed her arms. "The shirt you volunteered without asking."

Oh, crap.

"I can wear something else." I was already pulling the shirt back up and looking for something else to put on.

"No." Ash shook her head. "I want you to wear the shirt."

"But—"

"She," Ash interrupted me, pointing at Megan, "has been stealing my clothes for years. *Years.* Now she's stealing them for someone else."

I untucked the shirt again.

"Stop. What are you doing?" Ash waved at me to tuck the shirt back in.

This was not the drama I expected tonight.

"Okay, so basically you want me to wear the shirt, but you wish you'd thought of it or I'd asked, and not that Megan had just told you to go get it?"

"Right." She gave a quick nod before turning it into a side-eye glare at Megan.

"While I'm out tonight, you guys should get some roommate therapy or something."

The buzzer sounded by the door and I thought, *Literally. Saved by the bell.*

"Okay, well, thanks for distracting me with your own personal issues and neuroses while I waited."

I grabbed a sweater while they continued to bicker. Those two were amazingly tight for people who seemed to have nothing in common.

I raced down the stairs, my heart pounding while I tried to figure out what to think. But thinking about thinking was giving me a headache fast, so I decided non-thinking thoughts would be good.

Which...Emily. Shut up.

I pasted on a smile and opened the door.

Sage stood there, back to the door, looking down the walkway like a man not sure he was in the right place.

And then I saw them.

A tiny pack of tiny dogs being walked very slowly by an elderly woman.

"We can wait here till it's safe." I tried to keep the laughter out of my voice, but...seriously. Tiny dogs. The guy went head-to-head with rock stars on a daily basis and was afraid of things that couldn't even reach his knees if they tried to hop.

He gave me such a look of pure disgust, I wanted to point out that *I* was not the one afraid of tiny, fluffy creatures whose most dangerous aspect was the fact that they might cuddle you to death.

And, honestly, if I had to pick a way to go, cuddle death doesn't sound too bad.

"I think I'll be okay."

"Are you sure?" I asked, getting a kick out of teasing him for once. "Because there's four of them. I'm not sure I can protect you. If she only had three, I know I could take them all, but four...geez. Four is almost like a platoon."

Sage looked at me as if I were nuts.

Maybe I was a tad crazy, but I wasn't stuck on someone's stoop because there were cute animals that—

"Awwww. Look at that!" I pointed, and he turned to see a three-year-old who had rushed over and thrown himself down with the puppies. "Kids these days. No fear. No fear at all."

"All right. That's it." Sage stomped down the stairs, his steps slowing for a moment at the bottom, before he crossed the sidewalk to where the woman stood talking to the boy's dad as tiny dogs climbed all over him. "May I join you?"

The kid looked up at Sage, obviously wondering why anyone would ask to play with dogs. You didn't ask. You just did it. Especially if you were three.

Sage lowered himself to the ground, his head pulled back as if he were afraid someone would bite off his nose. From the look Sage got from the kid, my money was on him.

Sage reached out, curling his fingers in so no one could bite them, and kind of shuffled his hand across the back of one of the dogs. He nodded to himself as if he'd just cured cancer.

Then, he stood, wiped his hands off, and walked back to the stoop, glancing over his shoulder as he went.

"That wasn't so bad." He smiled up at me where I stood two steps up.

He looked so darn cute and proud of himself that I couldn't bring myself to tell him that was the weakest display of daring I'd ever seen.

"See?" I said. "We haven't even left the building and our get-to-know-you night's already a success."

"Date." Sage pointed to the right and fell in step next to me as I headed down the sidewalk.

"What?"

"Date. Tonight is a date."

I tried not to panic at the words.

"No. It's not." I was not on a date. No. I wasn't going from no boys allowed to dating. Too big a jump. Not gonna happen. "We're just hanging out. Getting to know each other."

Sage opened his mouth, then shut it, proving that, as compared to his behavior in regards to tiny dogs, he was smarter than the average bear...if bears feared things they could squash with one paw.

After half a block, he decided to open his mouth after all.

"So, not a date?"

"No."

"Hmmm..." He walked along beside me and, after a moment, took my hand.

It had been a long time since I'd had my hand held. I couldn't remember the last time. Troy obviously hadn't been a great hand-holder, or I'd remember. But Sage? His hand felt just right. Mine fit in his comfortably, the calluses on his fingers just grazing the back of my hand. Not too tight, like he was trapping me, tying me to him.

"But, I can hold your hand, right?"

Well, if he'd asked first, I'd probably have had to say no. But this was nice.

"Okay."

"And, I still get to feed you and make you laugh, right?"

"Well, yes. I mean, we're hanging out." Because that's all this was.

"Okay." He nodded to himself again, as if he were doing some complicated math in his head. "And, at the end of the non-date-hangout I get to kiss you good night?"

"Oh." Oh.

I tried to come up with something more than *oh*, but even my inner dialogue was failing me.

Sage smiled, a sly little grin that said he knew very well that *oh* wasn't *no*.

And as much as I tried to keep it in check, my heart gave a happy little hop. Down, heart. Down. I glanced back at him. Nope. There would be hops.

# Twenty-Two

## SAGE

Sage lost himself a moment in the feel of her hand in his. He slowed his steps just a bit and took a deep breath.

First dates.

He hadn't been on a first date in too long to know if this was normal. Maybe the warmth that spread up his arm from their point of contact was what everyone experienced on a first date.

He glanced at her just as she was looking up at him.

No, this was special.

It had to be.

If this were normal, then people would be happier in relationships. Divorce wouldn't be such a huge business, and people wouldn't be so discontent in their daily lives.

That thing that everyone was always talking about finding? Sage was pretty sure he may have just found it. It wasn't a grand explosion, it didn't move the earth beneath him, it didn't cause the earth's rotation to stall. It was the simple joy of holding the hand of a pretty girl. Not just *any* pretty girl.

Emily.

Maybe there wasn't a lot of power in just saying her name. Another person might overhear Sage's thoughts and shrug with indifference. But to Sage...it was Emily.

He sucked in a breath and held it. "I was thinking, if you're good with it, I'd like to make you dinner? My parents are still outta town. And I know how early '90s teen movie that sounds, but I promise nothing untoward will happen. I'll make dinner, hopefully provide somewhat charming conversation, and then bring you home."

She thought it over and he waited. Wow, he was so bad at this. Dating was stressful, he'd never realized that before.

"Well, you don't seem like the murdery type," she said, a teasing lilt in her voice. "I suppose I could trust you this one time."

Sage grinned and opened the passenger door of his truck. He helped her in with a hand, then jogged around to his side.

"So," she asked, watching him curiously from her side of the truck. "What are you going to make for dinner?"

Sage reached for the knob on the radio and flipped it on, filling the cab with the quiet background vocals of Tom Petty. "I have a dish."

"A dish?" she repeated, sounding as if she were trying to hold back a laugh. "Like a signature entrée?"

He glanced over and tossed her a wink. "All guys have at least one dish. Don't you know that?"

She let out a small laugh. "No. I didn't know that. So if I ask Officer Max what his signature dish is...?"

Sage exaggerated a grimace. "Now, see, I don't know #OfficerMax well enough to know if he would tell you his signature dish. But you could ask."

She laughed louder that time. "#OfficerMax? Is that what you call him?"

He shrugged one shoulder. "It's how we were formally introduced. On Twitter. I'm a loyal follower of all things #OfficerMax."

"You're a dork," she said, her voice trembling with humor. She covered her smile with a hand and looked out the window.

Sage grinned, pleased with himself. He didn't mind being a dork as long as the payoff was a relaxed and happy Emily.

When they pulled into his driveway, his stomach tightened with apprehension. Hopefully his awesome idea wouldn't backfire big time. He parked the truck by the side door and hopped out, hurrying around to her side. She'd already had the door open, but she allowed him to offer a hand and help her down. He kept hold of her hand all the way to the house, releasing it only to unlock and open the door.

He showed her through the mudroom and into the open-plan kitchen. She sucked in a soft breath and he grabbed her hand again.

"Your house is fancy," she said, voice strained.

He squeezed her hand and nodded. "My dad would love to hear you say that."

She glanced at him, a soft frown drawing her eyebrows down in question.

"When my dad bought this house, it was so dilapidated. He got it for a prayer and song. He's spent a decade turning it into this." He pointed at the cupboards and the filigree carved into the trim. "All of this. Counters, too." He ran a hand over the dark granite, feeling that sense of pride that he always did when he could show off his dad's work. "He purposely found a house that needed more work than it was worth, and turned it into the house he wanted it to be."

Next, Sage showed her the rest of the main floor. The living room, formal dining room, the bathroom. He explained how his dad even did the plumbing and wiring.

They paused at the bottom of the wide staircase, more of his dad's custom designs carved into the banister.

"The bedrooms are all upstairs," he said with a head tilt that direction, continuing to lead her back to the kitchen.

"Is that where your apartment is?" she asked.

"Nope. My apartment is above the workshop out back. And don't even ask if you can see it. This is a first date."

"Not a date," she said automatically.

Sage just shook his head. "Even more of a reason to not ask to see my place. Way too presumptuous. Can you sit here to give me a hard time, please?" he asked, gesturing to one of the high-backed stools at the granite bar.

She hopped onto the seat. "I still don't know what you plan on making."

He opened the refrigerator and pulled out two beautiful T-bone steaks. He turned around and held them up for her.

A laugh bubbled out of her. "Steak is your signature dish?"

"Hey." He tried to look offended. "Do you know how easy it is to wreck a steak? And I have a side dish, too." He opened the pantry door and pulled out two sizable potatoes.

"Meat and potatoes; I should've known."

"I'm about to blow your mind," he promised.

While Sage prepared the steaks for grilling and sliced the pineapple, they talked. Easy. Open. Relaxed. He'd never really had this before. Again, he was struck with the knowledge that this wasn't normal. Not in his world. He'd had girls he liked and girls he was just friends with. Something different happened with Emily where she was both. He was attracted to her, he loved her laugh, he liked to hear her talk, he wanted all of those things. Except more.

"Did your dad do your apartment, too?" she asked, twisting the lid off the water he had handed her.

"No. Actually, I did my own apartment. Took me four years, but I like how it turned out." He rolled the potatoes in tin foil.

"So carpentry was just part of your life, not necessarily your dream," she observed.

He nodded and reached into the spice cabinet for the black pepper grinder. "Dad was a single parent all of a sudden and he had to make some big decisions. He was bringing me to job sites with him before I was even a year old. I literally learned to walk next to a running power sander."

"But the music is where your heart is," she said softly.

He lifted his eyes to connect with hers and smiled. "Yeah. But I'm glad I have a trade. It means I'll have a job if this music thing never amounts to much."

"You're producing an album for a major rock band. I think it's safe to say the music thing is amounting."

"I think it's safe to say my every dream is coming true. It's also safe to add if I suddenly wake up and it's all gone, I'll be devastated." He shook his head and took the plate of prepared steaks in one hand and the plate of sliced pineapple and tin-foiled potatoes in the other. "Would you please be my lovely assistant and open the door for me?"

She hopped off her stool and followed him through the dining room to the sliding glass doors that opened onto the back patio.

Again, it was another beautiful piece his father had created with his own two hands—stone patio with a gas grill built into stacked river rock off to the side, and comfortable furniture his mom picked out decorating the stonework.

"Who's your gardener?" she asked, taking a seat in one of the chairs as he set the plates down and opened the grill.

"My mom. She won't let anyone else touch her lawn." He lit the gas, put the potatoes in first, and closed the lid. He turned his body and rested a hip along the side of the stacked stone, giving her his full attention. "What got you into photography?"

Her smile changed again. Bright and hopeful. He was cataloging all of her smiles. She had about a zillion. And he loved each and every single one. He wondered if she knew how expressive her face was. Every smile conveyed something different, and the more time he spent with her, the easier they were to read. He liked that.

She spoke of her photography, slowly at first, and then with increased confidence, even passionate excitement, when she spoke about taking pictures with Zelda.

"And, I mean, you get to capture the truth. No one can rewrite your vision with photography. It's just really…true." She let her hair fall forward, blocking his view for a moment. "It's your truth. No one can take that."

Sage glanced at her, hiding from him behind a screen of blonde hair, and realized Emily could do anything she wanted with her life. But she had no idea. Her clarity in her art told him everything he needed to know about what she was capable of. He hung out with artists for a living. And now he was falling in love with one.

Sage added the steaks to the grill, then the pineapple. When they were finished cooking, they went back inside where he set the bar with plates and napkins.

"This is the part that's going to blow your mind," he said, opening the foil on the potatoes.

He sliced open the skin of the spuds, added a dollop of real butter, a sprinkle of brown sugar, and topped it with the grilled pineapple. Then he presented it to her beside her grilled-to-perfection T-bone.

"There's no way that's healthy," she said it like he was adorable.

"It's a date, beautiful. It's not about being healthy."

He rounded the counter to take a seat on the stool beside her. "What?" he asked, when he caught her staring at him.

She shook her head and glanced away. "Nothing. Uh, thank you. This looks delicious."

He nodded once and dug in. He didn't know about her, but he was famished. Getting ready for a date with a girl who was in denial about being on a date was calorie-depleting.

It didn't take long before he was shoving the last bite into his mouth, a little ashamed that he had eaten so fast. One glance at Emily's plate and he no longer felt guilty. His eyes darted up to her face in time to see her hide her full and still-chewing mouth behind her napkin.

"That was really good," she said. But her mouth was still full, so it came out, "Law wah ooly gooh."

Sage threw his head back and laughed. She finished and swallowed, and set her napkin down.

"Thank you," she said, her eyes dancing. "That was quite fulfilling."

Sage reached up and tucked a strand of golden hair behind her ear. "Thank you for giving me a shot."

Her smile turned shy as a faint blush touched her cheeks. He hadn't dropped his hand from her hair. Instead, he gently twirled a lock around his finger, watching the way it shimmered and reflected in the light of the setting sun.

"Would you be interested in dessert?" he asked, his voice low.

"Uh, sure." A breathless quality in her tone had Sage's eyes drop to her mouth. He had already told her he was going to kiss her at the end of the date. Would it be wrong to kiss her now?

Suddenly, the side door to the house crashed open, followed by sounds of a struggle in the mudroom. Sage let go of Emily's hair and stood up, ready to take her hand and rush her out the front of the house.

But no, it wasn't any kind of an intruder. That would have been better than what actually happened next.

Sage's parents came stumbling through the doorway of the kitchen, their hands all over each other, their mouths fused together. Awful, wet kissing and moaning sounds filled the room.

"Hello?" Sage yelled, to get their attention and make them stop doing whatever it was they were doing.

His parents stopped making out and turned their heads slowly to take in Sage and Emily sitting at the bar. His mom detached herself from his father first, immediately running her hands down her overly rumpled clothes.

"Hey, Sage, baby," she greeted with a smile, ignorant of the fact that her lipstick was smeared all over her mouth. "Who's your friend?"

"Are we just going to ignore what happened here?" Sage asked, incredulous. Awkward embarrassment coursed through his body. No guy wanted to catch his parents making out, but no guy especially wanted his parents making out in front of the girl he was trying to woo.

Emily slipped her hand into his and he glanced down at her shaking body.

"You're laughing," he deadpanned. "At this, my life. It's making you laugh."

She turned her crimson-red face into his chest to hide. He cracked a smile as his empty hand came up to cup the back of her head.

"Are you on a date?" his dad asked, looking around the kitchen.

"Uh, I was," Sage answered, hoping his dad would read the tone. Dad just grinned. Of course he did.

"Don't give me that look," his dad said, ignoring the tone entirely. "How was I supposed to know you were on a date? You never date. This is great, actually. Happy for you."

"I can make coffee," Mom offered. "Would anyone be interested in some coffee?"

Emily's shaking continued and Sage hoped she was laughing and hadn't switched to crying. He let go of her hand and wrapped his arm around her back, holding her to him protectively. Her arms encircled his waist and she held on.

"No, thank you, mom," Sage replied, trying to keep the edge out of his voice.

"Bea," his dad said, taking his wife's hand. "I think they want to be alone."

"Oh, oh yes, of course." His mom lifted her eyebrows and smiled as if she were in on some big secret.

His parents left the kitchen and went into the den. Sage didn't move until he heard the TV turn on. He took a deep breath and pulled Emily away from his chest by cradling her face in both hands.

"Is there anyway for me to regain whatever cool I had established with you?"

# Twenty-Three

### EMILY

"YOU KEEP ASKING ME ABOUT recovering dignity and cool...and I keep wondering when you thought you lost them."

"Or had them, apparently," Sage mumbled under his breath.

The proximity of him—of everything—dawned on me in a sweeping moment. I took a step back, bumping into the island in the middle of the kitchen, and all but rebounding back into Sage.

"Hey, now." He took my hand and smiled down at me, not stepping in again, but certainly not letting me go, either.

I looked up at him, the light hair flopping in his eyes, that easy smile, the soft way he looked at me and wondered...what the *heck* am I doing here?

I glanced around, looking for the door and wondering if hitchhiking were illegal in this state.

"Stop that." Sage cut into my thoughts, pulling me in this time to wrap his other arm around me, trapping our hands over his heart. "We were having a good time. No panicking. You just saw that I live with a pair of teenagers trapped in fifty-year-old bodies. Now we have dessert, you let me hold your hand, and I kiss you good night."

I was still trying not to panic when he waggled his eyebrows like some tacky '70s actor. The snort slipped out without me even realizing.

"Sage!" a voice came from the other room. "Will Emily be here for breakfast?"

"Kill me now." He glanced toward the ceiling, as if it might fall in on him.

I liked him like this. The edges of gloss I'd painted over him rubbed away. He wasn't a spoiled mama's boy or a guy using his role in celebrity to get what he wanted.

He was sweet and funny and awkward. That last one won me over a bit.

He walked me back around the counter and pulled out the stool for me before rounding the bend to the fridge.

"So, dessert?" Sage pulled open the freezer, glancing in it with a nervous look. "Dessert. Right."

I rested my chin on my hand, watching him try to figure this out. I mean, *he* said dessert.

"How about some...no." He pushed the freezer door shut and pulled the fridge open. "We could have...oh. Yeah, no."

Straightening, he ran his hand through his hair, still glaring at the refrigerator as if not having dessert was its fault.

"What if we get ice cream on the way back to your place?" he asked—as I could have *sworn* he sent a glare toward the living room.

"Actually," I gave him my disappointed face. "I hate ice cream. And cheese."

"You hate ice cream?" He sounded more shocked than I expected.

"And cheese."

"Ice cream and cheese?" He turned back around, obviously trying to come up with a plan B while I tried not to giggle.

"Also, kittens and rainbows." I went on. "Oh, and philanthropy. I'm so anti-philanthropy I thought about starting my own anti-philanthropy philanthropy."

He spun to look at me, gaze narrowed. "You're joking."

I did my very well-rehearsed blank face and asked, "Am I?"

We stood, facing off over the kitchen island, until he broke and started laughing.

"There's no way you hate ice cream, kittens, and philanthropy."

"Don't forget cheese."

"Well, good thing I'm not going to ask for cheese on my kittens." He grabbed his keys off the counter, giving the kitchen a last glance to make sure he'd put everything way. "Hold on a second."

He headed down the hallway toward the sound of the TV, and after a minute I heard, "My eyes! My eyes! Can't you two act your age?"

I laid my head down on my arms where they rested on the counter and lost it.

This family was nuts. I thought the crazy thing about him would be he worked for rock stars, but apparently Sage was a crazy magnet.

A moment later, he breezed out of the hall and toward the door as if a cave troll was chasing him.

"Ready?" he asked, holding it open, obviously looking to escape the House of the Aging Lovebirds.

I gave him a smile and a little pat on the arm as I went by. The poor guy was embarrassed by the love fest, but honestly? It was the cutest thing I'd seen in my life. Who didn't want that? To still be making out like teenagers when you were old enough to be parents.

"I think they're cute."

"Shhhh." Sage pulled the door shut behind us. "If they hear you, next time they'll do it on purpose. Actually, they'll probably do it on purpose next time anyway. So, I'm thinking about moving to Antarctica. Anything new with you?"

He opened the door to his truck and waited while I climbed in.

Before he closed it, I asked, "If you move to Antarctica, can I have your parents?"

He stopped, hand on the doorframe, and glanced away. "I'm such a dick."

"What?"

"The parents thing. I mean—"

"Hey. No." I turned back, blocking the door from closing with my foot. "I didn't mean it like that, and you should *never* feel bad for having a great family. And you guys had your bad stuff, too. Count your blessings. It's not like your blessings steal my blessings."

Sage stared at me, his gaze so focused I wasn't sure what he was thinking, until he said, "You're amazing."

Oh.

"No." I shook my head, not wanting anyone—especially Sage—to mistakenly put me on a pedestal. "No, I'm not."

"I think you are." He leaned in. "Don't panic, but I'm going to kiss you now."

"Why would I panic?" I mean, besides the fact he was going to kiss me and I wasn't sure I was ready.

It's not like I was unkissed. But I hadn't been kissed since Troy, and that explosion of life-altering awfulness wasn't exactly high on my repeat list.

Of the guys I'd kissed before, I'd never felt this rush of expectation in that moment. I'd felt excitement or nerves, but this time it was something different. It was as if I was giving him something he wouldn't let me take back—but he was doing the same thing.

And then his lips brushed over mine, lightly, testing. And they were soft, and feathering, and my heart nearly broke from it. Then, as I feared he'd just give me that gentle sweep of a kiss, his hand slid up my neck, wrapping his fingers through my hair, and my heart dropped right through my body and halfway to the center of the earth.

# Twenty-Four

## SAGE

EMILY LET OUT A SMALL gasp. Sage felt the gentle sound hit him squarely in the chest. Her hair was pure silk where it wrapped and tangled in his fingers as he attempted to hold her.

But she was holding him.

Right at the edge of everything he had never felt and nothing he ever knew existed. The wind of the unknown whipped up the side of the cliff face where they were metaphorically standing, and her soft lips were the solid place his mind became tethered.

Maybe it was because he'd been anticipating this moment, fantasized about it, since the first day he'd met her. Or maybe it was because every time he was with her she opened his heart and his head to a new point of view that was so gloriously unexpected...

He'd lived a happy life. A good life. A great life, even.

But for the first time in that happy/good/great life, he was experiencing blissful need.

Her mouth reciprocated in pressure and her hands slid up his chest to press against the place his heart hammered. He braced his free hand against the doorframe to keep it from reaching into the truck and pulling her against him. Instead, he focused all of his energy on where his mouth was moving against hers.

She parted her lips just slightly and he accepted her invitation, deepening the kiss. He touched his tongue to her bottom lip for the barest of tastes, and then he ended the kiss.

He pulled away from her face a few inches to take a deep breath and see her in the starlight. Her eyes stayed closed and she let out a soft sigh, her cheeks freshly pink.

He'd done that.

That calm beauty that rested on her expression with such ease.

And he'd do it again. Soon.

Her eyes fluttered open and she smiled. Another new smile. Not shy, not blinding, something more than happy. This one was just for him. A smile that perhaps hadn't existed until he'd kissed her. A smile he helped create.

Together they had very carefully and slowly built a new language between the two of them. Like the shaping of wood that becomes an instrument to be held and played by a master musician, they were together shaping an instrument meant to be played by only them to make music only they would understand.

He grinned and bit down on his bottom lip before closing her door and jogging around to the other side of the truck.

They weren't even out of the driveway before he reached for her hand again, holding it on the seat in between them. He didn't want to sever the connection he'd found.

The sound of her sweet voice reached his ears in small stages. Light and soft, and then all at once clear as she sang along with the radio.

Train's "Drops of Jupiter."

It was one of those songs everyone knew, and impacted everyone differently. Where her head was, he had no idea. Her eyes were on the stars, her lips moved to the words, and her voice was crisp and melodic. He squeezed her hand at the same time as he joined his voice with hers. Because who didn't know every single word to this song?

She faced him, her smile wide. He returned it. Their volume increased until he could no longer hear Patrick Monahan and it was just Sage, Emily, and rising violins.

The song ended and she chuckled. "That was awesome. I love that song."

Sage filed that away for all time and pulled the truck over at a small ice cream place.

She ordered chocolate with sprinkles and he tried to order his sundae with extra kittens. To which the dude working behind the counter looked disgusted. But it made Emily laugh, so it was well worth the look of disdain.

He dropped the tailgate on the truck and they sat on the open gate, legs swinging as they ate. Well, Emily ate. Sage mostly forgot his ice cream in favor of peppering her with ridiculous questions.

"What other things besides cheese, kittens, ice cream, and philanthropy do you dislike?"

She nodded seriously as she swallowed. "Italian food."

"Yeah?" He lifted his eyebrows, trying desperately to make his face as sober as hers.

"And old pickup trucks."

He glanced over his shoulder and made a face. "That's not good."

"Boys with floppy hair and green eyes."

She looked up at him through her eyelashes, her lips quirking on one side.

"I'll get a haircut tomorrow," he said, his focus dropping to her mouth again.

"Good." She nodded curtly and looked away. He leaned forward and took her dish of ice cream out of her hands. "Hey!" Her laughter died when she realized how close he was to her face. She swallowed as her gaze landed on his mouth.

Sage hovered just out of reach, their lips a fraction of a centimeter from touching. She looked up at him, expectation and hope swirling through those baby blues.

Then he kissed her. Short, soft, and with just enough pressure so that when he leaned away again, she followed for a beat.

He grinned and gave her back her ice cream.

"I don't like your kisses, either," she said, clearing her throat and stirring the last little bit around in her cup.

"Right. And I'm going to start breeding yorkies tomorrow."

She snorted.

He eyed her melted ice cream and realized it was getting late. Especially for her. She probably had work right away in the morning and he was taking up all of her time.

Hopping down from the tailgate, he offered her his hand. She glanced up at him, a small flash of disappointment touching her features before she covered it. Good. She wasn't overly anxious to get away from him.

They tossed the rest of their dessert into the trash receptacle before pointing the truck toward her apartment.

The drive was quiet, but not in an awkward "what the hell do I talk about now?" kind of way. It was the kind of quiet that settles over people who just aren't ready to say goodnight yet. As if the silence were assisting them in soaking up every little detail of the evening.

She waited for him to come around and help her out of the truck. He grasped her hand and as she started to walk toward her door, he pulled her to a stop. She looked up at him with a soft frown. Taking a deep breath, Sage slipped his other arm around her waist and pulled her into his arms.

"What are you doing?" she asked breathlessly.

"Making a very important memory." Sage began to sway their bodies to the rhythm in his head. He waggled his eyebrows, then began singing the chorus to "Drops of Jupiter" one more time.

He spun her out and back in again, dancing with her on the city sidewalk. Easily the best first date ever. She was smiling, blushing, and holding tight to his hand by the time they got to her door.

She turned to face him, as if she were going to say goodnight on the front step.

"No way," he said firmly. "I'm walking you all the way to the door. That's where I give you your goodnight kiss."

She sucked in a breath and her voice came out in a stammer. "But you've already kissed me."

"Bonus kisses," he said, tucking her hair behind her ear. "The goodnight kiss is at the end. Everyone knows that."

"Oh."

He grinned. "Yeah. Oh." He loved it when she said "oh." It said everything.

For three flights of stairs, her hand was trembling in his and he couldn't understand why. Surely she knew that the next kiss could only be better than the first two. Which meant it was going to be pretty freaking unbelievable.

They stopped at her door and she turned to face him.

"Well, good night," she whispered.

He got the distinct impression she hadn't meant to whisper. He cupped her face with both of his hands and leaned in. Her hands rested lightly on his waist.

"It was a great night," he corrected her, his mouth brushing against hers. Her body sagged forward and he took one final second to admire her closed eyes; her plush, expectant lips; her pink cheeks. "Most beautiful girl in the world," he murmured right before he slanted his head and took her mouth with his.

She let a soft sigh and he wondered if she knew she did that when he kissed her. He moved his lips over hers, lightly at first, and then increased in pressure when her hands slid up his chest to his neck and finally in his hair.

She was everything bright and beautiful and good in the world. A shooting star, exploding light all over his life without even meaning to. She could destroy him with her brilliance, bring him to his knees.

But she didn't.

There was no fiery explosion, or pain, or dismemberment.

Just a kiss.

And yet the effect was the same.

He was physically intact, but his world had been blown away.

# Twenty-Five

## EMILY

THE DOOR CLOSED BEHIND ME and I turned around, my whole body soft with happiness, to find Ash and Megan standing in the hall looking at me as if I were nuts.

"Where have you been?" Ash asked. If she'd had on an apron and been waving a wooden spoon around, she could have been a '50s mom.

"Is he a great kisser?" Megan jumped in.

"Do you know what time it is?"

"He's surprisingly hot for a slacker guy."

"Do you have your work bag together?"

"Did he ask you out again?"

"You've only got ten minutes to hoof it to Michael's."

I watched the two of them, my gaze bouncing back and forth like a deranged tennis match.

"Oh." I ran a hand through my hair, pushing off the greatness of the night. "Is it that late?"

I pushed past them, tugging off my shirt as I went and grabbing a T-shirt. Luckily, my bag was packed and by the break in my furniture-wall.

"Yes."

"This is why I should be an Uber driver." Megan crossed her arms and nodded…bringing everything to a halt.

"No."

"Never."

I glanced at Ash, glad we were back in accord about something.

"What?" Megan sounded totally shocked by this. "Why not?"

"Because we've both ridden with you," Ash pointed out. "And there's no way Uber could afford the insurance on that."

"You're both wrong. Think about it," Megan went on. "I could be driving Emily right now, and she wouldn't be running late."

I almost replied that the stress of running late was nothing to the life-threatening stress of riding with her. But, wisely, I just grabbed my bag and headed for the door.

"Gotta go! You ladies fight this out amongst yourselves."

I pulled the door shut behind me and rushed down the stairs and out onto the sidewalk, only to slam right into Sage.

"Hey there." He grabbed my arms to steady me. "Miss me?"

I laughed, because if I thought of it, I might have—you know, between the dog and pony show that was my roomies.

"Sorry! I'm late for work."

He looked at me as if I were nuts.

"You're late for work?" He frowned when I nodded. "At The Brew?"

"No, at Michael's." I tried to pull away, because I was going to be *so* late, but Sage just held on and my body didn't seem to be fighting him overly hard.

"The crafty place?"

I stopped laughing, because—really, why not. Retail was the one place I didn't have a job.

"No. I do overnight child care for a single dad who's a doctor."

"Of course you do." Sage stepped back, immediately making me miss him, and gestured toward his truck. "Well, let's see if we can get you there on time."

He pulled the passenger's side door open and gestured for me to climb in before rushing around to his side.

"Just tell me where to turn." He glanced over his shoulder and pulled back out onto the street while reaching for my hand.

I was beginning to love a man who could multitask.

This was like Date Night 2.0.

"What were you doing on my landing?" I asked, because that was a little weird. Okay, a lot weird. I couldn't have changed that quickly, could I?

"Your banister is starting to get some rot. I was thinking of fixing it."

Oh, how cute was that?

I smiled to myself, glancing out my window so he couldn't see how incredibly happy something so silly made me.

I directed him as he wove through traffic, getting us to the ritzy area of town where people actually had little driveways to park in, and pulled to a stop.

I glanced at my watch, thrilled to not be late.

"Two minutes to spare."

I smiled up at him, about to say thank you, when he beat me to it, saying "Perfect" before reaching for me.

If I'd thought his kisses before were a lark—an accident of fate or maybe beginner's luck—boy, was I wrong.

He pulled me into him, more sure now that we were on Non-Date 2.0 than I'd been before—more sure of me or himself, I don't know. But the confidence was so darn attractive I went willingly.

I slipped into the comfortable bliss of him, happy and relieved and free like I hadn't been in so long. Years. Maybe my whole life.

It wasn't just a girl kissing any boy. Sage was more.

I felt safe—*he* felt safe.

As if he were my happy place and my shield and sword, all at the same time.

"Ahem." A throat cleared just outside my window.

I turned, to see Michael standing there, looking highly amused.

"So, are you babysitting from here tonight?" Michael glanced past me at Sage.

"Sorry." I grabbed my bag and pulled the handle to open the door. "I'm *so* sorry. I just—"

I motioned at Sage as if I had words that would make this less embarrassing.

Sage, for his part, was sitting there looking amazingly smug.

Not helping there, buddy.

He must have read my mind, because if anything he looked *more* smug, and gave a little laugh.

I hopped out of the truck, pulling my overnight bag with me.

"Hi, I'm Michael." Michael reached across the seat to offer Sage his hand.

"Sage." He did *not* sound happy about the meet and greet, which was totally not like him.

"Nice to meet you." Michael stepped back and turned to me, hiking his messenger bag up on his shoulder. "They've had baths already. Basically, they need to burn off all the sugar I let them eat knowing I wouldn't have to deal with them."

"Gee, thanks." I knew Michael tried to make every night he was home special, so I wasn't surprised. Since they lost their mom, they'd become a hyper-unit of three, only letting me in after months of babysitting.

"No problem. I know you like a challenge." He headed toward his car, waving at Sage as he went.

"*That's* your boss?"

"Yes." I thought that was obvious.

"And you sleep here?"

"Only when he works overnights."

Sage harrumphed like an old man. I glanced at the townhouse, wondering how long I had to figure out the weirdness that was happening before the kids destroyed the house from the inside out.

"And?" I pushed.

"He's just...younger than I expected." Sage glanced down at his radio and fiddled with the dial.

"Younger?"

"Yeah...you know, what is he, like thirty-five?"

"Thirty-one."

He mumbled something under his breath.

"What?"

"Nothing. Just that's kind of young to be a doctor and have kids and stuff."

More mumbling. This time I was pretty sure he said something like *McDreamy*, but that would be insane even for Sage.

"He married his high school sweetheart. She died in a car accident almost three years ago."

"Oh." Sage glanced up toward the house. "Oh, that's…"

"Right?" Because it was…it was just…

"Okay, so," he cleared his throat and glanced back my way, his gaze steadying when it found mine. "I'll call you."

Oh no. The *I'll call you* Date 2.0 ending. Not quite like the ending of Date 1.0. Crap. What had I done?

"Okay."

"Right. Well, have a great night." He waved as I pushed the door shut, pulling away from the curb and making me wonder what had just happened.

I walked up to the house, hoping I wasn't going to have an implosion of lost happiness, when my phone dinged.

I glanced down at the text.

**SAGE: They don't have little dogs in there, do they? You know…in case I need to rescue you later.**

# Twenty-Six

## SAGE

IT HAD NOTHING WHATSOEVER TO do with the handsome doctor whose house Emily was staying the night in. At least, that's what Sage told himself as he rubbed the threat of sleep out of his eyes.

He really had been making mental preparations to fix this banister when she had caught him. But it was meeting Dr. McHandsome Face that made Sage go home, dig through the better pieces of oak in the workshop, cut his measurements, sand it down, and drive back to the apartment when he was certain she would be at The Brew.

Was he a doctor? No. He was just a man with a trade who was all-in for a girl who hadn't yet realized she could do anything with her life.

Besides, making sure Emily didn't die from a tragic fall simply because her landlord was clearly disinterested in basic safety precautions for his tenants gave Sage a mission. Which he liked.

He finished prying off the end of the rotting banister and tossed it down into the landing. It broke apart on impact. Sweat trickled down the side of his face from under his hat as he eyed the wooden railings on the other two floors. He'd chosen to just fix the one floor for now; the other two didn't seem nearly as bad. But maybe he should plan to replace the entire thing.

Cleaning up the mess he made barely took ten minutes. Then he hauled the new railing inside. It wasn't fancy. Nothing like what his dad could do. But it was sturdy. He drilled fresh anchors into the oak beam, which he hadn't had to remove. Then he mounted his new railing and screwed it into place.

Nope. Not a doctor.

He bet Dr. Michael had his entire life all mapped out. He'd probably never missed a haircut. You know who would loooove the good doctor? Heather. She'd be all about the plan of success he'd probably drafted before leaving the hospital nursery thirty-one years ago.

He didn't want to be jealous of Dr. Mike. He knew Emily looked forward to her overnights there because she had a real bed and some time to herself. Those were things he didn't want to take away from her. But really, how long could a person last living the way she was living, burning the candle at both ends and showing very little, if any, fatigue at all? She took what life had handed to her and didn't just make lemonade, she made pie and sherbet and other lemony things. The last thing she needed was the guy she was seeing to be a dick about one of the jobs that gave her rest and peace.

And this was why he worked with his hands. Somehow, in the process of building and creating things out of wood, his worries and thoughts worked themselves out into manageable pieces in his head. Seeing all the parts and pieces in his hands made him realize how small his problems really were. Everything could be fixed, or mended, or improved, or polished. He was never stuck with something broken.

He took the soft towel out of his back pocket and ran it over the freshly-sanded wood, dusting off the excess. He'd have to come back and touch up the stain in a couple places to make it look more uniform, but otherwise it looked good. Satisfaction and pride in a job well done infused his chest.

No. He wasn't a doctor.

\*\*\*

"You look like crap."

"I've missed you, Abby," Sage greeted, adjusting his hat. Abby snorted while rolling her eyes.

Emily came out of the back and stopped short when she saw him. Several things washed over her face in rapid-fire succession as she took in his presence. Surprise, excitement, anxiety, hope, happiness.

Sage tried to give her his best smile despite the exhaustion hanging heavily on his eyelids. Maybe he should have gone home to clean himself up first, but he didn't. He wanted to see her. And by the look on her face as she approached him, she wanted to see him, too.

"Hi," she greeted, then bit down on her lower lip.

Sage reached across the counter and used his thumb to tug her lip out of her teeth. She leaned into the cradle of his hand. "Good morning." Then he stretched across the counter and brushed his mouth against hers ever so briefly.

"No PDA," Abby objected flatly. "And stay on your side of the counter."

"Sorry," Sage apologized. "I actually didn't plan on doing that," he admitted. Guess he couldn't help himself. He cleared his throat. "Would you like a ride out to Luke's tonight?"

"That's really out of your way," she replied.

"Let me rephrase. Where should I pick you up tonight to take you to Luke's?"

She shook her head but smiled. "My apartment, I guess."

"Then I'll see you later."

He lifted his coffee as a salute, his eyes darting to Abby. She probably wouldn't allow another kiss. So he shot his girl a wink and headed home to take a shower and a nap.

# Twenty-Seven

### EMILY

"MOST OF THESE WILL BE in black and white, so don't worry so much about balancing the color in the shot. Just focus on the light." Zelda blew a wild curl out of her face and frowned at her protégé. "Am I being bossy? I'm being bossy." She thrust the camera out toward Emily. "Take the pictures you wanna take. Forget what I said."

I took the camera and cradled it gently in my hands. "I still can't believe this is happening."

Zelda flashed a wonky grin at Sage, her own pleasurable disbelief in this moment very apparent. It was the most adorable conspiracy I'd ever been obliged to take part in.

"You can't believe this is happening?" Zelda snorted. "I've never been cool enough to need a second camera. This is awesome for me as well. We'll take some 'posed' photos"—she did the air quotes along with an eye roll—"I mean, as much as you can pose these yahoos. But we'll save those until later, when the sun is nearly set. For now, take pictures of them working and talking. Follow your instincts, and have fun."

I nodded. What else could I do? I'd just follow my instincts and I'd know when it was over if they stunk so bad I should change course or not. Win-win in a sad but saves-me-thousands-in-school-if-I'm-wrong sort of way.

"Hey! Check this out." Zelda held up a Canon EOS 5D Mark III. "This is my new baby."

She stroked the side of the camera as if it were truly a new pet. And who wouldn't? It was a freaking Canon EOS 5D Mark III. Basically, if I were going to have that kind of money, I'd have to not pay my rent or eat for eight months.

"It's so pretty." I reached out as if to touch it, then pulled my hand back. One did not just touch someone else's equipment.

Zelda didn't seem to notice. She was too busy staring at the camera as if she were going to marry it—creative bigamy, perhaps.

"I've wanted one of these since the model came out, and I've always put it off." Zelda looked through the viewfinder, snapping a picture of me. "I always figured something would happen. I wouldn't be able to afford it. I'm a live light, travel light girl. But now?"

I watched her glance down again at the camera.

"It's a beauty."

"We're going to take beautiful pictures together." Zelda grinned, looking as if she couldn't be happier. "She needs a name... Mjölnir. After Thor's hammer. Literally 'that which smashes.'" She held the camera close to her lips and whispered, "Because we're gonna smash the heck out this next session, aren't we?"

I glanced around, totally blown away anew about where I was and what I was doing, the Canon Rebel in my hands grounding me that this was real. That I was here to work.

Zelda wandered off, taking shots as she went—most of them just camera tests. I doubted she was going to use that picture of an ant she found wandering around the entryway. But, with her, I had no doubt if she wanted to, it would be art.

"Hey." Sage stood just behind me, watching me watch Zelda. "Watchya looking at?"

"Zelda has a Canon EOS 5D Mark III." I could hear the reverence in my voice.

"Sounds like something that can fly."

"No." I shook my head. "Better."

"Better than flight?" He shook his head at me as if this were unbelievable. "You're one of those girls who doesn't like Superman, aren't you?"

"Superman? For real? That guy is so boring it's like he was created to make every other superhero look badass."

Sage slapped a hand over his heart. "Say it ain't so."

"It is. It is so." I dipped my head toward Zelda, where she was taking a picture of a ceiling tile with her new super-weapon of photography. "Even I could be great with that. Do you know the amazing photos she's going to take? She's going to go from Über-Talented to Gifted—Bam."

He just smiled at me. I knew he got it. The guitar thing made him understand that artists were everything they did, and that the tools they had could make a difference they couldn't, even at their best.

Sage kissed me on the check and grinned. "Back to the grindstone. Work, work, work. I'll go make these sound good. You go make them look good. We have such difficult lives."

He wandered off as the band filed back into their sound booth.

Life didn't get any better than this.

I glanced at Sage, his head bopping to whatever was being piped into his headphones and—SNAP. Got it. The band might not want that one, but I was pretty sure it was a keeper.

And the pic might not be too bad, either.

# Twenty-Eight

## SAGE

EMILY SMILED AND LOOKED AROUND the studio. It was—as usual—full of rock stars. But she was more relaxed during this visit than all of the others. Sage wanted to take credit for that. But he knew it was just how Emily rolled. She adjusted to life's curve balls, making every moment work for her in whatever way she could.

She was the kind of person who'd be amazing to have at your back. Because no matter what came around the bend, she could handle it.

When had he realized that?

Sage took in a slow breath and swallowed. It was too early to start thinking in those kinds of terms. But that didn't change the fact that he was right.

Emily caught his eye and she made a silly face, sticking her tongue out and crossing her eyes. He grinned in response, because he knew that's what she was going for. But his gut was tight and his heart was racing.

The stakes were suddenly a lot higher than he thought they would be after a first date.

She made her way around the studio, taking test shots and moving into peculiar positions. On her way by him, he impulsively wrapped an arm around her middle and pulled her back to his front. He pressed a kiss to her neck as she attempted to wriggle away from him.

"You're amazing," he said in her ear before he released her.

She blushed deeply, but couldn't completely hide the smile on her face as she went back to her job.

"Sage."

He turned around to find Zelda with a hip out and her camera pointed at him. She dropped it to give him full eye contact.

"Don't distract my worker."

Sage nodded, suppressing a smile.

"But," she took a step closer and dropped her eyes to her camera. "That was a really cute shot. If you want a copy, let me know."

"You caught us?" he asked, surprise and warmth filling his insides.

She nodded. "I did. And it wasn't my first picture of you two."

His eyebrows lifted. "You're sneaky."

"I'm the sneakiest of hobbits," she whispered before moving away from him.

"Zeldy," Sage called. She looked back over her shoulder at him. He struggled with getting his voice to sound casual. "I'm gonna want copies."

She lifted her chin ever so slightly, a pleased glint in her eye. "You got it."

\*\*\*

Sage didn't understand about eighty-five percent of what Zelda talked to Emily about all evening. He hovered. He couldn't help it. He liked watching her. When she was talking shop with Zelda, she was all lit up. In her element, living the dream.

He did understand the compliments Zelda was saddling her with. He heard things like "natural, talented, had gorgeous instincts." And Emily would just shake her head as if she couldn't believe it. As if she wouldn't believe it.

The memory cards filled up one at a time as the day came to a close. Zelda sank down on the floor in the corner of the studio where she scrolled through the last memory card on the back of the camera Emily had been using. Emily sat down beside her and Sage stood with his arms crossed and a shoulder against the wall.

"Some of these are so good..." Zelda trailed off, clicking through the frames on the DSL. "Are you sure you're not a ringer?"

Emily laughed nervously. "I mean, I take glamour shots of dogs..."

Zelda was not amused. She thrust the camera at Sage. "Look. Look at what she captured."

Sage took the camera and studied the small display on the back. Even at this size he recognized what an excellent shot it was. Luke and Mike were talking, except Luke had his head back laughing, and Mike was grinning flat out at his best friend.

He handed the camera back to Zelda. "She's a pro, what can I say?"

Zelda snorted and muttered something under her breath about needing a bigger budget. "I have to check things." She stood up and stumbled over her bag. "I need to show people things. I'll be back."

Sage let his eyes drift to Emily, who was looking a little shell-shocked. He could understand that, too. It had been a very big twenty-four hours for her.

"Terrible day for you?" he teased.

Her expression remained flat and she nodded. "The worst. I hated all of today."

"People adoring you?" He nodded. "I can see how that would be annoying." He moved to take a seat beside her on the floor, bracing his back against the wall. He kept his feet flat and his knees pointed to the ceiling.

"You see these people all of the time," she said. It wasn't awe-filled or a question, just a statement of fact. "At first I thought maybe you didn't realize what an incredible job you have. But they're just regular people. Like working with Abby."

He arched an eyebrow and she caught it.

"Okay, no one is like Abby. But you know what I mean. They're people. And I got to see that in detail tonight. Observing, cataloging, learning." She sighed. "They're amazing people. Who work hard."

"Like you," he pointed out, bumping his shoulder against hers.

"I'm not—"

"Nope." He cut her off. "I'm not letting you do that. I get to call you amazing, because it's true. And you get to call me awesome, because that's true."

She sniffed a laugh. "Awesome and amazing?"

"Yep. The ultimate power couple."

# Twenty-Nine

## EMILY

I HANDED MR. NASH A lemon bar instead of his bran muffin, and you'd think I'd offered him arsenic.

Well, if you were anywhere near Abby, you'd think that.

"What is with you?" Abby demanded before rushing on. "I don't want you to go getting an ego or something, but you don't usually suck."

"Be still my heart. I'm not sure I can take this much effervescence from you." I gave Abby my best smile and considered pairing it with a hug just to totally freak her out.

"Yeah, well, today you suck. So your heart can be as still as you need it to be." She picked up an empty cookie tray and marched in the kitchen, leaving me smiling after her.

We were in the mid-morning lull, so I went out to the seating area and started putting everything to rights. It was amazing how messy a café could get in under twenty minutes. But, I liked keeping everything just right. I didn't mind that we were the place people didn't pay attention to their behavior. As long as I could make it comfy for the next folks, everything was good.

Because, everyone should have a place to relax, and—somehow, even with Abby running the joint—The Brew was that for a growing number of people.

I tried not to jump when my phone dinged, but my hands were almost shaking I was so excited.

It's such a cliché—the whole *I've never felt this way before* thing. But I really hadn't.

Of course, it had been years since I'd taken a chance on a guy. I don't think it was the timing, the moving into adulthood that did it. I think it was just him. Sage.

I pulled the phone out and was surprised to see it was from an unknown number.

**UNKNOWN: Hey! It's Zelda. Good to proof photos tonight at the studio. Six. Dinner here. K?**

I programmed her into my phone, trying to remember what the text said, but really just thinking, Omigosh, Zelda Fitzpatrick's number is in my phone. I have Zelda Fitzpatrick's number. I could *call* her. Not that that's stalkerish or anything. But totally I could. I have that ability. Just by hitting that little phone icon right there.

I was smiling down at my phone when Abby came out of the kitchen.

"You're not going to become that girl, right?" Abby set a rack of cookies in the pastry display and gave me a look that clearly said she didn't want to give up on me—but she would.

"What girl?" Was it that obvious? Did I have *stalker* written all over me?

"The one who carries her phone just so she can giggle over her boyfriend's texts?"

Oh. Phew. That was close.

"Nope. It was work." I stuck my phone back in my apron. "Zelda needs me at the studio by six to do proofs."

"Oh. Okay." Abby gave me A Look, as if to say that was okay, but she was watching me. "And the herb?"

"What?"

"The herb you're dating?"

"Sage?" I couldn't help laughing at that.

She nodded.

"We're not really dating." I glanced away, trying not to grin at the idea of dating Sage. "We're just...you know."

"Dating," Abby stated.

"No, we just went out on one date."

Abby tossed her hot mitts down and came around the counter, mumbling something that sounded like *just like the others*. But that made no sense.

"Sit." Abby pointed at the comfy chairs by the fireplace that was decorated for summer with cute little teacup-shaped candles. "We're only doing this once because I'm exhausted from all of you hopeless hearts who wander in here."

"I'm not—"

"Uht!" She chopped her hand through the air, effectively silencing me—and kind of scaring the snot out of me, too. "You two have been covertly dating for weeks. He comes in here, you guys have coffee and chat and flirt. Emily, for goodness sake! You work in a coffee shop. Dates are like half of our income. And then he's all going places with you and you're going places with him. This is called dating. Welcome to adulthood. There's no soundtrack."

"But—" This time Abby didn't need to move to silence me.

"Do you like this guy?" She waited, as if she didn't already know the answer. "Right. Obviously. Look at you. And you've been liking him and he's been liking you and you've been doing stuff to get to know one another, and now you're here without even realizing how, in a relationship."

She stood, her work obviously done as I sat in stunned silence.

"Okay. Good talk. But don't be one of those girls with the phone, or I'll put it through my blender."

She wandered off, leaving me sitting there stunned to find out she was right. I was in a relationship with a guy I really liked. I could feel my eyes narrowing. Sage. He sneak-attack relationshipped me.

Why was I not surprised?

But, if this is what being with someone like him felt like, I was willing to take the risk. How could it not be worth it when someone that sweet, that talented believed in you?

It suddenly didn't feel like much of a risk at all.

I pulled my phone out one last time while Abby was in the kitchen pulling out her next batch.

**EMILY: Hey. Going out to the studio to work tonight.**
**SAGE: Heard. Pick you up at 5:30.**

I smiled, trying not to be *that* girl, but not caring because that girl was so darn happy.

\*\*\*

When Sage got there I was waiting outside, admiring the new banister. Before he could get out to open my door, I hopped in, just plain happy to see him.

I glanced over, suddenly afraid Abby was wrong. That we weren't secretly in a relationship. That he wasn't sneak-attack-relationshipping me.

"Hey, beautiful." He reached out, pulling me to him for a kiss that was all too short, but that still had my whole body flushing hot.

"Hey." I grinned, so happy. A type of happy I'd never felt before. Not even when I'd thought I'd found a family of my own. All those other times had been *almosts* I always felt like something could go wrong at any moment.

But, sitting there with Sage, I felt so at peace with where I was at.

I was thinking nothing could make this better when he took my hand. And there it was. That connection I felt every time he was near, but magnified.

I sent up a mental thanks to Ash and reminded myself to buy her some Reese's Pieces on the way home.

"So." Sage cleared his throat. "You're ready to get famous?"

"Ha! Right. I'll be thrilled if she uses one or two of my shots for pics on the website."

Not to mention, they wouldn't even be credited. But, seriously. Who cared. The guys had all been awesome and signed a waiver Zelda stuck under their noses for the portfolio she said I could create. Nothing published, just shots to show school or potential jobs.

It was a dream come true.

And, because of all the work this week, I got to take off from Glamour Paws. Win-win.

We rode along, getting off the highway and winding through the leafy green back roads to Luke and Lenny's place. Sage was talking about a new guitar design he was thinking of trying, but he was afraid if Blake heard about it he'd want to—and I quote—buy it so he could massacre it onstage in a vengeful fit of creative destruction.

Or something.

We got to the studio and Sage gave a look, pointed at my seat, and said "Stay" before jumping out to run around to my door.

Before I could hop down, he brushed his lips over mine. I couldn't help it. I leaned in, wanting more. Zelda who?

His hand came up and wrapped around my hair again, holding my head gently but just how he liked kissing me, pulling me in, deepening the kiss until I was almost ready to just pull him into the truck with me and forget about my big night of proofing.

"Ahem."

Sage eased away and rolled his eyes heavenward before dropping them shut.

"I don't know who that is," he said, "but I'm getting really annoyed with all these people barging into my truck."

"Okay, dude. It's a truck. Not a building." Blake glanced around Sage's shoulder and winked at me. "And I'm just standing here. In a parking lot. Just hanging out."

"Whatever." Sage reached back in, took my hand, and waited while I slid out. "It's not like hanging out watching people make out is pervy or anything."

I snorted as Blake shrugged and turned to walk with us into the studio.

This guy really had no shame, and no problem with no shame. There was something kind of cool about that.

But, I was guessing you could get away with a lot more when you were a rock star instead of a barista-slash-nanny-slash-student-slash…geez. Even I was getting tired of all the slashes I had to do.

"You're here!" Zelda rushed forward, a camera in her hand. "I got some shots of the equipment this afternoon. A really cool one of their guitars lined up. You have to see it. It *screams* rock and roll."

I loved everything about Zelda. She made you want to fall in love with everything. That was the kind of heart I needed to work on having.

We sat down, glancing through the proofs of the week's work, her pulling up some of mine and telling me what she liked about them and where I might want to shift some of my shots.

She showed me the ones she'd earmarked for the website, and one she thought might be fun for the inside of the CD case. My palms were so damp at this point from having my work critiqued I was probably leaving handprints on my skirt.

Then, when I thought we were almost done, she pulled out four prints and placed them upside down on the table.

"I'm thinking these are our contenders for the cover." She grinned. "I'm kind of in love with all of them, so I'm always glad this part isn't my job. We'll give them to the band and their graphics guy, and they'll probably make the final call that way."

She turned over the first one, explaining how she took the shot, what she was going for, how close she got, and what she'd do differently next time. She did that two more times, then flipped over the fourth print.

"Oh!" It was mine. The print was mine! But... "You don't have to humor me."

Zelda smacked my arm. "I am *not* humoring you. I was actually pissed off I didn't think of this shot myself. From behind, with the lights shining on them like they're onstage? I felt so stupid when I saw it. It's amazing. Look how you got all of them in it, even Mike at the drums. It has a definite chance of being picked."

I looked at her, fighting back tears. I couldn't believe this. It was like all my dreams were happening at once, and I'd never even admitted I had dreams before.

Like someone said, *You know what? These are her dreams. We'll let her know about them when she's ready and it's time.*

"You can totally girl cry." Zelda wrapped an arm around me. "I'm all for a good girl-cry occasionally. They're power tears."

I couldn't wait to tell Sage. He was going to be so floored.

"Go on." She shook her head. "I already told Harrison you upped me for the last spot, so hopefully he kept his big mouth shut."

I rushed toward the door as she shouted behind me, "But hurry up. I'm putting the sandwiches out."

The rest of the evening was crazy. The guys looked over all the shots for the site and the interior while Zelda made a second round of sandwiches—or, as I was betting Harrison called them, tiny snacks.

They decided to think about the cover and come up with the name and vibe before picking the cover, but none of them said mine was out. So...life *made!*

I was just shiny with happiness as Sage bumped my shoulder when he reached for his soda, giving me a broad grin. It felt so good to have someone be that proud of me.

I glanced around as we cleared up after dinner. These guys, their girls, and their crew—they were a family. Or as close to one as you got. The idea that here I was, just some girl off the street, allowed into their tree house was amazing.

I was waiting for Sage to wrap up and store his stuff when Zelda stuck her head in the room.

"Hey, have you guys seen my new camera?"

"The Canon?" I asked, shocked she'd let it out of her sight long enough to misplace it.

"Yeah. I...I can't find it." Zelda looked as upset as I'd ever seen her—even more than when she'd fallen off a chair trying to get the perfect shot and snagged her *Doctor Who* T-shirt.

"I haven't. Where did you see it last?" I hoped off the counter I'd been sitting on, figuring we could find it before Sage was ready to go.

"I'm not sure. Before we cleaned up for dinner."

"Don't worry. We'll find it."

I glanced toward Sage, still hard at work, and caught his eye.

"Yeah. Go find the camera that could fly. I have stuff to wrap up and let Luke hear before we clear out."

"Great." I kissed him on the cheek, trying to solidify this whole We're a Couple thing.

He grinned before snagging me around the waist for a much better We're a Couple kiss.

"Emily!" Zelda shouted from the other room. "Stop kissing the help, and come be my search-and-rescue dog...photographer."

I wandered off, lucky I didn't walk into the door I was in such a daze.

Zelda and I looked for fifteen minutes before we both started to get frustrated. About that time, the band wandered back in, and Harrison immediately realizing something was wrong with his woman.

"My new camera is missing. We've looked everywhere."

He wrapped her in a big hug, pulling her up to give her a kiss on the nose. "Well, you didn't look everywhere, because you haven't found it."

"Also," Blake chimed in, "I don't see a stepladder, so you didn't look anywhere above the three foot height."

"Ha ha." Zelda glanced at me and we shared a short-girl eye roll.

Everyone joined us, looking everywhere we could think of—bathrooms, vehicles, the garbage in the kitchen. No one was finding anything remotely like a camera—let alone the dream camera.

"Hey." Sage pulled me into an empty room and closed the door.

"Hey." I glanced around, thinking this was so not the time for more kisses—but of course I wasn't going to say no to them, either.

"So…" Sage glanced toward the door before pulling me to the far side of the room. "I won't be mad. I promise, but…"

I waited, trying to figure out what had happened that he wasn't going to be mad about.

"If you took it, Emily, I'll cover for you. We'll just say I found it."

"What?" I couldn't believe he just said that. I had to have misunderstood.

"Look, I get it. Dream camera. Maybe you just wanted to play with it a little, take a few shots. I'm sure if we just bring it back, everything will be fine."

I watched his face, trying to figure out what he was saying—because I honestly couldn't believe he was accusing me of stealing. From *Zelda*.

Sage, of all people, was the one person who knew what honesty, family, and freaking not breaking the law meant to me.

When he didn't say anything, I shook my head, fighting to find the words. Fighting to stay calm. "I didn't take it."

"Emily, it doesn't matter to me."

"Then you won't mind if I ask you to stop accusing me of *something I didn't do*." I stepped back, trying to get my indoor voice back under control. "Not only would I never steal, but from Zelda? After what she's done for me? I can't believe you'd think that."

Sage stepped back, putting even more distance between us as we just stared at each other.

"You're serious." My heart dropped to my shoes. And stayed there. It didn't bounce back and start beating again. There was no rapid flutter. It just…died, I think. "You think I took it."

"No. I mean, if you did, I would take care of it."

"You'd *take care* of it? You mean, you'd cover for me. You'd lie to them?"

Part of me realized what he was saying. That he'd protect me from my own actions. But most of me was focused on the part that he thought I was a lying, betraying thief.

"I'd—I'd talk to them. I'd make sure nothing bad happened."

I raised my hand, needing to look at something that was me. Needing to understand if this was real—if for the second time in my life the guy I thought cared about me was ready to throw me under the bus for something I didn't do.

I almost physically felt the shields I'd let down slam back into place.

I turned, throwing the door open with so much force it bounced off the wall.

In the main room, Zelda stood, wrapped in Harrison's arms while he said, "No problem. This is what insurance is for."

I knew it was a big deal, though. Her memory stick was on there, and it was The Camera. And a brand new one, at that.

"I didn't take it." I just blurted it out, not knowing what else to do. "I didn't take it."

Zelda pushed out of Harrison's arms. "Of course you didn't."

But, as soon as she said it, I swore a shadow crossed her face for the barest moment.

"No. You didn't." She shook her head, looking determined. "You absolutely didn't. Why did you feel like you needed to even tell me that?"

I could feel the blood rushing to my face, painting my neck red and heating my whole body. This was almost as bad as Sage accusing me—telling other people he did.

Telling other people that the guy I'd been falling for—that I'd thought was worth all the risks—thought I was a thief.

I pressed my lips together, not sure what to do.

"I need to go" was what I came up with. I dumped my tote on the table, grabbed my wallet and keys, and hurried out the door, brushing the tears I'd been holding in off my cheeks.

I felt sick, so sick I stopped and leaned over, bracing my hands on my knees, afraid I was going to hurl right there in the driveway.

Every time—every *single* time—I let myself believe in something outside of myself, it just, BOOM! blew up.

I straightened, wondering how I was going to get home, knowing there was no way I was getting in a truck with Sage.

I didn't care that he was going to "take care of it." I'm sure he thought he was a great guy for overlooking my horrible habit of larceny, but—

I backed away from the thought.

I thought he'd known me. Me, who I was. No one who knew me would have done this.

I leaned over again, fearing that the need to hurl was rising back up.

When I just stood there, hunched over, I finally realized I had to get out of here—had to get as far from *him* as possible. I just wanted to be home in my dining-bedroom, stretched out on my mattress, pretending the rest of the world didn't exist, and maybe, maybe, if I thought about how I was nothing I for long enough, I could just...

fade...

away.

# Thirty

## SAGE

Sage's eyes darted from the door falling shut behind Emily to the people around him. He sucked in a harsh breath and cursed as blood roared in his ears.

This was why he'd wanted to have the conversation with her in private. He didn't want her to have to say that to those people. He knew how much she admired and respected Zelda and the band.

Throwing the door open literally and figuratively on their conversation would only complicate her situation.

*Their* situation.

Shit.

He closed his eyes against the memory of the look on her face when he'd presented his solution.

Instead of relief or irritation, she'd turned ghost white, as if someone had just stuck a knife in her belly.

He swallowed hard as his stomach turned over.

It was the look of complete betrayal.

No. She didn't think he would do that. He'd been trying to help her.

His eyes darted to the closed door again and realized she hadn't come back inside.

"You're gonna go after her, right?" Zelda asked sharply.

He stared at her, frozen in place by the fear curling like a snake in the pit of his stomach.

What had he done?

A cold chill crawled up his spine.

What if he couldn't fix it?

"Dude," Blake muttered. "Your girl."

Sage swallowed the sour taste in his mouth and made deliberate strides to the door.

He had to get to her. Talk to her. Explain...everything.

The rush of fresh air hitting his face didn't help the queasy feeling building in his gut. He clenched his stomach muscles to push it down.

Because this wasn't as bad as the gnawing in his gut was telling him it was.

It couldn't be.

Emily righted herself from her hunched-over posture and his chest tightened uncomfortably.

She moved down the driveway, solid, purposeful steps carrying her away from him.

Sage broke into a jog. "Emily, wait!"

Her stiff shoulders got even tighter as she heard his approach, which spiked the panic already spreading into his limbs.

"Emily," he panted, slowing to match her pace. "Where are you going?"

She stabbed the buttons on her phone in frustration. "Away."

Sage tried grabbing her bicep to get her to stop and look at him. She yanked her arm out of his grasp, as if his touch burned. A hole opened up in his gut, making the queasiness rise up in force.

"Wait—let me explain. You're taking what I said all wrong. I didn't mean it the way you heard."

Emily snorted. "Right."

This wasn't happening. It couldn't be happening.

He had been trying to *protect* her.

"Please tell me what to say to make it better. Tell me how to take it back." He choked on the last word as his throat constricted with rising desperation and helplessness.

She whirled on him, pain clear as day slashing through her eyes. The tears falling unchecked squeezed his heart painfully.

She swiped at the wet falling on her cheeks. "You think—" She shook her head and looked to the sky as she struggled with the words. She sucked in a shaky breath as her gaze reconnected with his. The distress in her eyes almost knocked him backward. "Like I'm a *stranger* and not someone you know. But I guess I really am that stupid. Because I thought, of all people, you would never think I'd *steal*."

Sage stepped forward and moved to touch her, but stopped himself. "I don't. Emily, I don't think that about you!"

"And not only that, but you were going to cover for me?" She shook her head, face twisted in painful disbelief. "That's not me, Sage!"

He stared hard into her shattered gaze, searching for the words to explain what had happened. She didn't understand. She couldn't.

Time was moving too quickly. He'd do anything to slow it down. He needed a minute to *think*.

"You think I want to believe you took it?" he asked instead.

"I don't want to think that about you."

Her eyes filled with fresh tears and she tilted her head to the side. "You really think I took it?" she whispered brokenly.

Sage placed both hands on his head and squeezed, trying to relieve the pressure building. "No! But it makes sense, doesn't it? You're the only one with access to it who knew what it was worth—"

"And I'm the girl with the troubled past, making me the obvious thief."

"No!" Sage yelled, dropping his hands to his sides. "It had nothing to with you! I was just trying to..." His voice trailed off as what he'd done started to become clear.

Super clear.

Sickeningly clear. Yeah, he thought she'd taken it.

His second instinct had been right—to protect her.

But it should've been his first.

Which wouldn't have led him to think that about her at all.

This was *Emily*. She wasn't that person.

Desperation rushed through him.

He needed her to stop trying to leave.

Stop trying to leave him.

"You have to believe me, please." He grabbed her arms, his chest filled with a dreadful panic as reality began to set in. She was *leaving*.

"*I* have to believe *you?*" He could hear the shock at the obvious irony in her voice. She placed her hands on his chest and gave him a hard shove. "Let go of me!"

He let go instantly and sucked in a deep breath. "Please let me fix this."

"Stop trying to fix me, Sage," she said, her jaw trembling and voice breaking. "I'm not broken."

Everything was breaking.

Sage shook his head. "That's not what I meant."

"Yes, it is." New torment cracked across her expression, hitting him again. "This is my fault. I shouldn't have risked it. Other people are just..." Emotion filled her voice and broke it. "You won, though. You got what you wanted: my trust. Good job with it."

Sage ground his teeth together and pressure built in his chest, threatening to push his heart right out of his throat. "Tell me how to fix it."

"You don't get it." She blinked slowly, her lids pushing out the most beautiful tears he'd ever seen and sending them down her cheeks. "You don't trust me. And that means I can't trust you. Not anymore."

The pain her words carved through his insides was too much for him to manage. He heard the truth of what she was saying, of what his thoughtless accusation had done.

But he rejected it.

He pushed it aside, using the only defense he could think of.

"No, I think maybe I do get it," he said, cutting through the noise in his head and getting to the problem as he saw it. "I think maybe you like to be the victim and you have no intention of letting it go."

She huffed in surprise, more wet gathering in her eyes.

But no words. A thick silence swirled in between them.

"Just forget it." He waved a hand up and down, indicating all that was Emily, his Emily.

He'd only been trying to save her, and all she wanted was to turn it around and into something worse.

"Forget all of it," he repeated, feeling the rough texture of his words as they fell from his lips.

Her face crumbled, but he wasn't going to stand there and watch it happen.

He turned on his heel and stalked back to the house. She wasn't meant for him. If she were, it wouldn't be this hard. She'd know he'd been doing the best thing for her. He wouldn't need to be explaining this crap to her.

He wasn't doing it. Not anymore. It was too hard, and he had no pride left to fight for anyway. She could do her thing, he wasn't going to hold her up through it.

"Where is she?" Zelda blocked the door with her arms crossed.

Sage jerked his head in the direction of the road. "Walking home, most likely."

Her eyes narrowed at him. "You just left her out there?"

Sage turned to the side and swept an arm out. "She's not my problem anymore." The sting of his own words zinged through his chest and lungs.

He brushed past Zelda into the house, grabbed his keys, and headed back out to his truck.

"McNabb!"

Sage closed his eyes and halted. He didn't want to get a lecture from any of them. Just because they had perfect marriages and lives didn't mean they had the responsibility of handing out advice when he didn't want it.

He turned to see Blake had followed him outside. Behind Blake, Zelda was backing out Luke's truck. Probably to gather her protégé off the side of the road.

"What?" he asked the guitarist.

"You made it worse?" Blake asked with a knowing eyebrow arch.

Sage released a stunted laugh and closed his eyes. "Make what worse? This is her issue, not mine. I tried to help. She doesn't want me to." He shrugged emphatically.

"Oh, dude." Blake shook his head and slid his bottom lip through his teeth. "Let me buy you a drink. Maybe this old dog can share some of his hard-earned wisdom."

Sage sighed with impatience. "I know you wanna help, and I appreciate it. But I think I'm just gonna take a drive to clear my head."

Blake nodded and stepped back, giving him clearance.

Sage got in the truck, started it, and turned the opposite direction of Emily.

He'd take the long way home.

His touchy radio buzzed to life.

"Drops of Jupiter."

Of course.

# Thirty-One

## EMILY

I STARTED DOWN THE DRIVE, wondering how I was going to get home, thinking maybe Megan could do her Uber thing and come get me when a horn honked from behind me.

Zelda—in a truck that was way too big for either of us—pulled up and rolled down the window.

"Hey, hot stuff. Looking for a ride?" She grinned at me, forced in a way that told me she knew how bad things were.

I glanced down the drive, wondering if there was even a gas station within a mile to hike to.

"Listen," she said, putting the truck in park and sliding over to open the door. "You need a ride home. Let's get you somewhere you feel safe and worry about the rest of this crap later."

Textbook Zelda. But, I also knew she wouldn't go back on that.

We rode, the music playing softly in the background through the back roads toward town. I leaned my head against the window, trying not to cry, figuring I'd have plenty of time for that once I got home.

We pulled up to the front of my place, and Zelda threw the truck into park.

"Ok, my little hobbit, listen, and listen carefully." Zelda turned toward me before I could jump out and escape to the secret sanctity of my dining-bedroom. "I know you didn't take anything. I trust you explicitly. Boys are idiots."

I snorted through my almost-tears at the last one.

"We're good. And that's all that matters, hear me?" she asked.

I nodded, not trusting my voice.

"I'll talk to you tomorrow," she went on, giving me her signature Zelda grin.

I nodded again, pretty sure that's all I was capable of at the moment.

I jumped out of the truck, nearly spraining my ankle, and wondering which guy drove this. Zelda had basically picked the vehicle not blocked in, and rolled her eyes at the fact that they all left their keys wherever they left the cars.

I climbed up the front stairs to the old oak and glass door, not really wanting to go home. Then, in one of those catch-you-off-guard moments, I saw my reflection in the window and became disgusted with myself.

*Of course* Sage didn't believe me. Why would he? I was just some girl. Some girl who had a bad past and a near miss with prison. He was Mr. Music from the perfect home.

I suddenly was so sick of being me I didn't even have words for it.

I spun down the stairs and marched down the street, knowing exactly what I needed.

A change.

***

"Oh, Emily." Megan stood in the hallway, looking at me as if I'd just lost my beloved puppy in a horrific nuclear accident. "What have you done?"

"Nothing?" I tried to sound sure, but wondered if I'd gone nuts…and when. Today, or a few weeks ago, when Sage walked into The Brew.

We were standing there, facing off—her still in her club clothes, me in my now stained pajamas. She shook her head.

"Oh, honey." She dropped her bag on the floor and came and wrapped me in a hug.

I wasn't sure what to do. I just stood there, my arms limp at my sides, trying not to feel anything.

"What happened?"

I opened my mouth, still unsure what I was going to say, when I heard the key in the door behind us. We both turned, waiting for Ash to wander in.

She did, trying not to make any noise before she realized we were both standing in the middle of the hall. As soon as she saw me, she pushed the door shut with a slam.

"What the hell did he do?"

I tried again, my mouth opening with no sound coming out.

Then, before I could stop it, I was near shouting at her, "This is all your fault!"

"My fault?" Ash looked shocked. "I'm not the one who chopped off all your hair and dyed it…what color is that? Is that black, or a really dark purple?"

"Ash." Megan gave her the *What are you doing?* look.

"*Take a chance*, you said." I pointed at Ash as if she wouldn't know I was talking about her. "*Go out on the limb*, you tempted me."

"Wait." Megan waved a hand. "You asked Ash for guy advice?"

"She was here."

"Does *no one* respect my specialties?" Megan waved her arms as if there was a crowd offstage she needed to attract.

"You have a specialty?" Ash asked, looking confused and annoyed.

"Boys. Boys are my specialty."

"I thought Ubering was going to be your specialty."

"That was going to be my job—in which I would probably offer boy advice."

Ash snorted, and I glanced between them, a sick, annoying tennis match of an argument.

"Hey." Megan took a step forward before turning on me. "I can't believe you went to her over me."

"I'm perfectly good at giving advice," Ash stated.

I was trying to figure out what was going on when Megan all but shouted, "You asked the lesbian for boy advice." She crossed her arms, then undid them to point at herself. "Me. I don't have a bunch of talents, but she can't have boys, too!"

"Relationship advice. And I'm great at relationships."

"You suck at relationships."

"I'm sorry, when was the last time you had a boyfriend?"

"Oh, as if your serial three-week monogamy spurts count."

"More than Ms. I Dance You Buy Drinks See You Later."

I'm sure Megan had a great comeback, but I tuned them out as I wandered into my dining-bedroom and crawled onto my mattress.

"Emily?" Two bodies collapsed on top of me, squishing me under my secondhand comforter.

"Yeah?"

"What happened?" Ash asked, pushing the spiky bangs I'd tried to give myself out of the way.

"He accused me of stealing from Zelda."

I didn't look up, but I could feel them silently communicating.

"Okay." Ash pulled the comforter down—which was for the best, because it was getting hot under there. "Let's fix your hair and you can tell us what happened as Megan—who has more talents than just boys—will clean up this cut you obviously gave yourself, okay?"

I climbed off the bed and into the shower they shoved me in, thinking nothing was ever going to be the same. That everything would *always* be the same. That I'd just keep living in that dining room working a bunch of jobs to squeak by, and never letting anyone else change that path.

\*\*\*

"We don't have any hazelnut soy milk. You're going to have to live without it. Maybe find a hipster place that serves overpriced specialty drinks that are too sweet and trendy."

"Okay." Abby took the guy's money and shoved his drink toward him. "That's enough of that."

The guy sprinted toward the door, probably never to return. No big loss.

I snorted. "That guy is not a Brew customer."

"Not what I'm talking about." Abby crossed her arms and gave me a look. "And what's up with your hair?"

"I chopped it off and dyed it black like my soul." I really didn't feel like having a soft-and-mushy with Abby.

It had been two days since The Accusation, and I still didn't want to talk about it. Ever again. Ever.

"Yeah. So, I'm pretty sure your soul isn't black. It's more like baby blue with sunshine yellow hearts all over it." She waved away one of the regulars who came up for a refill. "What did he do?"

I knew she meant Sage, obviously, but I just didn't want to talk about it anymore.

But, as Abby stared me down, I knew I wasn't getting out of at least a perfunctory explanation. "He accused me of stealing."

"He *what?*" The outrage in her voice was so thick it almost made me cry. Even Abby didn't think I'd steal, and she's the most cynical person on the planet.

Just as I was getting ready to explain, the door opened, sun shining in, momentarily blinding me, and fell shut behind Sage.

"Hey." He shoved his hands in his pockets, looking somehow both nervous and annoyed. His gaze traveled up to my hair, giving it an odd glance.

My hands started shaking and I wanted to run—wanted to hide. But where was I going to go in this tiny café?

"*You* are not welcome here." Abby stepped between us, crossing her arms.

"It's a free world." Where had Belligerent Sage come from?

"No. It's not. It's private property, and we have the right to refuse service."

"On what grounds?" His cheeks were getting pink, but he didn't look as if he were 100% ready to take on Abby.

"Didn't you see the sign out front?" She pointed toward the door. "No Shoes, No Shirt, No Soul, No Service. Don't make me call Max."

Oh. Wow. She was threatening to bring in the big guns.

"It does not say that." Sage really did not have a self-preservation bone in his body.

Abby spun, pulled the Sharpie out of the can next to the register, and marched to the door. Flinging it open, she dropped to her knees and added *soul* to the bottom of the No list.

"Yes. It does. Out you go." She held the door open, waiting for him to march out of it.

Sage glanced my way, a near plea on his face. "Emily?"

I tried not to blink back the tears that threatened to fall, instead turning and heading into the kitchen where even Sage wouldn't dare try to follow.

"Fine."

I heard the door fall shut before Abby stuck her head in the kitchen.

"Okay, he's gone." She stuck the Sharpie in her pocket. "Here's the deal. Enough with the grumpy, and you can't get any tattoos for at least three months."

With that, she turned and headed back into the main room, accepting as always in her own Abby way.

# Thirty-Two

## SAGE

Sage let the door to the garage slam behind him. He ignored the stares of the five guys in the studio and sat down heavily in his chair at the soundboard.

Today sucked.

Today could kiss his ass before going straight to hell.

It was, believe it or not, worse than yesterday. And yesterday had been a real bastard.

"Did you talk to her yet?" Mike asked. The spokesman had been chosen.

"Nope." Sage sighed, trying to block out the image of her face behind the counter at The Brew. She looked like she hadn't slept in days. At first, he was hoping that was a good sign. Because he also hadn't slept in days. Maybe she'd give him a chance at extracting his enormous foot from his mouth. It would be hard, since his foot was in his mouth and his head was also up his ass. The removal process was bound to be painful and lengthy.

"Why didn't you talk to her?" Mike asked cautiously.

"Because apparently I have no soul." He flipped the switches on the console with more force than necessary. "Abby even added it to the list of requirements on the door. I've been banned from The Brew. Emily won't take my calls, and I'm pretty sure if I show up at Emily's apartment again, Megan will castrate me with a shrimp fork. I'm officially out of options." He shrugged, sardonic amusement coloring his speech. "Unless of course I go full John Cusack stalker mode and just embrace the coming restraining order."

"They banned you?"

"Yep."

"Didn't you explain you were just a dumbass, like I told you to?"

Sage had had about enough of everyone meddling. They all had an opinion on what he could and should do to fix this shit storm. His frustration in the situation and in himself came to boil. It may have taken him a full twenty-four hours of replaying all of his stupid remarks and reliving her heartbreak at his callous words, but it eventually sunk in. Good for him, he could be taught.

"You know what?" He stood up with enough force to knock over his chair. "I'm not a rock star, okay? I'm just an average Joe idiot who caught a really lucky break. I had the girl of my dreams in my reach and I screwed it up. This is real life. *My* real life. My apologies are too little, too late." He tore a hand through his hair and paced across the room, breathing hard.

"Dude, calm down. You're gonna get the chance to make this right. That's how love works." Sway looked so sure of himself. All smug in his perfect marriage, with his perfect hair and his perfect chill.

They didn't get it. None of them were going to get it.

The door to the garage opened up and Zelda stepped through. Their eyes connected. Hers narrowed, his rolled. Awesome. He'd introduced Emily to his boss's wife and now they were besties. This couldn't get any better.

"Can I talk to you?" Zelda asked.

Sage sighed. Again. Because what else was he supposed to do at this point?

He stepped out the door and Zelda followed, pulling it closed behind her.

Zelda started in on him right away. "I don't know what your girl's story is—"

"She's not my girl." Sage cut her off.

Zelda glared and rolled her eyes. "Right."

"She's not!" Sage exclaimed, throwing his hands out to the sides. "I *wanted* her to be my girl. I wanted it so bad I could taste it! I was willing to do anything to make her my girl, but I blew it."

"Well, clearly, suspecting her of stealing was not the way to go."

Sage's mouth fell open in shock and he struggled for words. "You think I don't know that? With what her shitty fake family did, and that twat monster of a boyfriend? The last thing I wanted was for her to group me in with them! But I went ahead and did it all by myself." He stomped over to his truck and kicked the tire in frustration. "She was always looking for a reason to not trust me, and I went ahead and served it right to her. On a freaking silver platter."

"Sage!" Zelda's head shook in short, jerky motions. "You can't tell me stuff like that! This!" She used her index finger to make a circle including the two of them. "Right now, what you're doing, telling your girl's secrets, that's a *big* no. Huge!"

Sage grabbed his head with both hands, at a loss. "See? I'm the worst!" He swallowed hard and dropped his hands to his sides as it all became very clear to him. Emily's smile, her laugh, her shine—it was all out of his reach now. "She's not my girl, Zeldy," he said slowly. "I did that."

Zelda didn't argue with him. She took a deep breath and let it out. "She's kind of amazing, you know. I adore her just a little bit."

His smile was void of humor. "Right?"

He'd just wanted a chance. And right when she'd finally given it to him, let him inside for one glorious moment, he'd taken her trust for granted. It was that simple and that awful. He'd messed up.

Not just messed up. Mess wasn't a big enough word.

He'd wrecked it.

He still couldn't believe he'd actually accused her of taking it. Couldn't believe the thought had actually come out of him. What kind of an idiot does something like that?

It had been a huge moment for them.

A moment that mattered more than all the others.

She thought he'd had her back, and instead he'd stabbed her in it.

All while selling it to her as if he were going to be her hero.

She didn't need a hero.

Here was a girl who had long ago learned how to fly with one broken wing; she didn't need the added weight of a guy who wasn't going to pull his own. Who couldn't be on her side when it counted.

He'd failed her.

It would be easier if Abby were right. If he had no soul.

Because then maybe it wouldn't hurt this bad.

# Thirty-Three

### EMILY

D## AY FOUR WITHOUT SAGE.
How had it gotten to this? I'd caved so easily. I was such an idiot.

I'd spent years making sure things were safe. Even with the roomies I'd been careful—or as careful as someone could be with Megan, who wouldn't notice a brick wall if she'd built it herself.

But here I was. Let someone in—some *guy* in—for the first time since my brush with boyfriend betrayal. And, as soon as I fell to the trap of wooing, BAM!

I ran a hand over my pixie cut. On the upside, I was going to save money on hair products.

"You know, those glasses look even cuter with the hair." Megan tossed herself down on my mattress and started folding my clothes with her extra energy. "If I got ticked off and did that to my head, I'd look like an alien."

The snort escaped before I knew it was there. Only Megan would see this as comfort. Of course, it oddly was.

"So, here's the new plan…" Megan sat up, setting my laundry to the side.

"Does it involve you becoming an Uber driver?"

"No…well, kind of. But no."

Usually I'd worry, but I couldn't figure out how it could get worse. Unless, of course, Sage convinced everyone to press charges about the missing equipment and the cops picked me up. On the upside, I had the wrongfully-charged-with-lawbreaking thing down pat at this point.

"First," Megan went on as if this were an adventure, not my life, "we're going to text Officer Max and ask his advice."

"Except we don't have Max's phone number." And wasn't Max a lucky man that Megan didn't have him on speed dial?

Megan waved a hand, as if this were inconsequential. "Abby does. Then after we inform him of the wrong that has been done to you, we ask him how to get Sage arrested."

She said this so calmly, like having someone thrown in jail was just the logical next step. It dawned on me I never asked about Megan's family connections.

Note to self: do that.

"Ummm…" Brokenhearted I may be, but vengeful wasn't really in my makeup. Life was hard enough. I could only deal with my own emotions, and right now those were getting over Sage and moving on.

"After Sage has spent some time in the slam*mah*, we'll find out who really took the equipment and have them prosecuted to the fullest extent of the law…and then some." She looked oddly like an avenging kewpie doll, all dark curls and pink, round cheeks.

"When did you get a city accent?"

"After that, we'll let Sage out of jail only after he grovels." She nodded like this plan made sense.

"Okay, Nancy Drew, that's an interesting plan." Then because I really couldn't deal with this, I added, "Why don't you run it by Ash and get her to help us out."

She hopped up, nodding. "We're going to need all our resources, and that girl is tricky."

As soon as she'd headed back to their room, I collapsed where she'd been stretched out on my bed.

Today I had a Glamour Paws photo shoot. Usually just the idea of getting to play with photography equipment filled me with joy, but suddenly the idea of touching anything electronic or artistic made me nauseated.

I packed my run-around tote and headed out the door. As I walked to the studio, I called Abby, knowing it was a slow time.

"Hey. It's Emily."

"You're not calling out. I have plans."

"Fine, thanks. How are you?" I asked, ignoring her Abbyness.

"Fine, fine. I'm good. You're miserable. We both already knew that." Abby sighed on the other end of the line. "Are you maybe less miserable today?"

She sounded so concerned I made an *uh-huhn* sound to try to convince her that things were already looking up.

"I'm not calling in, but I wanted you to know Megan is going to call you later. Do *not* give her Max's number."

"Why would I give her Max's number?" She sounded more suspicious than normal.

"She has this absurd plan to have Sage thrown in jail and solve The Case of the Missing Light Meter."

"Huh," Abby said. "So...just out of curiosity, what's this plan look like?"

"No one is going to jail. Do not help her with this scheme. She'll probably end up being deported or something."

"Is she undocumented?" Abby was sounding more and more fascinated.

"No. But if there was ever a citizen who could get deported by accident, it's Megan. Her heart is always in the right place, but she has no idea of moderation...or a stop button."

I waited for Abby to agree on the other end of the line, but no affirmation came.

"Abby."

"Fine, fine. I won't give her Max's number." She sighed, as if this were just one more way I put her out. "But there's nothing I could do if Max was here when Megan stops by."

"Right." I tried to make my tone sound as fierce as possible, but I doubt Abby noticed as she hung up.

\*\*\*

My boss did a double take when I pushed through the front door, but didn't say anything about my hair, which was a nice change.

I stared at the cameras we locked up at night in the cage, my hands trembling at the sight of them. Maybe I wasn't cut out to be a photographer.

It had been a stupid idea anyway. I should have been working as a temp and trying to make a career—not to mention, having my benefits covered. It had been so stupid for me to think I could be something more. That path was for people who had a team, who had support. Who deserved good things.

I figured I owed Michael at least two weeks' notice.

Tomorrow was Saturday, but I'd call the school Monday and see if I could get my deposit for my next class back. Then I'd call a temp agency and see what I could do about becoming a corporate drone.

Life could be worse. There was always worse.

I grabbed the camera, forcing myself to enjoy the feel of it in my hands. Maybe one day I'd get to do this as a hobby. But, for now, it was time to stop being a dreamer and become an adult.

I stuffed some dog treats in my pocket, pasted a smile on my face, and headed out to enjoy the sunset of my dream.

# Thirty-Four

## SAGE

THE THICK GROWTH SAGE WAS sporting on his jaw and neck was stiff under his fingertips. The whiskers caught on his calluses and kept the movement from being fluid. He stared at the lights on the console, but he didn't see them.

She'd cut her hair.

And dyed it black.

Was that symbolic for cutting him out of her life? Like the song "I'm Gonna Wash That Man Right Outta My Hair," though perhaps Sage wouldn't wash. Perhaps he had to be cut out. Was that a good sign, or should it make him feel even worse?

Could he actually feel any worse?

He lost track of how many days it had been. It felt like years. It also felt like a bad dream that he couldn't wake up from. Every day had that foggy, discombobulated look to it.

Mrs. Callahan had come back and Sage finished her dining room. That's where he'd come from today. The final touches and payment were taken care of. He'd stood outside The Brew for twenty minutes when it was over. Wanting to see her, not wanting to see the pain slash across her face.

He wanted to go back. Fix it. Take it back to the workshop, strip it down, make it better. Make it new.

Relationships didn't work like that.

The more time he had to go over what had happened, the more he understood exactly how epically he'd screwed up. Emily should have been his first thought, not his second.

Sage was vaguely aware of the meeting taking place behind him. The entire band and Zelda were in the small room. He was supposed to be listening, but he wasn't. He was marinating in his own heartache. He was brokenhearted soup.

"I want Emily to be my second on this."

He jerked his head up and around, honing in on her name. Zelda's eyes flashed at him from her perch on the arm of the sofa.

"She has a gift, and frankly it would be stupid to not bring her."

"Can we afford her?" Luke asked.

Zelda scrunched up her nose. "My own business is growing to an extreme. I have to turn down more jobs lately because I simply don't have the time. I want to bring her on to work for me full time. If she says yeah, then she'd be covered under my own fee since she'd be my employee."

"Can we afford you?" Luke changed his question. Zelda grinned.

Sage cleared his throat. "Uh, what tour?"

"Garage tour. Small bars, clubs, lounges, things like that for a couple weeks. To try out the new stuff before final mixing. You know, work out the kinks." Luke dipped his head Sage's direction. "I expect you to be the one running the sound. We'll need you there to make sure it sounds the way we've got it nailed down in here. Plus, with you doing the mixing when we get back, you'll know better how to handle it. I want this tour to be as clean as this recording has gone. Which means you have to come with. No excuses."

Sage pressed his lips together and looked directly at Zelda. "Go on tour with Emily for a couple of weeks?"

Zelda tried to look innocent, but her sneakiness was obvious. "What? Why are you looking at me like that?"

Sage arched his eyebrows, and Harrison knocked his shoulder into Zelda, urging her to come clean.

"Okay, geez! So what if I think the solution is obvious. We all fell in love on tour. It's the perfect place to put this whole situation back to rights. So sue me for being a romantic."

Sage shook his head. "She won't go for it. She's too smart for your schemes."

Zelda crossed her arms over her chest in defiance. "Well, I'm not going without Emily."

"Shit," Luke muttered, rubbing the back of his neck.

"As Zelda goes, so goes my nation," Harrison said.

Luke looked to the ceiling. "Lord, save us from a fangirl's good intentions." He dropped his gaze to Sage. "If she comes along, will you be smart and not make it worse?"

"I don't even know how to make it worse," Sage muttered. Luke narrowed his eyes. "Of course. I'll be on my best behavior, but she won't go for it."

"I'll talk to her," Zelda spoke up.

The conversation drifted into logistics and possible venues. But Sage wasn't listening again.

He was stuck on the glimmer of hope he could have another chance. He didn't deserve it, not by a long shot. But he might actually get it. It had been hard to get in there the first time, but he was pretty positive he could do it again. He would throw himself at her feet over and over again. On tour he'd be able to show her he was sorry, he had her back, he would do anything for her. On tour, he had a chance.

A small, tiny, nearly nonexistent chance.

For the first time in a week, Sage wasn't hopeless.

# Thirty-Five

## EMILY

"So, that's not extreme or anything."

I glanced up to see Zelda standing on the far side of the café, grinning at me like we'd been apart for years.

"Yeah." I rubbed my hand over the back of my neck, still not used to the short fuzziness there. "It was a moment."

"Had 'em." She crossed the room, coming up to the counter and reaching across to pull me into a counter-encompassing hug. "Got a minute?"

I did a quick glance around the café. Everything was stocked, clean, and ready to go in the morning. The guy who was probably my last customer had left about fifteen minutes ago, leaving me with plenty of time to get the world in order.

"Sure." I rounded the counter to join her, motioning to the comfy chairs. "What's up?"

"Stop." Zelda shook her head, giving me a significant side-eye. "Stop thinking horrible things."

I took a deep breath and let my shoulders drop back. I'd been afraid Zelda was not only dropping me as a friend, but had changed her mind since the camera hadn't shown up. Everything shifted back around to not-horrible, and I slouched back in the chair.

"Well, I was going to call you this week anyway." I took a deep breath and sat forward, and spilled the beans. "I'm giving up photography. It just doesn't make sense."

"*What?*" Zelda's voice jumped so many octaves I thought wolves might howl in the distance.

"Yeah. I've actually given notice on all my jobs. And," I took a breath before rushing on, "I got my tuition for my next class reimbursed. I'm starting at this office gig over in Cambridge in a week."

"Doing artsy marketing stuff, right?" Zelda's brows were drawn down in what I swear were little cartoon *V*s.

"Actually, I'm going to be the admin to the admin to the sales manager." I still didn't know what that meant, but I knew it paid more than minimum wage and was on an easy bus line, and I could keep my job with Dr. Michael's kids.

"No. Absolutely not. I forbid it." Zelda stood up and marched across the room only to turn and march back. "No."

"You said that."

"And I meant it!" She pounded her fist into her other hand.

"So, yeah." I gave her a smile, feeling the love under all the anger. "I can't do this much more. I've been at it for five years, and I'm tired, Zelda. I need some stability, and I need to know I won't be homeless or a step away from homeless for the rest of my life."

"But, I have a better offer!" She sat back down. "You're going to work for me."

Oh, well, that was adorable. Between the two of us, we'd make a full person in height and probably break half of the planet in klutziness.

"That's a very kind offer—"

"No, it isn't. It's why I drove in today." Zelda settled back down, looking her version of professional. "I'd like to hire you on full time. You'd work for me. You'd be my second on all major shoots, not to mention building your own clientele as you see fit. Of course, Double Blind is our major—and most important—client. They pay the bills. Which means it's a good thing you gave notice, because we're going on tour!"

Leave it to Zelda to see fate in my decision to move on and become an adult.

"Right, so—" I cleared my throat. "Yeah. No."

"What? No, what?"

"Zelda," I softened my voice. "I can't."

"Yes, you can." She sounded so sure.

But, I'd already given up the dream. And, to have it again, only to know it would probably be snatched away would kill me.

Not to mention, Sage. There was no way I was traveling and working in close quarters with him for however long and however often.

"I need to let go of the dream. It's not going to happen long term, and I need to be planning for my future."

"This *is* your future." Zelda wasn't going to let this go without a fight. "You're incredibly talented. You have a gift to see things and capture moments. I feel so much joy in your photos. And, light. Geez. You play with light like Arthur Griffin. I'm not offering you a hobby. I'm offering you a job—

no! A *career*. Which starts with *car*, so it obviously means you're going places."

I opened my mouth to try to interrupt.

"Plus!" She jumped up, looking more excited than even a moment ago. "There's a two-thousand dollar signing bonus."

Wow. That was a lot of money. I could pay off the last of one of my credit cards with that.

"Equipment is included." She kept going, counting off perks on her fingers. "Health benefits."

I was beginning to consider it. Heck, I was more than beginning to consider it. I was practically sold.

"And super-fun world travel with rock stars!"

Oh. Yeah. The band…and the band people.

"Zelda—"

"Don't say it!" She shook her head. "We'll make it work."

"I can't. I'm sorry. I know you're offering me the chance of a lifetime, and, to be honest, I could use a break. But the truth is, I honestly don't think I could work like that. I don't think I could give you anything you'd use. I'm just…"

I tried to figure out the right word to make her understand. I just couldn't be near him. He not only broke my heart, but he represented everything I knew was a dreamland I'd let myself slip into. It was good to know. It was smart to realize it now.

A girl could only count on herself and the world wasn't going to cut her any breaks.

"Listen, I get it. I even love the adorable Audrey Hepburn circa *Sabrina* thing going on." She smiled while I ran a hand over my dyed pixie cut, thinking it was supposed to be rebellion, not retro class. "But you can't do this. I did this. I thought I would make sandwiches for a living and give up

Harrison. But you're going to make copies. That's worse! That's like heart-killing! You need to create!"

I gave her the best smile I had, knowing that with Zelda I'd at least have one more friend when all this was over. "Well then, I guess I'll create copies."

\*\*\*

## SAGE

"You!"

Sage glanced up as Zelda barged into the studio, wrath and fury coming off her in waves.

"You have broken my fangirl. You have ravaged the soul of my soul sister. You have demolished the cheer of my little hobbit. You are dead to me."

Behind him, he heard a gasp and turned to see Harrison going pale.

"Zelda," Harrison breathed out, a rush of shock.

"No. No. Emily is beyond all of our reaches now. She's done the unimaginable."

Sage jumped out of his chair, tipping it over as he did, heart racing. "Is she okay?"

What could she have done? Was she hurt?

"No. She is not okay."

Sage reached for his keys, ready to drive them to the nearest hospital.

"Zeldy, what's happened?" Harrison took her hands, trying to slow everything down and absorbing a bit of her anger. "What horrible thing has Emily done?"

"She...she..." Zelda sucked in a breath. "She quit life and got an *office job,* and it's all your fault."

The band all turned and looked at him, expecting him to fix it. To make everything better. Hell, he didn't even know how things had landed here.

Step one: Meet the girl of your dreams.

Step two: Woo her.

Step three: Destroy everything in a crash of destruction so horrendous no one can find the bodies.

Sage sucked in a breath.

"I can fix it."

"How?" Zelda glared, clearly not believing him. Sage didn't blame her.

"It's what I do. I fix things. This...I can fix." He turned to Luke, feeling the weight of what he was about to say grow heavy in his chest. "I'm not going on the tour."

Luke's eyebrows dipped severely. "I think you misunderstand the importance of having a sound man."

"Get Greg or Trey. I heard Sandy O is back from Vegas, call her. I don't care."

"But we picked you for a reason, Sage," Luke said gruffly.

"Doesn't matter. I've already gotten a taste of living my dream. You've already given me more opportunity than I deserve. This is Emily's shot. The one thing in the world that puts that light on her face, and I'm the a-hole standing in the way?" He shook his head. "I won't be that guy. I'm not that guy."

"You're in love with her," Zelda said, wiping a tear off her cheek, her anger dissolved.

"Yep," Sage said, the small confirmation burning his chest. "Lot of good it does me now."

***

## EMILY

My phone beeped as I lay in bed looking at the ceiling, wondering if I should just give up and wear those clippy bows in my hair if I couldn't even manage rebellion girl right.

I doubted that would look professional enough for my new job. I was going to head down to the thrift store tomorrow to try to get some work outfits. Things that would blend with the classy office-chic girls I would have to work around.

I rolled over and grabbed the phone, not sure I wanted to check the text.

**ZELDA: We're good to go. Sage has to build stuff and is not going on the tour.**

Wow. That was…convenient.

**ZELDA: We'll call this a test run. Bc it's short term, signing bonus $3k.**

I looked at the amount, knowing it was more than I make in a month with all the jobs. I felt an urge to reply, to accept. But it felt like falling for a trick. Like going down the rabbit hole with Alice when you'd both already been there once.

Adulting.

I was supposed to be Adulting.

**ZELDA: All pics not including rock stars are yours to keep, sell, Whatevs**

Geez. She was just hitting below the belt.

**ZELDA: So, that's a yes. Right.**

I sighed, texting back my answer, and slid into bed wondering if any choice could have been the right one.

# Thirty-Six

## SAGE

H E RAN HIS HANDS OVER the wood, feeling the flaws, the imperfections that were as close to perfect as he had ever found. The ridges he would sand down and polish. The ripples and swirls that would become the bloom of his creation.

If only everything in life were this simple to read. If only he could take moments and hold them in his hand, feel their edges and perfection. If only he could show his love as easily as he could carve out sound holes.

If only.

His phone buzzed on the tabletop, and he chucked his pencil across the room, where it hit the wall and clattered into the pile of discard. Wow, he was stupid. It had taken twenty minutes to find it last time.

He picked up his phone and swiped at the screen.

**Luke: Do you still have those pedals we picked up in St. Louis?**

Sage squeezed his eyes shut as he thought about it.

He hadn't slept in days. Not for lack of trying. Every time he lay down, he heard her voice as it broke and cried. Saw her face as it reacted to his thoughtlessness.

In his mind, he did it differently. He reacted better, anticipated the question, rose to the challenge, proved he was worth the trust she'd placed in him.

But none of that was possible now.

He had to keep his distance. It's what she wanted. And he was desperate to give her everything she wanted.

So he'd spent hours going through the scrap pile, trying to find broken pieces he could give a second life to...a second chance. Just because something was broken didn't mean it was useless.

Like the pedals he'd repaired and stored for Luke. His eyes flicked to the back row of cabinets he kept locked.

**Sage: Yeah. They're here. You need them?**
**Luke: Affirmative. We leave tomorrow.**

Finally, a task.

Probably the final farewell in the lingering good-bye to the band and the life he'd started for himself there.

It was good, though. This was good.

He needed to learn this lesson. He'd lived too charmed of a life and it was his turn to grow up now. It was fair.

He went to the cabinet, found the pedals, and headed to Luke's.

The driveway and front yard were filled with extra trucks and trailers. Some of the regular crew humped amps into the back of a large van and Sage's gut tightened with tour anticipation. The small shows were the best shows. More energy, more risk, more reward.

And he was going to miss it.

"McNabb."

"Greg," he greeted the longtime sound man.

"Are you coming with us? I sure could use your skills."

Sage let go of Greg's hand and ran a hand through his hair, feeling the sting of his words and the practiced lie he was about to utter. "Nah, I couldn't get the time off." The last thing Sage wanted Emily to discover was that he'd bowed out. He was afraid she'd think it was some kind of a tactic and still not go. The real reason he wasn't going was between him, Zelda, and the band.

"But this is dream making," Greg argued, confusion clouding his expression. He would know. Greg was one of the few who knew what Sage really wanted out of the Double Blind experience. The sound man had taught him more than he realized, had even allowed him to run the main board multiple times on the road.

"Can't you just quit your job?"

Sage chuckled nervously. "Some things are more important, Greg." He hefted the box under his arm. "Is Luke inside? I have something he needs."

"Yeah." Greg jerked his head toward the garage.

Sage nodded his thanks and headed inside. The pedals they'd picked up in St. Louis way back when were old school, found on an adventure at a flea market. They hadn't worked at the time, but were perfectly designed for small shows and the blue beast Sage had built for Luke years ago. Sage had taken them home, rebuilt them, then stored them. Waiting for their next call for use.

In the back of his mind, he'd always figured he'd be the one to hook them up. Not only was he not getting a chance to run sound on a tour, he was giving up his spot as guitar tech.

A whole mess of good-byes in one fell swoop.

He paused in the studio. Most of the instruments were already packed and loaded. Mike used a different drum kit for the road than he used for recording, so all of his stuff was still there. Empty mic stands, tangled cords, and crumpled recording notes littered the floor. The image resonated deep inside Sage's chest. It was like looking in on what was left of the dream.

Pieces.

Scraps.

A moment that was close to almost.

He'd almost done it.

It was fitting, really. He had no business making music with legends like these. For some reason, it had just taken longer for everyone to realize it. Like finding a stowaway on one of the crew buses. He was getting off at this stop.

The box of pedals tucked under his arm was an appropriate symbol to signify good-bye. The manipulation of sound, the connection to a unique world. Rebuilt, renewed. Given new life, and letting go of the old.

He found Luke upstairs.

"Here you go, boss." He set the box on the table.

"Sage." Luke nodded, glancing at the pedals. "Can you listen to this for a second?" He stood from the chair at the board and handed the headphones over.

Sage frowned, but took the headset. "What am I listening for?"

"You tell me."

Luke flipped the switch and music filled the headphones.

Sage closed his eyes and focused. His senses were flooded with everything that had gone into making the album. He smelled coffee, sunshine, and excitement. Blue eyes and dresses, smiles and hesitant kisses. It was like a sucker punch to his already exhausted faculties.

The rush of Emily that would always and forever be associated with every song on this record. The first one he'd ever produced. Maybe the only one he'd ever produce. If that were the case, he was okay with it.

It was the perfect soundtrack for what relationship they'd had. It rocked. It had passion, soul, art at its most raw. Forever these songs would shake him at his core.

If only he'd realized sooner what had been at stake.

The song ended and he removed the headphones. "Sounds really good to me. What were you hearing?"

Luke's serious face broke into a grin. "Butch Vig you're not, but damn if you're not on your way."

Sage's lips twitched. "What?"

"That's all you." Luke shook his head. "I don't want you to miss this. Reconsider. Come on the road. Be the guy who makes this great." He stood up and grabbed Sage by one shoulder, pulling him closer with a stern look. "I keep telling you we picked you for a reason, and I get the feeling you're not hearing me." He shook Sage by the shoulder. "This is it. Put your name on this record. Finish it with us."

Sage rotated his shoulder out of Luke's grasp and shook his head. "You don't understand. If I go, she doesn't go."

Luke crossed his arms over his chest.

"Luke, I wanna go. I do. This album has more of me in it than anything I've ever made. But there'll be other opportunities for me. This is her one shot."

"You said that already."

"It's true. She's had a shit life, and no one has ever cared about her. Not really, not about her heart. I screwed things up for us, but I can fix this one small thing for her. I can take care of her heart's needs." Sage closed his eyes as all that he'd been avoiding thinking about pressed its entire weighty reality on him.

"I'm really sorry I'm bailing on you guys. Of all the things in this world to bail on, I never thought it would be you. Or this." He waved a hand, indicating the upstairs rooms. "I mean, shit, this is it. I used to sketch pictures of myself in rooms like this when I was in high school. Being a part of the process, making music, creating the very stuff I've always wanted to live and breathe... Luke, I'm not an idiot. I know exactly what I'm walking away from."

Luke nodded solemnly. "I can't promise you get to come back. You must know that."

Sage could only nod. Because he did know. He knew it the minute he quit.

"We're on a timetable. If you're not coming with us to hear the changes live on the road, there's very little reason to bring you back to finish up. And not finishing..."

"I know."

He knew Luke wasn't trying to be a dick. He was trying to tell Sage what he already knew. If he walked away, it was permanent. No coming back. Not just in the studio. Chances were slim to none they would take a risk on him again.

Luke shook his head and then offered his hand. Sage took it.

"I hate to see you go. You've been a part of this family for a while. It'll be hard not having you around anymore."

"I'm thankful for the experience."

More thankful than he could accurately express. This band was more than a job. It was more than a lucky break. This band was an answer to a prayer his mom had prayed for him. To be able to live a dream while not having to face the very thing that had taken his birth mom away from him..? It had been everything.

Luke nodded, expression grim. He wasn't pleased. At least that was something. Sage would always have the knowledge one of his idols and his favorite band of all time had thought he was good enough to produce an album with them.

Those things, along with knowing his actions meant Emily might be able to live a dream she had thought was too big to dream...well, it helped.

It still hurt.

Right exactly in the spaces between his ribs every time he took a breath. He imagined that feeling would eventually fade.

All at once, he was losing two impossible things. The band, the girl.

What had he told Emily? *I'm glad I have a trade. It means I'll have a job if this music thing never amounts to much.*

He'd be able to build. He would always have that.

He jogged down the steps, anxious to get out of there before he had to talk to anyone else. Knowing his time in this world was over, he didn't feel like sticking around for more punishment.

The studio below was empty. Except for two females trying to reach something a foot above their reach on the shelf above the soundboard.

"Maybe if I give you a boost," Emily suggested, bending to shove a shoulder into Zelda's rear end.

"Yeah, do that," Zelda agreed, her hands straining for the box. "Give it all you got. Throw me into the atmosphere, if you can."

Sage had about a half a heartbeat to decide if he should save them from certain injury or if he should try to find someone else to save them. But his body was already moving their direction.

"Please don't die," he said.

The sound of his voice caused Emily to go rigid. He ignored it and reached past Zelda to get the box. As he tugged it off the shelf, it caught on something, yanking it down on top of them. Zelda's hands came out and grabbed hold of it before it hit anyone.

"Mjölnir!"

Sage's eyes went to Emily. Every feeling he'd been trying to avoid hit him in the chest like a nine-pound hammer. There she was. The only girl he'd ever loved. Within arms' reach. And between them was the object that had been the catalyst for tearing them apart.

"I guess it was here all along," Zelda said weakly.

Emily didn't say anything. She stared at Sage; the guard he'd worked so hard to get behind was back in place and reinforced more than ever before.

It was odd; the measure of time it took to look at her somehow didn't reflect the magnitude of everything he saw.

Every laugh, every inside joke, every touch, every word. Every little moment she had risked a piece of herself for him.

He saw it all. The fear that faded to the background, the kisses, the fun, the conflict, the chance she took on him.

Girls like this didn't just happen. She was one of a kind. Impossible to find ever again.

As much as it sucked walking away from the band and the music, losing her was somehow worse.

A moment so close to almost, he could still see it.

An echo fading in her eyes.

"I'm sorry," he said, pushing the words out despite the dryness in his throat. "I know it doesn't...matter." He swallowed hard and licked his lips. "I know I can't fix it. I know it's my fault. I know what I did, and I am so...sorry."

He scanned her new haircut. The blonde was gone, replaced with a jet-black that was striking on her pale skin. It made her blue eyes stand out intensely. Still, she was Emily. Through and through. She had the kind of light that couldn't be hidden.

"Most beautiful girl in the world," he murmured.

He pushed the box into Zelda's arms, deciding he'd had enough torture for one day. He yanked his keys out of his pocket and headed to his truck.

# Thirty-Seven

## EMILY

I glanced around, listening to Zelda chatter at—I mean, *educate*—me.

I'd thought this trip was going to be a voyage of sadness, but no one had let that happen. I'd been put to work immediately, and the busy rush of things helped move life forward.

"And that is why there are different actors playing the Doctor." Zelda looked at me expectantly, like I was supposed to have an amazing revelation about life from this.

"But what about the other characters?" Because this made sense, but it also didn't make sense. Of course, the show had been on forever, so maybe a "quick overview" had been too much to ask.

"Well—" Zelda broke off as the van pulled through the gates. "We're here!"

I glanced over, trying not to grin so wide my mouth broke. It was our half-day off, and we were in the best place ever for it. Outside one of my dream photography museums.

"Dorothea Lange." I breathed it out like a prayer to the gods of Shades of Light.

"Right?"

Together, we hopped out and headed toward the museum after letting Zed know when to pick us up.

"She was like…a rock star." I breathed out heavily as we stood in line, too excited about the fact this traveling show was here the same time we were.

"A groundbreaking, feminist, world-traveling, artist rock star."

"So that."

"Right?"

The guy in front of us turned around and gave us a weird look. But, if you're not excited about art, why would you be in line to get into a museum?

Zelda reached out and grabbed my hand for a moment. "I'm so glad you came. I know things have been a little weird for you, but having you with us has been the best."

I stood, stunned for a moment, finally realizing she wasn't humoring me about all the friendship stuff.

"It's been the best for me, too."

"Don't get me wrong—I love all the girls. They're *my* girls. But having another artist—*visual*—artist and nerd with me…it's been so fun."

I blinked, trying not to tear up. It had been more than fun. It really had been the best.

\*\*\*

"What did you say your names were again?"

"I am The Doctor, and this is my companion, Donna." Zelda looked at the man with a completely straight face.

So I was Donna today. Yesterday I had gotten to experience life as Clara. Zelda was always The Doctor. At first, I had no idea what she was talking about with the aliases. Apparently Doctor Who was one of my missing fandoms. Harrison and Zelda were correcting posthaste my ignorance of all things Whovian. Who said there was nothing to do on a bus between venues?

I was thinking there was no way those names would clear with security when he nodded and said, "Yup. Here you are on the list, Doctor and Doctor Donna. Set up wherever you need. Sodas on the house for roadies. Beer is for the talent only."

"Got it. Don't spoil the help." She winked at him and wandered into the small, darkened club looking around the area for the best shots.

Besides making everyone call her Doctor when she was working, Zelda had also been demanding everyone recognize us as sisters since we hit the road. About halfway through the mini-tour, I'd heard her and Harrison arguing about my sister status.

"She's coming to live with us."

I stifled a laugh, because really.

"Zeldy, she's not a puppy. She has a place to live."

"But she's my soul sister, and she needs to be with family."

"Zeldy." I could hear Harrison working on his patience. "Emily has a life, and just because you've decided to adopt her doesn't mean she wants to give up that life."

"But what about holidays and birthdays and important days?"

"Well, of course she'll come stay with us. Just like any sister would. But, we're not here to take over her life. Just join it."

"Fine." I could hear Zelda huff a little that she'd made a plan that didn't work out—shocker. "But she gets the pretty room with the view of the meadow."

"Of course she does."

I glanced around the bar, smiling at the memory. Zelda was nothing if not the most loyal person on the planet. And, I'll admit, loyalty was a new thing to me. And family—it was the only thing I'd *really* ever wanted. When Sage had asked about my dreams, all this other stuff was awesome. But just the idea that I might belong somewhere? That was the dream.

Later that evening, she sat me down and asked how I felt about changing my last name to Fitzpatrick while Harrison stood by looking incredibly amused.

But even the band had started referring to us as The Sisters, so I guess it was a done deal whether I decided to change my name or not.

Part of me worried this was going to make everything harder when we got home, but I realized it didn't matter. For the first time in my life, I felt like I *did* have family. That Zelda wasn't going anywhere. She made sure I felt that way every day.

I had a feeling Sage had slipped something to her, so I sat her down and told her about my past, figuring they probably did a background check on me anyway.

Irate, meet Zelda.

She'd already announced we were sisters, but that's when she called her parents about the adoption, and I had to ask Harrison to put a brake on that chatter.

"Hey, Donna!"

I glanced up after a second to the sound of my newest alias.

"Can you see about getting the lights on the stage set up so I can see what we're working with?"

"I'm on it!" I jumped up and headed for the bar to get the lights adjusted.

At this point, our habits were pretty set. Zelda wanted shots at every show. She'd put me in charge of the Instagram page, which meant before pictures to go live twenty-minutes after the show started. I could give hints, but nothing too obvious.

It was the best job I'd ever had. Nightly scavenger hunts? Yes, please!

There were a few lucky stragglers who always figured it out—or gave up trying to guess and picked a bar—each night after I let the town out of the bag. So, the band always did their opening song, then took one request. The fans *loved* it. Okay. I loved it. It was pretty darn cool.

And, tonight was no different.

I'd given some great hints and had told them I'd accept bribes. One girl told me her brother's roommates brother's best friend was on a Certain TV Show, if I was interested.

I played along; that was my job, but no. I wasn't. And I doubted I'd ever be interested again.

But hey, my life was more than I ever thought it would be.

Sage broke my heart, but he gave me a family.

\*\*\*

"Whatcha doin'?" Zelda leaned over my shoulder as the bus pulled out, glancing at the photos I had separated out on my laptop. "Oh! I love that one."

She pointed to one of my favorites. It was all the guitars lined up along the side of the stage before the show started. I'd shot it before the lights had come up, so there was a great moody feeling to it.

"I wanted you to clear these pictures for the photo site." I was thrilled and nervous about the whole thing.

It had started with the idea that I'd post my extra non-people photos on a stock photo site and start building a reputation and some cash. But then everyone had gotten involved—because, that is, apparently what they do—and POOF, I had a website.

Not only did I have a website, but I had business cards. Business cards you could pick up at the merch table if you wanted to purchase a Special Behind the Scenes Double Blind Photo.

So, yeah.

"Are there people in them?" Zelda asked.

"Well, no. But—"

"That's your contract. No people, you're clear."

She walked away before I could argue. I was stalling. It was true. But, I was afraid of what would happen if I put my work out there and no one bought it. *Especially* with how much the band had been pimping me. If they couldn't sell pictures of their own tour I'd taken, that meant…well, nothing good.

"Hit publish!" Harrison called from the other room.

So I did.

And then I sat staring at the computer…and hitting refresh.

And then I hit refresh.

Then I hit it again.

Then—the laptop disappeared from my little table.

"This is going somewhere you can't get to." Zelda did something before shutting it down and handing it to Harrison. "Also, I changed your password, so don't even try it on your phone. Now. Get some sleep. One more week of this, and then you can sleep in a real bed."

I didn't have the heart to tell her I slept on a mattress on a dining-bedroom floor. She'd probably have a bed sent. Both she and Harrison were caretakers. It felt like my job, at the very least, was to protect them from the world. They needed an emotional bodyguard, and that was me.

The girl without a heart.

Sage had finished the job, and now the best thing I could use was my ability to lock down emotions to make sure the people who loved me best were free to love everyone they wanted...safely.

I was a very special kind of superhero now, with a power I wouldn't wish on anyone else.

I climbed into bed, not wanting this trip to end. The band and the girls and the travel, they were amazing. I felt like I had a place in the world. My job with Zelda was a good one—we did great work together—and one that made me feel...well, not *important* but something good. Something close to that. Almost, *almost* like necessary.

I closed my eyes and, like every night, tried to push thoughts of Sage away.

Even three hundred miles away he was still very present. The guys talked to him and about him. There were calls made and questions that needed to be answered. Apparently Sage was the guy.

You'd think this would be a great way to get used to him being in my life without *being* in my life. But, not so much.

I lay there, eyes closed, trying to think of anything but Mr. Floppy Hair and Gorgeous Hands, but all I could think about was the hard lesson that every betrayal scars you in a different way.

# Thirty-Eight

## SAGE

"A RE YOU LOST?"
Sage grimaced and hefted the toolbox in his hand. "I know you know why I'm here."

He'd left a note the day before, explaining his plan. If they didn't want him to do it, all they had to do was text him and tell him so. He had received no text.

Megan cocked her head to the side and crossed her arms over her chest. "I didn't actually think you'd show up yourself. I thought maybe you'd send a lackey or something."

Sage nodded. He figured he'd have to take his lumps. "I don't have lackeys. It's just me."

She stared at him for a full minute before opening the door and letting him into their small apartment. *Small* was an understatement.

He came into the cramped quarters and looked in on what was Emily's "bedroom." It wasn't a bedroom. She didn't even have a bed.

He pushed aside the renewed anger at the circumstances and her shitty foster parents, and set down his toolbox.

"How long is this going to take?" Megan asked.

Sage measured the space with his eyes, making initial calculations in his head. With the band on the road and no projects lined up at the moment, not to mention his complete inability to sleep, it wouldn't take long at all.

"I'm gonna have to build a wall here...and partially here." He showed her with his hands. He shifted to look at Emily's stuff again. "Can you pack her stuff a little? I have some tarps in the truck I'll bring up for you to cover anything you don't want to get dust all over."

It wasn't exactly conventional what he was about to do. On a matter of impulse, fueled by pent-up energy and an aggravated mental state, Sage had decided to build Emily a room and a bed.

It wouldn't take him long at all. Not even when he knew he'd go over the bed frame again and again to be sure it was exactly perfect.

"I'll be done before she comes back."

Megan measured his response, her distaste obvious. "I don't like you in our space."

Sage faced her directly and took a deep breath. "Okay."

She narrowed her eyes. "Okay? That's all you have to say for yourself?"

"Megan—" Sage stopped himself. He wanted to say a dozen different things to her, but knew it wouldn't matter. She had her girl's back. For that, Sage was thankful. At least Emily had good people in her life who would fight for her.

He heaved out a sigh. "I'll be right back." Then he jogged back downstairs to get the tarps.

\*\*\*

It was day four in the apartment, and Sage was feeling good about his progress.

Thankfully, the girls had been working for a good portion of day one and two. He already had the drywall taped and sanded. He would paint last, on a day when they were both working again.

On day three and four, he had watchdogs. They hovered, made cutting remarks, and criticized everything from the color of his boxers to his ability to use a tape measure.

Honestly, it didn't bother him. He deserved worse. At least they weren't throwing rotten food at him.

"I know I've been watching you make things out of wood for four days," Megan said, reaching a hand to the headboard he'd carried in that morning, "but I think it's just now registering to me that you made this. Out of a tree."

Sage grunted. "It's not like I cut down the tree myself and hauled it from the mountains."

"But you did haul it." Megan jumped in. "From the lumberyard or something."

"Yep."

He pulled his hand chisel from his tool belt and scraped off a small ding along the joint he must've missed last night. He'd done the major carving in the workshop and would finish the smaller details here with his hand tools. Then he'd let the girls pick what kind of stain they thought Emily might like best.

"Do you mind if I listen to some DBS?" Megan asked.

Sage froze. He stared at the tool in his hands, feeling like he'd forgotten how to process the English language.

"Sage?" Megan asked.

"Uh," he squeezed his eyes shut.

"You know what?" she said. "Never mind. I think I'll read instead."

"Okay," he said, knowing he sounded relieved, but not being able to help it.

It's not that he didn't want to listen to them. It was just hard at the moment. He couldn't listen to music at all. He kept trying and would only end up unplugging it.

It hurt to hear music. His brain couldn't disguise it as background noise. It stung. Salt. Open wound.

"Do you think you could get me an early release of the album you're working on?" Megan asked, nose still in her book.

"Probably not." He stood, lifting the headboard and moving it to its back on the floor. Then he went back to his knees again and pulled his hand tools closer to him.

"Do they have rules for that?"

"Uh, I don't know." The design he'd chosen to carve into Emily's headboard was one he'd been saving. He had come up with it the week he'd met her. He'd been at The Brew, and she'd made a joke about the "flowery notes" used to describe the coffee roast that day.

He'd covered a page in his notebook with flowers that morphed into musical notes. It was his favorite. And it could never belong to anyone else. At least this way, it would be used.

"What other jobs are you on right now?" Megan asked.

Megan liked to make conversation. Sage had picked up on that right away. As long as she wasn't being mean, he obliged her.

"Just this one."

He opened his notebook to the page he needed and bent over the headboard.

"Are you looking forward to getting back to the studio?"

Sage cast a small glare to Megan, but she missed it. He turned his ball cap backward to keep his hair out of his face and the bill from bumping into the headboard. He also didn't answer her.

"You seem sad, Sage," Megan said conversationally.

"That's the unfortunate byproduct of grief, Megan," he responded, focusing on the curve of the petal.

Megan sat, cross legged, back braced against the far wall studying him—eyes narrowed in what he was suddenly realizing was a far more aware glare than he'd ever given her credit for.

"But you'll get to go back when they get back. It's one tour, right?" She leaned forward, studying him intently. "How much are you really missing?"

Sage blew the wood shavings gently off his workspace.

His phone rang, and he pulled it out of his pocket.

"Hey, Dad," he answered. Because...saved by the bell.

"I have a client who needs some demolition work done in a couple weeks. Will you be around?"

"Uh, yeah." He sat back on his heels and rubbed his forearm across his brow. "Yeah, schedule's wide open. Whatever you need."

Maybe this was why he had ended up in Emily's life. Maybe he wasn't meant to be her happily ever after. Maybe he was simply meant to make her life a little bit better with the skills he'd been gifted. Get her to the next stage so she could go off and shine, making the world a better place.

There were worse things to be in the world.

# THIRTY-NINE

## EMILY

I SAT QUIETLY IN BACK of Harrison's Volvo, leaning against my window and watching him run his thumb back and forth over the back of Zelda's hand, where they were joined on the armrest. Quietly, "You're My Best Friend" played along, bringing us all down from the adrenaline junkie rushes of the tour.

He got off the Pike and started weaving through the side streets to my college-student overrun neighborhood.

In front of my place, Harrison double-parked and got out, pulling my things out of the truck while I thanked Zelda for the one thousandth time for the opportunity.

"Oh, please!" Zelda hugged me. "We're not to your door yet."

"Zelda, you do *not* have to walk me to the door." Because it was several flights up and late at night. "You guys still have a big drive out to your place. And, I'll see you tomorrow."

"You're right. You should totally just come home with us tonight!"

There was a subtle throat-clearing from behind us.

"Right." Zelda blushed. "I'll pick you up at the train station tomorrow."

I laughed, trying not to give her an I Know What You're Doing Tonight look. I'd just lived with the practically-still-newlyweds on a bus for two weeks. I'm sure getting some *alone* time was high on the to-do list.

"Let me get that for you." Harrison hoisted my bag as if it were filled with cotton balls and headed toward the front stairs.

Zelda followed along after him, her camera bag over her shoulder.

"Tomorrow we're going to start sorting through from the beginning. Sometimes pictures you don't love on their own fit great into the narrative we're going to create."

"The narrative of We're Awesome," Harrison added over his shoulder.

"Right." Zelda smiled up at him completely unironically.

At my door, I squeezed by Harrison to try to sneak into my apartment without waking up Megan and Ash. Gentleman that he was, he followed me in, carrying my bag the whole way.

I rounded the corner to my dining-bedroom only to—hit a wall. Literally.

I stopped. Stepped back. Looked back at the door.

Had we magically gotten into the wrong place?

"I thought you lived in a dining room." Harrison looked past me at the wall.

I moved past the wall and into the room where there was…a bed. I would have thought it wasn't my bed, but it had my comforter on it. So, I now had a bed. And a wall. With a little half-wall that broke out to an entryway.

And, hanging from the ceiling, a bar all my clothes hung from.

"What the heck happened here?" I glanced at the room that had a modicum of privacy now, the bed that wasn't a mattress on the floor, and my clothes stored in something better than milk crates.

I glanced at Harrison and Zelda, both of them looking at me as if I were nuts.

"I swear, this is a totally different room." I waved my hand, trying to demonstrate the breadth of the change.

"It is." Zelda look as amazed as I felt. "It's like *magic*."

I glanced back, exhausted and ready to collapse, and thought…maybe it was magic.

\*\*\*

I woke up, stretching after a great night's sleep. It was good to be home. I planned on taking the longest shower in the world. Maybe even followed up by a bath because I couldn't remember the last time I saw a full bathtub.

Maybe I'd head to The Brew and force Abby to wait on me before I got on the commuter train out to Zelda's.

I couldn't help but wonder if Abby had replaced me. Maybe with someone cynical and ready to abuse those who laid their money on the counter for coffee and pastries they deemed worthy of the snark.

But, my hope was that no one had worked out. As much as everyone liked to look at Abby as gruff and unfeeling, she was secretly a marshmallow and I was hoping she still had a place for me.

I rolled over, opening my eyes, only to be met by huge blue ones staring right at me.

"Holy mother of all stalker crazy people!" I jumped up, backing away, then remembered I was in an actual bed.

Which was still a mystery. One I hadn't questioned too heavily at 2:00 a.m. after seven hours on the road. But still, a pretty confusing one.

Megan sat, pink fluffy robe around her, cup of tea cradled in her hand, in the old beanbag chair she usually kept next to her bed.

"*Finally.*" She set her cup down and leaned forward. "I've been waiting for you to get up for like twelve hours."

I glanced at the clock, wondering just how late I'd slept.

7:42.

"Megan, I only got home like five hours ago, so unless we totally overlooked you sitting there creepily staring at my empty bed…hyperbole, much?"

"Right." She waved a hand. "Whatever. I've been waiting. That's the main point."

"Yes. I can tell it's been hours by the steam still coming out of your coffee cup."

Megan glared at the mug like it was a deceiving liar.

"So?" Megan smiled at me, her big full-wattage smile, and I realized how much I'd missed her.

"So, what?" I also missed driving her crazy. Playing dumb usually hit her right in that hot button.

"Your room? It's no longer a dining-bedroom! It's a mostly-bedroom now. We couldn't put in an actual full wall or it changes code or something." She grinned. "And it's blue. Well, almost blue. Apparently this is called eggshell white. But, you can totally see the blue. I *demanded* blue for you. I also had the idea for the little sliding things under your bed."

The what? I leaned over the side of my bed and saw little rolling storage bins that would work like drawers.

"Brilliant, right?" Megan all but high-fived herself.

"It is." I sat up, looking around again in the full light of morning. The room was pretty amazing. It was almost like a bedroom. Even without a door, it felt more closed off, private. And there was definitely way more storage than my nine different outfits would need. "You did all this?"

"I was instrumental." She nodded.

"You were not, you pain in the rear." Ash shouted from the other room. "Why the heck are you waking us all up on our day off? Go away!"

I tried to cover my laugh with a yawn at the look of outrage on Megan's face.

"Oh!" Ash shouted again. "Welcome home. Now, shut up."

"But—"

"Go shower," Megan cut me off. "I'll take you to The Brew where you can tell me all about your new celebrity status."

And she could tell me about my new room…whether she liked it or not.

\*\*\*

"It's about time." Abby was standing behind the counter, glaring at us when we walked in, as if I were late for my shift instead of having been gone for two weeks.

"I'm not working today. So stop glaring at me." Megan glared back, the two of them giving each other quite the looks.

"Wait." I stopped, turning to Megan. "You took my job?"

"Well, you did quit it." She sounded more than a little defensive.

"Right. I know." I glanced around, feeling out of sorts.

"And it's only a couple hours a week." Her defensiveness continued.

Abby and The Brew were mine. It wasn't as if Megan wasn't welcome here, but it was just that this was part of my new world. I guess I'd always assumed I could come back. Even if John hired someone else—and who knew if Abby would let him, or if she'd want to go back to working herself to death—I thought I'd at least be part-time help.

But if Megan had "taken my job," then that probably meant there was no job left for me.

"Did you get your application in?" Abby wiped down the counter and gave Megan a look that clearly said she doubted she had.

Of course, I had no idea what application she was talking about.

"Yes." Megan gave her a little smile. "It's in. Thank you."

Abby softened before she said "Whatever" and turned to me. "You're back."

"Yup."

"Are you staying?"

"There's no tour for a while, and I'm not sure if Zelda has us going anywhere, so I assume so." I got a little sad about the no travel thing.

As much as being on the road was hard, they'd become part of my family. Especially Zelda—and by extension, Harrison. Now I was home, and my other family had reunified themselves differently.

"Good." Abby nodded as if this was great news. "You can work three morning shifts a week and every other Sunday."

"I...I can?" I wasn't even sure I could, but I suddenly wanted to throw my arms around Abby.

"Yes." She stepped back. "Stop looking at me like that."

"Like what?"

"Like you're going to hug me or something."

"Jenna hugs you all the time," Megan chimed in.

"Yes, but Jenna's a hugger."

"You hugged Hailey that day when she got her new contract and cried happy tears."

"Happy tears need hugs."

I watched this bouncing back and forth.

"I think Emily deserves a hug so she knows you missed her."

"You missed me?" I couldn't help how hopeful I sounded.

Abby looked completely put out by this. "*Of course* I missed you."

I looked at Megan, who wore a smug smile of satisfaction. "She followed your Instagram. Got the app and everything."

Abby nodded, looking uncomfortable.

"Tell her what you told Mr. Watson." Megan nodded her head at me as if Abby might not know who she was supposed to talk to. "Tell her."

Abby sucked in a breath and looked at something just over my right shoulder. "I told Mr. Watson he should follow you because you're extremely talented."

"And..." Megan urged as she went around the counter and started making our drinks.

"And I missed having you around." It was like Abby had completely given up trying to be a bad ass.

"Oh!" I threw my arms around her. "I missed you, too! I really did. Thank you for saying that to Mr. Watson, but I knew you were on my team."

Abby looked stunned, and it dawned on me I'd never told *her* she was important.

"I'm glad to be back," I finished as I pulled away.

"Okay." Abby nodded, as if we'd just finished an important conversation. "Megan said you'll need to finish up road stuff with Zelda. Let me know when you're ready to start your shifts."

With that, Abby gave Megan a nod and headed back into the kitchen.

"So." Megan grabbed the comfy seats and gave me her brightest smile. "You're back. This is so great."

She asked about the tour—because, hello; fangirl—and then, after I'd told her enough funny stories to last a lifetime, I shifted to her.

"How did you end up working at The Brew?" I figured it would help out with rent, but I was still paying my part even while I was gone.

Megan stilled and set down her mug. I wasn't sure I wanted to hear what she had to say.

"So, Sage—"

"*Sage?*" I wasn't even sure where the sentence was going, but I didn't know if I had the emotional energy yet to go with it.

"Em, just listen, okay?" She leaned forward and took my hand. "Sage is the one who did your room."

"Oh. Wow." I closed my eyes, picturing it. Amazed and...annoyed.

"I mean, I *totally* helped. Like with the design and the painting and putting your stuff where you'd want it, but the building stuff? All him." She looked nervous, like she knew this was a big deal. "At first, I didn't want to let him in. But Joey—"

"He went through our landlord?"

"Yeah. And free labor? Like Joey was going to say no to that."

We both snorted. Joey was running so many slightly-illegal apartments it was lucky his picture wasn't on the post office wall.

"So he was there, and then I came in here and he was here." She waved toward the counter. "Fixing something for Abby. And I had to *wait* for coffee. So I told her she should hire me. And she did. And then he went and built your room."

"What about his job?" I asked, trying to find the logic behind all of this.

"Still doing it." Her voice had softened.

Darn it. Sage had won her over, too.

"Yeah, well it's not like we don't work more than one job."

"But none of them have power tools."

I jumped at the idea of him drilling into himself with something electric and sharp.

"Fine," I conceded, because what else could I do?

So, Sage had taken care of some stuff while I was gone. Whatever.

I tried to slow down the flutter of my heart. No one had ever done anything that big for me before. But, it felt like…a *thing*. A thing that was supposed to heal a hurt. I didn't know if it could.

You can't buy trust.

We sat there a minute, just the two of us thinking our own thoughts when Megan took a deep breath and gave me a look I knew I wasn't going to like.

"I think you should talk to him."

I sighed, closing my eyes and collapsing back in the chair.

"Yeah. Of course. I won't be able to avoid it now that we're back. I'm sure when we're at the studio it will be unavoidable."

"So, see, that's the thing?" she hedged. I wasn't sure what she was avoiding, but I was sure I wasn't going to like it. "I don't think he'll be at the studio."

"Why not?" Did he get a job and leave? Was he on tour now with someone else? Was that why he wasn't at The Brew at his regular time?

"I *think*—I'm not sure...Sage isn't very chatty, ya know?" Megan looked at me for assurance, but all I could picture was Sage listening to Megan go through story after story without giving him a chance to jump in. "So, I *think* he might have lost his job."

"What job?" Was he done with that woman's dining room?

"His job-job. The one with the band." Megan looked pained at having to spell it out.

"Why would he have lost his job?" That didn't make any sense. He said he was just going to stay here and finish the dining room for that lady and then everything would be fine.

"I don't know. I'm not sure I get it, but I guess this tour is like a test-their-sound thing. And they figure out what they want to do, so that guy has to be on the tour. Almost like a band guy. Like he does the sound and makes notes and takes care of Luke's guitar and basically is like the band guy behind the band."

That weirdly made sense to me.

"So, if he's not on the tour, he can't do the record?"

Megan nodded. "Or CD, or whatever you call it now. I think that's the deal."

We sat there, staring at each other, trying to figure it all out.

"Luke kept giving Asa and Greg notes and saying *when we get back*. I guess I just assumed that was to work with Sage."

"Maybe I'm wrong." But, she didn't sound like she thought she was wrong.

"What does this mean?" My head couldn't keep up with my emotions.

I was angry and frustrated and hurt. He'd lied. He'd said he'd never lied, but if this was true he had.

But, he'd lied for me. He made sure I had my shot at something good.

Or, maybe they'd fired him. Zelda could be a little intense about things, and once she decided we were soul sisters, I could see where that might go bad.

But I can't see her doing something that could damage the band, so no...

"You're thinking a million things at once," Megan jumped in. "Just, maybe, you know—ask him."

But, ask him what?

I didn't know if I could trust him. This still felt like him trying to buy my trust—of course, you can't buy something if the person doesn't know about it, so maybe not.

I still felt betrayed. It wasn't like him assuming I was a thief was no longer an issue.

But I knew one thing.

I was getting to the bottom of this even if I had to rent a Zipcar and let Megan drive me out there herself.

# FORTY

### SAGE

A WEEK'S WORTH OF DEMOLITION work and he'd managed to accomplish it in three days. His muscles screamed at him every time he moved. But still, it wasn't enough to exhaust him so he could sleep.

He was at the point of crazy tired where he was certain a quarter of his day was spent ignoring full-on hallucinations. And his caffeine addiction was concerning. It was so bad Abby was keeping tabs on his intake. She said she had a strict policy for "over serving."

Just the day before, he'd stumbled over a large dog in a fedora smoking a cigar. It had happened in The Brew, and Abby saw the entire thing. Even the part where Sage tried to bravely pat the dog on his shoulder in a sign of peace.

There was no dog.

It was a basket filled with Brew T-shirts...or *tea*-shirts, as John called them.

Sage had been patting the sign.

Abby had questioned whether or not he was safe to drive home. He was just thankful she let him buy a coffee so he could get to his next job site.

Staying busy had been his only hope. If he stopped, even for a moment, the empty future loomed before him. No music, no girl.

All the pieces and scraps he was able to turn into something usable, and he couldn't pick up those pieces. They hid in discarded piles of sawdust all around him. He had turned off the radio in his truck weeks ago. The silence of the workshop was only noticeable when the tools stopped running.

So he never stopped.

All of this meant he ignored the Zipcar that careened to a stop outside the workshop.

But he couldn't ignore the pixie-haired, stardust-covered apparition that blew through the doors of the workshop.

"Nope," Sage said, focusing on the groove he was carving. "You're not here."

"Oh, really?" Emily sounded equal parts confused and annoyed.

"I'm sorry, Sage," Megan said, scurrying in behind Emily.

His eyes flicked up to her. "You're not here, either."

"Are you kidding?" Emily asked, eyes narrowed. "I take my life into my own hands by having Megan drive me out here—"

"Hey!"

"And you're going to ignore me?"

Sage dropped the chisel on the table and placed his fists on his hips. He cocked his head to the side as he glowered at Megan. "We had a deal."

Megan rolled her eyes dramatically and tossed her hands in the air. "Did you really expect me to keep a secret from my best friend?"

Emily stiffened and turned toward her. "I'm your best friend?"

Megan grimaced and jerked her head at Sage. "Focus on one epiphany at a time."

"Right." Emily nodded and went back to Sage. "You're going to explain to me what exactly is going on."

Sage shook his head and looked to his boots. "No. Because you're not here."

Emily huffed. "Fine, Sage, I'll bite. Why am I not here?"

His gaze bounced between her eyes, and even though he didn't want to, he still felt it. The rush of seeing her, the peace that infused his tired limbs. All he had to do was see her, be near her.

"Because I can't handle it," he forced out of a dry throat. "Because if you were really here, I'd be liable to embarrass myself."

Her eyebrows dipped. "Embarrass yourself how?"

His shrug was more of a shoulder twitch.

She pressed her lips together and crossed her arms over her chest. "Did you build me a room and a bed?"

He didn't answer, except to flick his eyes over to Megan.

"No, look at me, Sage," Emily commanded softly.

He did, but it hurt. A slash right through his gut.

When she realized he wasn't going to outright answer her question, she squeezed the bridge of her nose and sighed. "Why are you here and not at the studio? I went there first."

Megan may have told Emily what she knew, but the band wouldn't do that. Not even if she bribed Harrison with a thousand chocolate donuts. Which meant Sage could deny whatever it was Megan may have implied.

Except, he didn't want to. He hated lying to Emily. It felt like gravel in his veins and cotton in his lungs.

"I don't work there anymore."

She tried to read him, measure his words, come to a discernible conclusion.

"Why not?" Her voice just above a whisper.

"Because I don't."

"But—" She shook her head and took a step toward him. "You love working there. I've heard you talk about it. I've seen you do it."

"Some things are more important." He blinked, the burn of fatigue making the blink feel thicker and longer than normal. She was so close now he could smell her. The subtle and delicate fragrance that was all her. And all too much. If she didn't leave soon, he was going to start to beg.

"You lied to me."

"No. I had other people lie to you."

"Nice loophole."

"What? Do you want me to feel like shit about that, too? It's not enough that I lost the girl of my dreams and the job of my dreams, you want me to feel guilty about how I went about trying to rectify it?" He tried to control the edge of sarcasm that threatened to invade his tone. "Done. Sorry I lied. Sorry I asked others to lie. I'm so damn sorry, I don't even know what to do with myself."

Her jaw clenched, pressing her lips into a thin line. "Did you do all of this so that I would forgive you?"

Sage's tough facade crumbled. "No! Dammit, Emily. I get that I screwed up. I get that you had a shit life. But you make it so freaking hard to love you."

Her eyes went wide and she took a step back. He narrowed his eyes, knowing how she heard it and knowing what he actually meant. He moved around the worktable to stand before her.

"In my head, you were never gonna find out." He rolled his lips inward. "In my head, you get to move on and chase your dream, and finally, hopefully, have the life you deserve. I did those things because no matter what, I can't stop thinking about you. I can't stop wanting to be a part of your life, even if you never know it. I love you. And I care about you. And while those things seem separate, they tend to go hand in hand."

He threw a hand toward Megan. "You have the most amazing people I have ever met in my life at your back. And I'm not even surprised. Of course you do. Of course Abby would throw down for you, and Megan threatened castration.

"You inspire loyalty and devotion. And they *love* you. We all love you. All the time. But you make it so blasted hard. Not because you're hard to love. No, that part is easy. It's hard to get you to accept our love. You're so busy waiting for the other shoe to drop just so you can say you saw it coming the whole time. But Em, darlin', we're gonna love you anyway. Our love isn't contingent on your acceptance of it.

"Which is why I was trying to love you secretly. Because I knew you'd think there was an angle, or an agenda. And there's not."

He dropped his hands limply against his things. "I love you. That's the only reason I have."

# Forty-One

## EMILY

I STOOD THERE, LOOKING AT Sage looking at me and wondering, what the heck just happened.

"So..." Megan glanced between us. "You heard that, right?"

I nodded, still looking at Sage and trying to stop the panicked paralysis setting in.

"Soooo..." Megan nudged me.

I glanced at her, completely at a loss.

Sage was saying he *loved* me.

I don't know if anyone has ever said that before. Even Troy, the manipulative ass, never used those words to get me to do what he wanted.

I should have felt all that mushy stuff people talk about—the stuff I'd longed for. But instead, I felt a fast and dark fear reaching up to wrap its boney fingers around my ankles. I'd had people in my life who were supposed to love me and that had never worked out so well.

"How do you know?" I asked, not sure what this all meant, because I *wanted* this. I wanted him. More than I'd ever wanted anything before. I couldn't stand the idea of love meaning something different to him than it meant to me and losing him later.

"Oh, Emily." Megan gave me a hug and headed toward the door. "I'll be in our snappy hybrid Zipcar."

Even in an emergency, Megan got a car she loved.

The door fell shut behind her, and then it was just the two of us.

"How do I know," he asked. "How do I know I love you?"

I wished he'd stop saying that. I wasn't sure my heart could take much more. I'd lost him once—along with the only strip of pride I had.

Now I was willing to let the pride go, but him? I don't think I could get used to him being in my life only to lose him again.

"I know, for a million reasons, and none at all." He put down the towel he'd been holding and leaned back against the thing he'd been working on. "I know, because you make me feel like everything in my life focuses down to when I'm with you. Every moment I'm not with you are just the moments between. I know, because you don't care about what I build, but yours has become the opinion that counts. From the moment I saw you, you get more beautiful—inside and out. You bring so much joy to other people and I love that...I don't need it all for me."

I stared at him, completely lost by this picture of me he was painting. The girl I knew could never live up to that—or to his world.

"I know, because you're my music."

I heard my own small gasp, because there was nothing more precious to him than that.

We stood there, the two of us joined by the hand he reached out for. As soon as his strong, calloused hand wrapped around mine, I felt a connection I'd been fighting since he'd first walked in The Brew.

I gave a tug on my hand, trying to get it back. Afraid of the buzz that zipped along my whole body from the connection.

"When I'm building a guitar, I find the wood that's most easily going to create the best sound and work the shape I want. You shape and sand and fit and build and find the best components to fit it with.

"And," he continued, "if I do everything right, if I give this piece of wood and metal enough love, and attention, and care—the sound it makes will be perfect. That barely ever happens." He gave me this little smile, sad and a bit broken, that hurt me down to my soul. "But that's not what you are."

Oh.

I was melting. Melting in a way that meant I'd never have all of me back, no matter what happened next.

"Sometimes," he went on, "you build it and the sound is past perfect. It has flaws and tones that aren't like every other guitar. And it's beautiful. That's you, Emily. You're the beautiful sound I hear even in my sleep."

He stood there, one hand tucked in his pocket, looking at me as if I were something special. Like I was important.

And in that moment I knew we needed to get this right.

I boiled it down to the absolute truth.

"You hurt me."

"I know."

"In the worst way."

"I know," he repeated, more gently.

"I can't let people in who aren't going to stand by me. I can't have my life ripped away again."

I closed my eyes because he looked so sad. His sadness was obviously not for him, but for me. At it, a heat of anger burst through my heart I hadn't expected.

"And I don't want your pity." I pushed my gaze back up to meet his. "I don't want you walking on eggshells. I just want your trust and your loyalty."

"They're yours."

I stood there, trying not to shake. I felt fear and anger and relief and an emotion I wasn't afraid to name, but wasn't sure if it was true pumping through me like adrenaline.

Never before had I *wanted* like this.

I'd learned early in the system that wanting got you nothing but heartache.

"Emily." Sage took a small, soft step toward me. "I realize what I did. It was stupid. I thought—I thought I was protecting you. I wasn't thinking about *you*. Just, what's the worst thing that could happen, and how do I stop it. But, I should have thought of you—I should have *known*..."

I looked away, trying to compose my feelings. Taking a deep breath, I turned back to him. It was so much. Part of me knew what he was saying. The guys had talked him up nonstop on the tour. And, I guess I could understand the impulse to save me—even from myself.

I just struggled so much with the hurt that he thought there'd been a need for that.

But, he was right about something. Just like I needed him to trust me, I also needed to learn to trust him.

And, lowering my gaze and letting everything I was feeling wash over me, I realized...I had.

"But, I realized something." He took another step forward so his scuffed-up work boots stepped into view. "And, I'm not sure you're ready to hear it. But, I need to say it."

"Oh." I stepped back, pushing those boots out of view, pushing him out of view. Giving myself one more moment to catch up, because I had the worst feeling that *I* was the one ending us—for good. He was going to tell me we could be friends. And I'd smile and nod. At least I didn't have any more hair to cut off unless I was going to go for a close shave. "That's okay. I mean, I think we both know this had to be it, right?"

I wasn't sure what I was going to accomplish coming out here, but maybe it was just what I needed.

"Right." He stepped back in. "This is definitely it for me."

I nodded, wondering how to make my exit as graceful as possible.

"*You're* definitely it for me." Sage reached out and took my hand, gently trapping me there with him. "I don't care how long it takes. I know you're it for me. The only way I'll give up is if you can say honestly I'm not for you. I know you may need to take some time for that. I know I have to earn back your trust, but Emily, you're the best person I know. Which makes me the biggest idiot I know." He sucked in a breath. "That's a pretty big idiot with the people I know, so I'm sure I'll mess this up again. But—I love you. I *love* you love you. And, if you'll let me be near you—near your beautiful sound—I'll keep working to earn that trust and time and hopefully your love."

My heart pounded so loud in my ears, I was sure I heard him wrong until I looked up into his lush green eyes and saw it there...the same thing I felt.

Love.

I sucked in a breath, and with it, a sense of peace I'd never had in my life. I looked at this amazing man offering me everything, and knew—just *knew*—that without him my life might as well stop growing now.

"Sage?" I could hear the shaky uncertainty in my voice, knowing it came from a fear of not being enough for him, but being willing to try.

"You're my picture." I couldn't help but smile back as the slow, almost cocky grin spread across his face. "When the light is magic and the timing is serendipity, and I'm there and...snap. A moment so true caught that I can't even explain the goose bumps it gives me when I look at it. And to think, I'm there, just on the other side of it—somehow secretly *part* of it.

"When I look at you, I know I'm part of it because..." I sucked in another breath and he laughed, shaking his head.

"It's not a death sentence, gorgeous."

"Right. Not for me. But what about you?"

"What about me?"

"I'm—I'm not exactly a winning bet. I have no family and no background and no education. I'm still figuring out life." The fear rushed back up, and I knew what had been holding me back this entire time—from the beginning. "What if I'm not what you need?"

*What if I'm not good enough?*

"Emily, we'll figure it out together." He took my hand again. "And, because none of that is true. You've found your family. You've found your passion. Educations aren't certificates. And, because, without you, there's no music."

"I love you!" I blurted it out like there was no going back. Then, softer, "I love you."

His arm came around me, pulling me to him. "Most beautiful words from the most beautiful girl."

I let myself sink into his kisses, knowing that this was the best place, the picture snapped, the music made—the love found.

# EPILOGUE

*One Year Later*

I GLANCED AT THE USED RV and couldn't believe I was moving out of my dining-bedroom and into that. It might actually be smaller. But, it had a kitchen.

Well, kind of.

Of course, it looked even smaller than it was when lined up next to the five tour buses beyond it.

"Second thoughts?" Sage snuck up behind me and wrapped his arms around my waist, letting his chin rest on my head.

"Well..." I grinned, hidden as I was, and laughed when he tickled me in retaliation.

"No chance for that now. We're hitting the road, and there's no looking back."

I glanced up at him, that big, happy grin shaping his mouth in a way that meant I *had* to kiss him.

"That's enough of that!" Blake's voice shouted down the row at us. "What do you think you are, happily married or something?"

Sage just shook his head and kissed me again. It wasn't like we were going to escape these guys now that we'd be on the road with them for the next five months. But, the fact that we both worked for the DBS machine meant we were going together.

And, yes—I married him.

Of course, first I had to let Zelda's parents adopt me because she was sure we really were soul sisters, and I had to have her last name for a week before the incredibly small ceremony at Sage's parents' place.

I leaned back into the warmth that was Sage, happy with the picture I'd just taken of the back of our new home decorated with giant letters spelling out JUST MARRIED and knew that I wasn't alone—and I never would be.

"Okay, this isn't a vacation. Where is Sway?" Luke stormed by, followed by their new assistant manager, Fox Murphy. "What time are we supposed to leave? McNabb, everything's a go for setup for Connecticut?"

"Yup." Sage stayed, as always, cool under pressure, a character trait I was learning made life simple, easy, and happy.

I grinned up at him as he took my hand and led me toward the door of the RV. Just as we got there, he swung me up into his arms and turned sideways to step onto the slightly worn blue rug.

"How many honeymooners get to travel with rock stars?"

"Not rock stars." I gave him a last kiss before we buckled in. "Family."

Best honeymoon ever.

# About Bria Quinlan

RWA RITA award finalist and USA Today Best Seller Bria Quinlan writes Diet-Coke-Snort-Worthy Rom Coms about what it's like to be a girl and deal with crap and still look for love. She also writes books for teens that take hard topics and make you laugh through your tears. Some people call them issue books. Some people call them romantic comedies. Bria calls them what-life-looks-like.

Her stories remind you that life is an adventure not to be ignored.

# About Heidi Hutchinson

Heidi Hutchinson was born in South Dakota and raised the exact right distance away from the Black Hills. She had an overactive imagination very early on, and wasted no time in getting most of her friends in trouble due to her unrealistic and completely ridiculous ideas. Seeing as she was so lazy and also afraid people would think she was bonkers, she didn't write down any of the story lines that played out in her daydreams.

During her teens, she took pen to paper and filled more notebooks than she is proud of with angsty, depressing, self-deprecating poetry. This led to her writing down more things: notes, ideas, character bios, plot twists that had no plot yet to twist. After years of cleaning up her own scraps of imagination with nothing solid to hold on to, she sat down and wrote the story that had been in her head the longest. Fueled by coffee and her unwavering and perfectly normal devotion to Dave Grohl, she discovered a writer living inside her.

She still lives in the Midwest, though not as close to the Black Hills as she would prefer, with her alarmingly handsome husband, their fearless child, and rather large and spoiled dog.

Where her fuel is still predominantly Dave Grohl and coffee. And a whole lotta love.